Old Tippecanoe Club of Chicago

Dedication to Benjamin Harrison

Christian gentleman, patriotic citizen, brave soldier, wise statesman

Old Tippecanoe Club of Chicago

Dedication to Benjamin Harrison
Christian gentleman, patriotic citizen, brave soldier, wise statesman

ISBN/EAN: 9783337118853

Printed in Europe, USA, Canada, Australia, Japan

Cover: Foto ©Raphael Reischuk / pixelio.de

More available books at **www.hansebooks.com**

DEDICATION

—— TO ——

Benjamin Harrison

CHRISTIAN GENTLEMAN; PATRIOTIC CITIZEN;

BRAVE SOLDIER; WISE STATESMAN

—— AND ——

23d President of the United States.

THIS VOLUME
IS RESPECTFULLY DEDICATED
—— BY ——
THE OLD TIPPECANOE CLUB
OF CHICAGO.

PREFACE.

UNQUESTIONABLY the unique Presidential campaign in this country was that of 1840. A stupendous, peaceful revolution! When forty-eight years later the surviving followers of that gloriously successful chieftain, numbering no less than fifty thousand souls, received the glad tidings that the National Republican Convention had nominated his distinguished grandson, Benjamin Harrison, for President of the United States, they rallied as if by bugle call, formed themselves into scores of Tippecanoe Clubs, held spirited, soul-stirring meetings, as in days of yore, buckled on the armor, and unfurling their time-worn banner to the breeze, again marched forth to battle and to victory. Most of the veterans, conscious of having participated in their last Presidential conflict, were then ready to exclaim with Simeon of old: "Lord, now lettest thou Thy servant depart in peace, for mine eyes have seen Thy salvation."

It is improbable that similar coincidences will ever reappear in history, in that the identical principles sacredly maintained by so large a body of voters during almost half a century, notwithstanding the vicissitudes, oft times tumultuous, to which the republic had meanwhile been exposed, including the unfortunate canvass of 1884, should again be the battle-cry and win popular favor and endorsement—and that under consanguineous marshalship. Let it be recorded in history, and never forgotten, that every man who voted for the two Harrisons for President was loyal to the Union during the War of the Rebellion. If constant devotion to *principle* throughout a long and active life shall be held worthy of remembrance, esteem and emulation by the descendants of those who intelligently and patriotically practiced it—and if the perusal of these pages shall stimulate the reader of whatsoever party to an exalted sense of political duty, and consequent love of country, the object of this book will have been accomplished.

DECLARATION OF PRINCIPLES

——OF——

The Old Tippecanoe Club of Chicago.

. —— ...

At a regular meeting of the Club held at the Grand Pacific Hotel on the 29th day of December, 1888, the following among other proceedings were had:

RESOLVED: That a Committee of five be appointed whose duties shall be to draft a Preface or Historical account of the times and Biographical History of Chicago's Old Tippecanoe's from 1836, 1840 and including 1888, the same to be placed in the Register of the Club, and to be published under the supervision of said Committee.

Afterwards, to-wit, on the day and year aforesaid, the President appointed the following persons to constitute said Committee, to-wit: Hon. Cyrus M. Hawley, Henry Sayrs, Albert Soper, Wm. H. Bradley, Wm. S. Elliott.

Attest: H. M. GARLICK, Secretary.

To the Tippecanoe Club, of Chicago, Ill:

MR. PRESIDENT, LADIES AND GENTLEMEN.—Your Committee to whom was referred the duty to supervise the publication in book form of biographies of the members, and to prepare a suitable introduction explanatory of the purposes of this organization, have the pleasure to report, that they have received and examined about seventy-five biographical statements, and have directed them to be copied in proper form for printing, and expect that many others will be received by your Committee.

Your Committee further report that they have prepared the

said introductory explanation, or statement of the principles and purposes of this organization, to be printed with said biographies.

C. M. HAWLEY,

Chicago, Illinois, January 26, A.D., 1889.   Chairman.

This organization was formed on the fifth day of July, A. D., 1888, to aid in the election of Gen. Benjamin Harrison and Levi P. Morton to the presidency and vice-presidency of the United States of America. It consists of those who voted for Gen. Wm. Henry Harrison for president in 1836, and those who voted for and aided his election to that high office in 1840, including their sons, daughters, sons-in-law, and daughters-in-law.

Ex-President Gen. Wm. Henry Harrison was born in Berkeley, Virginia, near Richmond, on the 9th day of February, A.D., 1773. In June, 1793, with the rank of lieutenant, he was appointed aide-camp to General Wayne, though not a graduate from a military academy. He participated in the battle and victory against the Indians on the 20th of August of that year. He then was placed in command of Fort Washington, and continued in the same command until 1798, when he resigned, and retired to private life on his farm at North Bend in Ohio. But he was not permitted to remain long in retirement; for he was soon after appointed by President John Adams, secretary of the Northwestern territory, embracing what is now Indiana, Illinois, Michigan, Iowa, Wisconsin; and soon thereafter Louisiana was added thereto. On the 3d of October, 1799, the first legislative assembly of the territory elected him as its delegate to Congress, which office he filled to the satisfaction of his constituents and with credit to himself. In 1801, he was appointed Governor and Indian Agent of the Territory. In 1809, he negotiated the Fort Wayne Indian treaty. But the wily Tecumseh and his brother The Prophet, were not disposed to comply with the terms of the treaty, for they were intent on war. They made the attempt to combine all the Indian tribes and forces to overpower, kill, or drive out the settlers from the territory, notwithstanding their treaty obligations to live in peace. Their efforts to enlist all the tribes failed, but they succeeded in gathering a formidable army of braves of nearly 1,000, who stealthily, Indian like, rushed with a yell upon

General Harrison's camp before the break of day; but they were repulsed. The battle of Tippecanoe followed, resulting in the death of Tecumseh, and the triumph of General Harrison and his army. This victory excited the envy, or fears of the British agents, and they renewed their secret efforts to incense the Indians against the United States more openly, and to boldly invade the territory. In addition to these hostile efforts, on the 16th of May, 1811, the British ship of war, Little Belt, fired upon the United States Frigate, "President," in command of Commodore Rogers. This was one of the causes of the war of 1812 with Great Britain, in which Gen. Wm. H. Harrison was distinguished as one of the ablest of our commanders.

As commander of the Northwestern Army, he held the rank of Brigadier General. In March, 1813, he was promoted to the rank of Major General. In 1824, he was elected United States Senator from Ohio, and was appointed chairman of the military committee. In 1828 he was appointed by President John Q. Adams, Minister Plenipotentiary to the Republic of Columbia, and was received with marked attentions by reason of his distinguished character and ability. In 1836, he was nominated by the Whigs in several of the States for president, but was defeated by the election of Martin Van Buren. In 1840, he was nominated at Harrisburg, Pa., for president by the National Convention of the Whig party on a Protective Tariff and National Currency Platform, and elected by an overwhelming majority, and was inaugurated on the 4th of March, 1841.

We voted for, and aided in his election, because he represented our political principles, and was eminently qualified to discharge the duties of the great office.

His sentiments of protection to home industries, a home market for our productions, the development of our natural resources, in order to furnish remunerative employment for our citizens, to the end that they become prosperous and educated, not only in the common schools and colleges, but in schools of all kinds of industry; and his doctrine of a national currency for exchange and circulation commanding a par value in all parts of our country, drew to his support the most intelligent of our citizens. At the time, all our industries were suffering from the Calhoun free-trade slavery extension policy, which sought to benefit the slave-holding states at the expense of the free states and their manufacturing industries.

General Harrison's popularity was so great, that, when he left North Bend for Washington, his passage was lined by hundreds of thousands of admiring citizens, whose plaudits rang out as though the nation was celebrating its jubilee. His inaugural was patriotic and impressive in vindicating the principles involved in his election, and which he proposed to carry out during his administration. But while the people were resting in his purpose and fidelity, on the 4th of April, 1841, at thirty minutes past midnight, he was struck down by death, like the great oak that is scathed and leveled by the lightning. As he sank into the silent depths, he uttered this patriotic injunction, intending it for the vice-president; "I wish you to understand the true principles of the government. I wish them carried out. I ask no more." His every official act in war and in peace shed glory upon our nation.

His humanity on the field of battle is illustrated in his order directing his troops to take a town that was opposing our force. "Go!" he said, "and take the town. But let an account of murdered innocence be opened in the records of heaven against our enemies alone. The American soldier will follow the example of his government, and the sword of the one will not be raised against the fallen and helpless, nor the gold of the other be paid for the scalps of a massacred enemy."

At the date of the inauguration of General Harrison in 1841, the population of the United States was about 18,000,000 and the census now soon to be taken will show that under the wise and beneficient influence of our institutions we will have reached sixty millions. In her material prosperity, intelligence, institutions of learning, and industrial and moral development our people have kept pace with increase of population and territorial domain; and now, we present to the world a monument of civilization and culture of life, energy, fraternity, power, and magnificence which no other nation has attained.

Ancient Egypt, Greece, and Rome were once the glory of the world; but to-day they are the monuments of death. Our government being of, by, and for the people, it is considerate, wise, just, liberal, and strong with the people. The cohesive element of equality and unity, qualifies them to wield their power wisely, and to fill all stations, official and others, with ability and efficiency. This is the natural sequence to the enfranchisement of the people with free conscience, free speech, free soil, free labor, free men, free votes, and an honest count. No other people or government ever presented such a unity in equality. All the gates and avenues to success are wide open to all persons and classes; and every entry-port is fortified, if not by iron-clad forts and naval batteries, by the united will and combined energy and action of a free and determined people.

The only enthroned despot we ever had, was American chattel slavery, which, by its inordinate greed for dominion, and its treasonable acts, was dethroned and put to death by the sacrifices and valor of the loyal people supplemented by the voice and ballots of constitutional reform, and its oppressive and degrading remains committed to their grave beyond the power of resurrection.

And now, while we are not an ocean-bound Republic, though our shore is washed by the Atlantic, Pacific, Gulf of Mexico, and our northern sisterhood of waters, yet, it is within the providence of events, by the voice of the people interested, and in accord with manifest destiny, that, at some time in the near future, our country may become ocean-bound, uniting people and domain in one grand Republican empire, under one flag, and moving forward as one body, like the billows of the sea. Such a governmental power, united, independent, educated and harmonious, with a home market for its productions in all the lines of art, science, agriculture, manufacture, and raw material, would assure prosperity and peace at home, if not to the world at large.

It is the duty of our state and national legislative assemblies to aim at state and national independence in all branches of development and industry, to the end that the people have equal opportunities, and are educated in all industries, and are able to provide a pleasant home for themselves and families. In this day of progressive enterprise, and the ambition of nations, education and skilled labor in all possible branches of industry, are demanded for the safety of the state, and the protection of the rights of the people, or else, we will become weak and dependent.

We had a painful illustration of this condition when the great rebellion in 1861 broke in upon our fancied security, and found us strong only in patriotic numbers, fired with zeal and courage; but wholly destitute of arms, munitions and other equipments. Our forts were, also, either filled with traitors, or dismantled and destitute of provisions, our ships of war unseaworthy, or in far distant waters, our arsenals denuded, and our manufacturing industries in want of skilled labor, and were therefore inadequate to supply the needs of the Government in that emergency. Hence, it was impossible to move against the rebellion at once aggressively without involving our army in a sea of blood to no purpose. It was fortunate for the integrity of the union that the rebels were in no better condition to destroy the union than we were to maintain it. But, if we had then also been confronted by England or France in support of the rebel forces, the union might have been overthrown, slavery extended and perpetuated, foreign goods found a free market, and Mexico and Cuba, at an early date would probably have constituted integral parts of the slave-holder's "Confederate States of America."

The cause of these difficulties in equiping our forces, and of this great exposure, is directly chargeable to the Calhoun policy of slavery in union with free trade. The Protective tariff policy of Gen. Wm. H. Harrison, which was re-ordained in his election by the people in 1840, and became the law in 1842, produced changes under which the country became once again prosperous. Unfortunately the sudden demise of the President left his party compatriots entangled by the singular estrangement of John Tyler, who succeeded to the office of Chief Magistrate. In the meantime, the old scheme of John C. Calhoun, like the "Mystery of Iniquity," was industriously at work to circumvent what the votes of the people accomplished in 1840, and finding in Polk and

Dallas fit agents for the purpose, they were elected in 1844, and well did they perform the part assigned them to do, and the events which followed showed what they were to do by what followed, to wit: The repeal of the Protective tarriff of 1842, by the annexation of Texas, by declaring war against Mexico, by the extension of the domain of slavery; and as a consequence by the enactment of the so-called compromise in the interest of slavery, in 1850, the repeal of the Missouri compromise, which was in the interest of freedom, in 1854, and the slave-holders rebellion in 1861. This last blow at freedom, instead of breaking the loyal back, roused to action loyal millions; but not until Fort Sumpter was fired upon by rebel batteries were our forces called forth into lines of battle, and Congress summoned in special session to meet the emergency, which immediately enacted a Protective tarriff, provided for a National currency and adopted other measures to put down the rebellion. But it took about two years before our forces were prepared to move effectively by sea, rivers and land against the enemy, but when they were ready and did move, they were victorious. But by the prolongation of the war and the pressure of circumstances, and the demands of the people, the president, as commander in chief, as a war measure, issued the Proclamation of Emancipation of all slaves within the limits of those states and parts of states which were in rebellion. This was the severest of all blows to the rebellion: for it not only took from it needed support, but enlisted in the service of the Union army two hundred thousand colored soldiers who had been slaves, and they proved themselves as brave as they were true. And beside, the effect of the protective tariff was immediate. Manufacturing industries were revived, and new and more extensive enterprises entered upon. Ships of war, forts, and arsenals were constructed, skilled laborers increased in numbers, and although the war expenditures were counted in billions, our loyal people were prosperous; and when the war was ended, our soldiers, when they returned to civil life, found these increased facilities, and therefore plenty of remunerative employment, and our national debt in process of rapid extinction.

But not content with such achievements and financial success, the Democratic party, still hungering after the leaks and onions of free-trade, caused Mr. Cleveland, in his annual message in 1887, to recommend Congress to repeal the protective tariff, and return to the Calhoun free-trade policy, which was suited to the South only while slavery existed. In pursuance of this recommendation the Mills free-trade bill was finally passed through the Lower House, made the cardinal doctrine of the Democratic platform, Mr. Cleveland was again nominated for president, and he, in no equivocal terms, accepted the honor, re-affirming the sentiments of his former free-trade message, as well as the platform adopted in conformity with it.

This old issue roused the Republican party, which in national convention in Chicago in 1888, nominated General Benjamin Harrison and Levi P. Morton as its candidates for president and vice-president. This called out the Tippecanoe guard of 1836 and 1840, as before stated, which labored and voted to elect them, because they represented the political principles of the guard, which were antagonized by the British free-trade doctrines of the Democratic party platform. And we unhesitatingly affirm that no more capable and worthy men, and representatives of true Republicanism, of home industries, of free votes, and true counts, are to be found in the nation.

General Benjamin Harrison entered the military service of the United States as a volunteer, and raised Company "A" of the Seventieth Indiana Regiment, and was commissioned captain by Gov. Oliver P. Morton, July 2, 1862, and at once proceeded to the front with his regiment, and from that time to the close of the war, he was foremost in every battle in which he was engaged. Indeed, his bravery was so conspicuous that he did not seem to fear personal danger, however greatly exposed. His only care was to secure victory in the interests of a peace founded in union, liberty, justice. Such patriotism, ability and valor was soon recognized, and he, as a consequence, was promoted from rank to rank, to that of Major-General of Volunteers. While he was a strict disciplinarian, he was considerate and kind to his command—frequently, when he found a soldier weary and exhausted by long marches, mounted him on his own horse, while he himself marched on foot.

When the Union army was triumphant, and the Rebel army disbanded by surrender, and Jefferson Davis a prisoner in Fortress Monroe, Gen. Harrison, comprehending fully the necessities of the situation, advocated universal emancipation of the remaining slaves, and of universal enfranchisement of all citizens by constitutional law. Reconstruction of the Union on principles short of these would not comport with a truly Republican government of, and by the people of the United States. Such an enfranchisement alone constitutes a true Republican government. Anything short of it is an oligarchy of either small or enlarged representation in government of its citizens; but nevertheless, it is limited in rights and privileges to the exclusion of some of its citizens.

If anything is now lacking it is the want of a national free school system, obligatory in character, to make education universal, including in its curriculum the education of head, hands and conscience in every industrial pursuit and moral excellence. Equal opportunities cannot be extended to all classes of citizens short of this; nor can the nation and government be said to be independent unless our agricultural, horticultural, mechanical and scientific schools are universally distributed, and become inexhaustible fountains of science, art, and of skilled master mechanics. When such a summit of independence is attained, with equality before the law, and when the enfranchized can freely cast their votes according to their will, and when their free votes are truly counted, our people and government can then be said to be independent in fact as in name.

General Harrison, when he recently addressed "The Grand Army of Veterans," gave utterance to his sentiments in eloquent words, as follows: "I would like to hear a bugle call throughout the land demanding a pure ballot. This is a matter above and beyond any question of partizanship, and I feel that I express the sentiment of every comrade present when I declare that a free ballot, honestly expressed, and fairly counted, is the main safeguard of our institutions, and its suppression, under any pretext whatever, cannot be tolerated." And he is as emphatie in his advocacy of methods to promote general progress—the development of our natural resources, the protection of our home industries, the education of all classes in the schools—including science, art, mechanical and hand industries; and that of furnishing to all equal opportunities, and remunerative employment so far as possible. This " bugle call " of General Harrison is now sounding and echoes "throughout the land," and re-echoes from every hamlet and heart loyal to the principles of states and national constitutions, and unless heeded it will reverberate in thunder tones, and wake the sacrificial hosts of veterans who now sleep in rest, that they may again respond to this " bugle call " to demand a pure ballot and an honest count.

Our Tippecanoe Club has responded to this "bugle call," and to the sentiments of the Republican platform of 1888. This, and similar organizations, are to be congratulated that to some extent they have been important factors in the election of General Benjamin Harrison and Levi P. Morton to the presidency and vice-presidency of the United States.

Minutes of the First Meeting of the Old Tippecanoe Club.

On Monday, July 9, 1888, there convened 16 veterans at the Grand Pacific Hotel pursuant to a published call made on the day previous requesting all persons who voted for Wm. Henry Harrison in 1840 to report themselves or send in their names to be registered as members. The purpose of this meeting was for the organization of the Old Tippecanoe Club, to support General Benj. Harrison for President of the United States and Levi P. Morton for Vice-President.

The meeting was called to order by Enos Slosson, who stated its object. The first business being the election of officers for and during the Presidential Campaign, the following gentlemen were elected: Dr. D. S. Smith, President; Enos Slosson, Vice-President; Benj. Ackley, Secretary and Treasurer.

On motion of L. W. Garlick, a committee of three was appointed to draft a Constitution and By-Laws and submit same at the next meeting, and A. N. Raymond, Enos Slosson and W. A. Osborn were appointed such committee.

LIST OF ENROLLED MEMBERS AT THIS MEETING:

Enos Slosson, aged 71, native of Elkland, Pa.

Alanson N. Raymond, aged 70, native of N. Y.

Henry Tanner aged 75, native of Buffalo, N. Y.

Benj. Ackley, aged 72, from Milwaukee, Wis.

R. G. Askin, aged 71, native of Huron Co., Ohio.

Bernard Wegsilbaum, aged 78, native of Phila., Pa.

J. H. Colbarn, aged 72, native of Columbus, Ohio.

Daniel True, aged 76, native of Albany, N. Y.

W. A. Osborne, aged 69, native of Lee, Mass.

W. B. Ayers, aged 69, native of Utica, N Y
P. W. Blodgett, aged 79, native of Groton, N. Y.
Dr. David S. Smith, aged 72, native of Camden, Gloucester Co., N. J.
R. P. Pate, aged 71, native of Belfast, Maine.
Calvin Gifford, aged 71, native of Syracuse, N. Y.
L. W. Garlick, aged 73, native of Kent Co., Conn.
Walter S. Hinckle, aged 73, native of Buckland, Mass.
Adjourned to July 16.

Headquarters of the Old Tippecanoe Club.

GRAND PACIFIC HOTEL.

Extract From the Chicago Tribune,

OF JULY 10, 1888.

THE TIPPECANOE CLUB.

Organized by men who voted for Harrison in 1840.—It starts
with sixteen members and its motto is "Tippecanoe and Morton
Too"—Dr. David S. Smith is president—an idea that originated
with Enos Slosson, Esq., and which will cut some figure in the
November campaign.

The refrain of the happiest campaign song ever written has
been amended officially. The men, who in 1840 swept on to
victory singing:

TIPPECANOE AND TYLER TOO

will enter the list in 1888 shouting, with voices a little tremulous,
it is true, but none the less instinct with conviction—

TIPPECANOE AND MORTON TOO.

It was all arranged last night at the Grand Pacific, and a large
share of the credit for the scheme belongs to Enos Slosson, who
is a staunch Harrison man. The other day he fell to wondering
what he could do in a modest way, becoming an old gentleman
of moderate means and quiet disposition, to place a historical
name again in fitting company in the roll of presidents. This
thought reminded him that his first vote helped to elect William
Henry Harrison in 1840. Then he remembered that two or three
old gentlemen in Chicago of his acquaintance had always voted
the republican ticket, and straightway it occurred to him that if
all the old chaps in the United States who had voted for Harrison
in 1840 would organize and go on record for Harrison in 1888 the
example would at least be edifying. He consulted the other

two or three, and the result was the notice calling last night's meeting.

The notice was short, but response was prompt. Fifteen jolly, retrospective old boys came early, organized, appointed proper committees, and adjourned until next Monday at 3:30 P. M.

Dr. David S. Smith was elected temporary chairman, and the old boys would make him no concessions on any account.

A speech! a speech! they cried.

Dr. Smith was abundantly equal to the occasion, but several of the old boys had pronounced that their daughters or nieces drew the line at latch keys, so he cut it short.

"I appreciate the honor you have conferred upon me," he said. "Not many men have been equally distinguished. To have lived forty-eight years to vote for a second Harrison after living twenty-one before voting for the first president of that name, is an honor and a distintion also. In 1840 we elected our Harrison; let us do what we can to further the same worthy cause in 1888." (Applause and cheers.)

Enos Slosson, Alanson N. Raymond and Daniel True were appointed a committee on nominations. They reported in favor of Dr. Smith for president, Enos Slosson for vice-president and Benjamin Ackley for secretary and treasurer, and these gentlemen were elected by acclimation. When Messrs Raymond, Slosson and Osborne had been elected a committee on resolutions with instructions to report next Monday afternoon, the meeting was adjourned.

Several of the old fellows had their sons with them. One was accompanied by his ·grandaughter and one by his niece. The male members of the second generation manifested a strong desire to be admitted to the membership.

"This organization will be effective because it is unique," said the old boys. "If we let you young chaps in we shall degenerate and sacrifice our effectiveness. It must be a club of veterans."

"Well, that settles it," said a member of the second generation. "We shall have to organize as sons of veterans."

The oldest member of the organization so far is P. M. Blodgett.   He is seventy-nine and looks seventy.

" I voted for two presidents before Harrison," he said, "but I have forgotten their names.   They had to be Whigs, though," the old fellow added, with a chuckle.

It is expected that William Skinner, aged eighty-four, will become a member, as well as a great many others who were unable to attend last night.

" What shall we name our club?" asked one.

"Tippecanoe!" answered a chorus of ready voices.

"And what will its motto be?"

" Tippecanoe and Morton, too."

Continuation of Minutes.

The Club met pursuant to adjournment at the Grand Pacific Hotel, on July 16, 1888. Enos Slosson, chairman of committee appointed to draft constitution and by-laws, reported viz:

First, this organization shall be known as the Old Tippecanoe Club, of Chicago.

Second, the membership shall be limited to those who assisted or voted in 1840 for Gen. Wm. Henry Harrison, including also their wives, their sons, sons-in-law, their daughters and their daughters-in-law.

Third, the object of this organization shall be the furtherance of the election of the nominees of the Republican National Convention of 1888, viz: Benj. Harrison, grandson of the "Tippecanoe" Harrison of 1840, and Levi P. Morton, of New York.

Fourth, the officers of the Club shall consist of a President, First and Second Vice-Presidents, Secretary and Treasurer, and Sergeant-at-Arms. It shall be the duty of the President to preside at the meetings.

Fifth, the regular meetings shall be held on the first and third Saturday, at 3 P. M., of each month until election; but a special meeting may be called by any three members when any important business of the Club demands it. Twenty members assembled shall constitute a quorum to do business. One or more members shall have power to adjourn from time to time.

Sixth, the rules of order shall be the same as those governing the Senate of the United States. Officers here elected will continue in office during the campaign of 1888, or until their successors are elected or appointed. In absence of the President the First Vice-President shall preside. If both the President and First

Vice-President are absent the second Vice President shall perform the duties of the President. The Secretary and Treasurer shall keep a record of all meetings, serve notices on members and perform other duties pertaining to the office. He shall also receive and disburse all moneys collected and expended for the authorized use of the Club. The Sergeant at Arms shall assist the President in maintaining order and performing such other duties as may be consistent with his office under the direction of the presiding officer.

Believing as your Committee does that the fruits of the work to be done by this organization will be felt by the young and vigorous elements in this campaign, we pledge ourselves to assist and stimulate all persons who are known to have voted and assisted in the election of Old Tippecanoe in 1840 to join our ranks and go hand in hand to a triumphant victory with Young Tippecanoe and Morton too.

On July 21, the Club convened at its headquarters. The President in the Chair. The first meeting was the unfinished business of the last meeting, viz: Election of second Vice-President and Sergeant at Arms.

Whereupon R. T. Bennett was elected second Vice-President and C. R. Vandercook Sergeant at Arms. Dr. D. S. Smith, Enos Slosson and A N. Raymond were appointed a Committee to provide an appropriate badge for the veterans. R. T. Bennett and M. L. Prince were appointed to secure a Glee Club to attend the meetings and furnish Club with Campaign Songs. Dr. D. S. Smith here offered the following resolutions which were unanimously adopted. Resolved: That we tender to Col. John B. Drake, proprietor of the Grand Pacific Hotel, our most cordial thanks for his generous hospitality to us as a body, and placing us under still additional obligations by furnishing us larger quarters, sufficiant to accomodating the quadruple veterans of 1840. Resolved: That we tender to the general Chicago Press our thanks for the notices of our assemblages heretofore through their able and efficient reporters, and invite their future attendance and favorable consideration. The Treasurer reported $6.00 on hand. Many names were here added to the Club. Adjourned.

The Club met at its headquarters on August 4, the first Vice-President in the chair. Minutes read and approved. Committee on badges asked for and received further time to report. Committee on music reported that a Glee Club would be present at the next meeting and furnish music. On motion of J. H. Gill, of Mount Pleasant, Ohio, it was voted that the officers of this Club be authorized to enroll all applicants, if by letter or in person, who voted for Harrison in 1840, or assisted in that campaign.

On motion of the President it was voted that the Secretary be invited to procure a suitable book for the purpose of giving each member the opportunity of recording his authograph, his birth place, his residence, where he voted or assisted in 1836 or 1840, at the election of Gen. Harrison, with the request 'that at the closing of the present campaign it be placed in the vaults of the Historical Society of this City. Enos Slosson, Benj. Ackley and Dr. Smith were appointed a Committee to confer with Mr. Drake with reference to present headquarters. Several spirited speeches were made by veterans. On motion of Mr. Bennett the Secretary was authorized to have printed the Constitution and By-Laws so that each member might have a copy. Treasurer reported $20.25 on hand. A large number joined the club. Adjourned.

The regular semi-monthly meeting occurred August 18. The first Vice-President in the Chair, minutes of last meeting read, corrected and approved. Mr. Ackley reported that the book of record was ordered and would be submitted to the next meeting. Mr. R. J. Bennett addressing the chair appropriately urged the importance of swelling the ranks of the Club and then offered the following: Resolved, that the members of the Tippecanoe Club who voted for Wm. H. Harrison in 1836 and 1840 for President, and intend voting for Gen. Ben. Harrison the grandson of "Old Tip" in 1888 for the same office, do most cordially invite all others, who voted for any other candidate in 1836 and 1840 and vote at the coming election to join this Club. A spirited discussion followed by Jas. H. Gill, Philip Burroughs, L. W. Garlick, Judge Hawley, M. L. Prince and others, whereupon Judge Hawley moved amendments to the resolutions as follows: Be invited to meet with and co-operate with us during the present campaign.

The resolution passed as amended. Mr. Noah Scott and others recited their reminiscenses of 1840 and the good old times. Judge Hawley after finishing his able criticism of the Mills tariff bill extended a cordial invitation to the members of the Club to meet with the Hyde Park veterans in their Hall on the corner of 53d. Street and Jefferson Avenue, on August 25th. Accepted. It was voted that the Glee Club be invited to be present August 25th. at Hyde Park. Eight new names were added to the Club. Adjourned.

The regular meeting was held on September 1. The President on taking the chair remarked that while east recently he purchased a copy of rules for the conduct of public meetings, which he laid on his table before him saying, he proposed to be governed by them.

A poem dedicated to the Club by Clara Howard of Harvey, Wisconsin, was read and received with cheers, and the reporters were requested to print same in their respective papers.

The committee on badges having failed to act, Enos Slosson, Col. Mitchell and P. Burroughs were appointed on committee on badges to report at next meeting. John Gage of Massachusetts, made a donation of $10 for defraying expenses of music. Amount collected $16. Resolved: That the President of the Old Tippecanoe Club of 1840 be requested to appoint thirteen members of this club including its officers, who are hereby instructed to convey our congratulations to the nominee of the Republican National Convention, and ask him to deliver his first speech in the city of his nomination, before the Old Tippecanoe Club, who voted in 1840 for the first Gen. Harrison, and now stand pledged to vote for Gen. Harrison of 1888 for President of the first republic on earth. Also to confer with Levi P. Morton and ask him to accept an invitation to be present at the same time. The following were appointed said committee: Judge Hawley, General Hinckley, H. H. Williams, Thomas Mitchell, Captain Duray, P. Burroughs, and the officers of the Club. John C. Gage, Thomas Mitchell, and others, addressed the Club, awaking old time enthusiasm. Many new members. Adjourned.

The Club duly assembled September 15. Minutes of the last

meeting read and approved. Dr. Smith called the attention of the Club to an old silken banner which stood against the wall. "It is the property," said he, "of Rev. L. P. Mercer, whose father carried it in Pennsylvania in the campaign of 1840, and had kindly offered to loan it to the Club." The Doctor suggested that as the owner values the Banner highly it be left in owners' care. Mr. C. R. Van Dercook moved that L. P. Mercer be made an honorary member of the Club and carry the banner in the parade. Carried unanimously.

The committee on badges reported "the badges ready," as they were exceedingly appropriate they were duly accepted and the committee discharged. The committee on invitations was also discharged. The treasurer submitted his report which was accepted.

On motion of Mr. Van Dercook it was resolved that the chair appoint a committee of three whose duties shall be to act as the financial committee, to solicit subscriptions to meet the expenses of the club and to audit all bills and pass on same before payment, carried. The president announced that he would name the committee at the next meeting or through the press.

Mrs. Archibald Harrison a sister-in-law of General Harrison was introduced to the club, made a few remarks, was presented with a badge and enrolled an honorary member. The following named gentlemen then addressed the club: Wm. Hyde, George Paine Harris, Mr. Burroughs and Mr. Clement. Action upon a motion by Judge Hawley relative to visiting General Harrison at Indianapolis on October 6, was deferred until the next meeting. Adjourned for one week.

At the meeting of September 22, Rev. Henry L. Hammond at the request of the president offered prayer. The president then named the following as the finance committee: Albert Soper, Wm. Ripley and C. R. Van Dercook, and announced as the committee on invitations, Enos Slosson, Judge Van Higgins and Thomas B. Bryan, whereupon the committee on finance made its report through Mr. Ripley, which was accepted. The matter of the quartette club was referred to the finance committee with power to act. Mr. Ackley moved that the finance committee be instructed to procure the necessary music for the club. After considerable discussion it was moved that the club visit Indianapolis September 29. Carried forty voting to go. Mr. Vandercook offered to furnish a band of music for the occasion. Col. Mitchell moved that a vote of thanks be given by this club to the Hyde Park League for their invitations and our appreciation of their courtesies and that they be most cordially invited to go with us on September 29, carried.

The regular meeting of the club was called to order October 6. The president reported that some fifty or sixty members of the club made the excursion to Indianapolis and paid their respects to Gen. Harrison and had a most enjoyable time and all had returned safely to their homes. Enos Slosson offered the following resolutions: Resolved, that we tender our heartiest thanks to our fellow townsman George M. Pullman for the use of his beautiful and convenient palace car so opportunely furnished and fully equipped for our comfort without change while the Old Tippecanoe club was making its first pleasant and satisfactory call upon the next president of the United States—Benjamin Harrison. Resolved, that thanks be also extended to the Second Regiment Band for the music furnished on the occasion of our late trip to and from Indianapolis, also for the evening concert given by them from the balcony of the New Dennison House in Indianapolis, adopted.

The president intimated that contributions would be in order. The following gentlemen addressed the meeting: General A. M. Stout, Colonel Wiley S. Scribner and Henry Sayrs. Colonel Babcock here donated to the club $50.00 for which he received a vote of thanks. Great numbers of new members enrolled. Adjourned.

The club met on October 13, in regular session the president in the chair. On motion of Albert Soper it was voted that the club hold its regular meetings every Saturday afternoon at two o'clock until after the sixth of November next.

The following resolution was offered by Henry Sayrs: Resolved, that a committee of thirteen be appointed (of which the president shall be chairman)—to draft for publication an address to the young voters, said committee to report at the next meeting of the club; adopted. The secretary sent each member a written notice requesting his presence at the headquarters at the next meeting. A vote of thanks was here tendered General Leake for his very able address. Twenty-nine new members to-day.

The regular meeting of the club was held October 20, the president in the chair. Dr. Smith chairman of the committee of thirteen appointed at the previous meeting to draft an address to the young voters, reported that said committee met pursuant to notice and do most respectfully submit to this club for adoption an address prepared by Mr. Henry Sayrs, the same having been approved by the committee.

Mr. Sayrs proceeded with the reading of the address, which was received with cheers, and unanimously adopted and copies of the same were furnished the associated press and city dailies.

It was moved that a vote of thanks be tendered Mr. Henry Sayrs for the able address just read. Carried.

.

ADDRESS TO YOUNG VOTERS.

In the present crisis of our country the Old Tippecanoe Club of Chicago feels it incumbent upon it to present the following considerations to young voters: Modern Democracy bears even date with the Presidency of Andrew Jackson, under whose administration the annual ordinary expenses of the government averaged $18,221,686, against those of his immediate Republican predecessor, John Quincy Adams, of $12,625,487. Removals from office for political opinions under Washington were 8; John Adams, 9; Jefferson, 39; Madison, 2; Monroe, 3; J. Q. Adams, 2. Total removals by the the first six Presidents, 74. During the first recess of Congress, Jackson removed 176 high officials, and according to historian Parton, his removals numbered not less than 2,000, which shows the perfect consistency of the Democratic party then and now on the question of civil service reform.   This administration announced and enforced the pernicious un-American doctrine that "To the victors belong the spoils," and one of the first officials removed was "Old Tippecanoe," General William Henry Harrison, Minister to Columbia.

When Jackson became President, the country, under the benign influence of a tariff of adequate protection, was in a condition of unexampled prosperity, and seemed to so continue to almost the close of his career. The arbitrary and revolutionary assumptions, approved and encouraged by partisan adherents, touching great monetary and financial matters, and Congressional tampering with the tariff, ignoring by degrees the protective spirit, did not fully develop their disastrous tendencies until after the installation of his successor.

In his inaugural address, Martin Van Buren boasted that he would follow in the footsteps of his "illustrious predecessor." Very soon thereafter the country found itself in a deplorable condition. Consequent upon a low tariff, importations had been excessive, and the balance of trade was largely against us. Business became paralyzed, labor was idle, factories were closed, bread riots occurred, credit was ruined, all banks suspended, many of them failed, among them those with whom the government funds had been illegally placed. Gold was at a premium of twelve per cent. Under issuance of a "specie circular" the government received gold and silver only, leaving for the uses of the the people, banks, and individuals, shinplasters of every conceivable kind and denomination. Defalcations by government officials were of stupendous amounts and in great number.

To steal was to "Swartwout." At this time several of the Democratic States did not pay interest on their debts. Mississippi repudiated her debt altogether, and bonds of the State of Illinois sold at fifteen cents on the dollar. This pro-slavery administration, having annually cost $30,432,475 for ordinary expenses, was overthrown by the glorious election of gallant Wm. Henry Harrison in 1840. His assuring inaugural address and singularly able Cabinet inspired public confidence; an early session of Congress was called to provide ways and means to carry on the government. The president's untimely death caused universal mourning. His dying words to his successor were: "Sir, I want you to understand the true principals of the government. I wish them carried out, I ask nothing more." A general bankrupt law was passed to enable the people to commence anew, and prosperity shone upon business, revived under the protective tariff of 1842.

The peculiar election of Polk, a man unknown to fame, claimed as for free trade at the South, and as good a protectionist as Clay at the North, took the country by surprise, and when it was discovered that he and his Secretary of the Treasury, Robert J. Walker, were consumate free traders of the Cobden school, manufacturing interests became dazed, and when the partisan Vice-President, Dallas, of Pennsylvania, by his casting vote, insured the passage of the free trade or revenue tariff bill of 1846, confusion and indignation prevailed. While this administration cowered in the face of war with England, it did, with an eye single to the extension of slavery, go to war with Mexico under a resolution of the House of Representatives that "war existed by the act of Mexico." Henry Clay said his tongue would have cleaved to the roof of his mouth before he would have voted that lie. Such an administration naturally collapsed amid the plaudits of the people, and brave General Taylor became President. His reign was brief, however, for death for the second time in the history of the Republic, invaded the Presidential chair. His persistent determination secured the entrance of California into the Union as a free State. The administrations of Pierce and Buchanan were eminently Democratic, under absolute control of the slave power, leading directly and unmistakably to the greatest civil war known in the history of mankind.

The ratio of losses per $1,000 to the government on receipts and disbursements under Jackson were $7.52; Van Buren, 11.71. Under Republican Presidents: Lincoln, 76 cents; Johnson, 57 cents; Grant, 24 cents; Hayes, 8-10 of a mill. Those under Cleveland will not be manifest until after March 4, 1889.

The Democratic party is opposed to internal improvements by the general government; is in favor of free trade and opposed to the principles of protection. Vainly pretending not to know the difference between taxes and duties, it discriminates in favor of the former.

It opposes registry laws for the purification of the ballot. It would exalt the State above the nation. It causes our country to be represented at foreign courts by ex-rebels and worse—copperheads. It menaces the continuous loyalty of the Supreme Court. It embraces the worst elements of society, and is an omnipresent affinity of the liquor traffic. Its living principle is spoils, and it is "held together by the cohesive power of public plunder." Sympathizing with the rebellion, it is responsible for the creation of the public debt, and not anxious for its payment. Upon sixty millions of dollars loaned without interest to friends and coadjutors of the Democratic party, and many more millions lying idle in the treasury, the government is in effect paying interest in not using said money in payment of its interest-bearing bonds. Friends of a merchant who managed his finances thus would be justified in applying to the court for the appointment of a conservator of his estate. This money should circulate in all business channels of the Nation. Naturally the Democratic party is careless and indifferent as to the welfare of the disabled Union soldiers and sailors and their families. It is master of all the recent slave states, and the abject slave of every state that rebelled against the Union. President Cleveland, who has vetoed more bills than all his predecessors, holds his high office and the Democrats their majority in the House of Representatives chiefly by reason of frauds in the election in those states, and by the overwhelming vote of the slums in the city of New York!

Conspicuous among pleasant memories of duty performed during almost half a century, is having in our early life voted for General William Henry Harrison for President, and for the reasons herein set forth, and many others unnecessary to enumerate, we are fully convinced that continuous opposition to the Democratic party and its policy has proven true service to the country, so that when the life of the principle of protection of American labor is at stake we feel that we may with perfect propriety, appeal to the reason and patriotism of every young voter and invite them to unite with us in the endeavor to elect General

Benjamin Harrison, in whose valor, wisdom, honesty and patriotism we entertain the same confidence that we had in his illustrious
grandsire, President of the United States.

HENRY SAYRS,
D. B. FISK,
DR. DAVID S. SMITH,
   President of the Club,
JUDGE VAN H. HIGGINS,
WILLIAM RIPLEY,
JUDGE C. M. HAWLEY,
ALBERT SOPER,   } *Committee.*
T. B. CARTER,
SAMUEL C. GRIGGS,
NATHAN MEARS,
COLONEL R. M. HOUGH,
C. R. VANDERCOOK,
ENOS SLOSSON,

Here the president created a surprise in introducing to the
club the Hon. James G. Blaine. The way in which the latter was
received would give a lesson in enthusiam to any meeting. Mr.
Blaine said he was not a voter in 1840, but remembered seeing
the senior Harrison while on his way to Washington in 1841.
The scenes of that day were still vivid in his memory, and he
hoped to see before long another General Harrison on his way to
the White House. He was very glad, indeed, to meet so many
veterans.

Speeches were made by Dr. Brooks and Mr. Fontleroy.

It having been announced that seats on the platform in Cavalry Armory had been provided for the Old Tippecanoe Club, to
listen to Mr. Blaine's speech in the evening, the president requested all the members to meet at the Burdick House at 7
o'clock. Twenty-nine members were added to the club.

OCTOBER 27.—The regular meeting was called to order by the
president. C. R. Vandercook offered the following:

Resolved, That the club, as a body, have a street parade on the
31st inst., and that for that purpose all members be requested to
then meet at the headquarters.

The president stated that the club had just had an invitation from the Commercial Club and the Board of Trade Republican Club to join them in their parade next Saturday. It was decided to march as planned, and also accept the kind invitations. On motion of Mr. Burroughs, Col. R. M. Hough was chosen marshall of the day. Addresses were delivered by Stephen A. Douglas, Jr, Captain McHenry and others. On motion of Mr. Ripley, Mr. Douglas was elected an honorary member by a rising vote, and the president presented him with the club's badge; whereupon Mr. Douglass proposed three cheers for Harrison and Morton, which were given with a will. New members, 39. Adjourned.

The regular meeting was held November 3. The president stated that the veterans had assembled to take part in the great parade of the day. The marshall stated what he would expect of the boys. That the lines would form on La Salle and Quincy Streets. It was then voted that the regular business be suspended and that club adjourn for one week.

November 10, meeting called to order by the president after first congratulating the club in his pleasant and appropriate manner on the successful termination of the campaign. The finance committee asked and received further time in which to make its report. Philip Burroughs submitted the following: Resolved, that the Old Tippecanoe club of Chicago hereby extends its warmest thanks to the Commercial club and also to the Board of Trade Republican club for their invitation to join them in the march as well as for the honor shown by placing us at the head of the column. Resolved, that we also tender hearty thanks to General Joseph B. Stockton and the chairman of the central committee for their many courtesies and generosities shown the old boys of 1840. Adopted.

Mr. Albert Soper presented the following: Resolved, that a committee of three be appointed whose duties will be to revise the minutes of the meetings and reports of officers of the club, and prepare an introductory preface, to be placed in fore-part of the register; committee to be appointed by the chair. Carried. The chair appointed H. M. Garlick, Albert Soper and Henry Sayrs.

Resolved, That the members of this club do most heartily extend their sincere thanks to John B. Drake and Samuel Parker, of the Grand Pacific Hotel, for the use of this parlor during this great political campaign. Long may they live, prosperous and happy, are the wishes of the veterans of 1840. Adopted.

The following resolution was unanimously adopted:

Resolved, That the Old Tippecanoe Club of Chicago, in meeting assembled, do hereby extend to Dr. David S. Smith, President; Enos Slosson, 1st Vice-President; R. J. Bennett, 2d Vice-President; Henry M. Garlick, 1st Assistant Secretary; C. R. Van Dercook, Sergeant-at-Arms; Col. R. M. Hough, Marshall, and the Finance Committee our warmest thanks for the very able manner in which they have discharged their respective duties, and in their devotion to the interests of this organization, all tending to the great victory on November 6.

On motion of Mr. Enos Slosson, a committee of three, composed of Thos. B. Bryan, Enos Slosson and Nathan Mears (appointed by the chair), was designated to draft suitable resolutions to be forwarded to General Harrison, Levi P. Morton and the Gov-elect of Illinois. Said committee retired, and prepared and submitted the following, which was adopted by a rising vote:

Resolved, That we, members of the Old Tippecanoe Club of Chicago, some four hundred in number, many having cast our first vote for Wm. Henry Harrison, and because of our extreme age probably our last vote for his illustrious grandson, the president-elect, now unite our voices in heartiest congratulation to the President, Vice-President-elect, and the Governor-elect of Illinois, and commend them and our beloved country to the blessing of Almighty God.

Mr. Thomas B. Bryan moved that each member of the club be allowed to put his own autograph on the roster.

Although a civilian, Mr. Bryan was unanimously elected a member of the Loyal Legion, of which the late General Sheridan was commander-in-chief, in recognition of Mr. Bryan's faithful services in maintaining the honor, integrity and supremacy of the government of the United States. His identification with the Harrisons has been intimate, dating back to his residence in Cincinnati, when, as legal adviser of Mr. Scott Harrison, he assisted in the settlement of President Wm. Henry Harrison's estate. The convention which nominated General Harrison in 1840 was presided over by Gov. James Barbour, of Virginia, an uncle of Mr. Bryan.

Mr. Phillip Burroughs presented the following on permanent organization, which was adopted:

Resolved, That the Old Tippecanoe Club of Chicago shall continue its present organization so long as five members attend the meetings, and for that purpose they adopt the following rules:

ART. I.—The club shall meet the first Saturday after the first Tuesday of November of each year, and as much oftener as may be necessary for business.

ART. II.—The membership of this club shall be limited to those who assisted or voted in 1840 for the distinguished General Wm. Henry Harrison, and includes their wives, their sons, sons-in-law, their daughters and daughters-in-law.

ART. III.—The present officers shall hold their terms for one year, or until others are chosen in their places.

ART. IV.— The annual election for officers shall be held the first Saturday after the first Tuesday in November, in 1889, and yearly thereafter.

ART. V.—Five members of the club may call a meeting, and the highest officer present shall preside at all meetings. If no officers are present, then the oldest member shall preside.

Mr. I. A. Fleming, representing the Chicago Printing Co., stated that as it had been suggested that the club have catalogues, to contain names of members, their residence, and a brief biography of the club, he, on behalf of his company, would furnish the club with 1,000 printed copies free of charge. The proposition was accepted with thanks and cheers. The following gentlemen addressed the club, eliciting round after round of applause, viz: Hon. Thomas B. Bryan, Gen. J. B. Leake and J. B. Patterson. Gen. Leake dwelt mainly on the question of fraudulent elections in Southern States, handling the same in a masterly manner. In answer to a dispatch by Mr. P. M. Blodgett, the following telegram was received.

INDIANAPOLIS, Nov. 10, 1888.

P. M. Blodgett, Tippecanoe Club, Grand Pacific Hotel, Chicago:

Please convey to the members of the club my high appreciation of their efforts and cordial support during the campaign.
The evidence given me of their respect and confidence has been
very gratifying to me.   BENJAMIN HARRISON.

On November 24, the meeting was called to order by the First
Vice-President. Minutes of last meeting read and approved.
The following preamble and resolution was presented by Henry
Sayrs:

WHEREAS, It is desirable and important that the volume now
being prepared for the purpose of being placed with the Historical Society, to contain an account of all the proceedings in 1888
of the Old Tippecanoe Club of Chicago, shall embrace the autograph of every member of the club.

Resolved, That Secretary Garlick be, and hereby is, authorized
to procure printed postal cards and thereby notify and request
all members who shall on December 15th next not have signed,
to call at his office, No. 39, 116 Dearborn Street, and affix their
signature to the record, the expense of said postals to be paid for
by the treasurer.   Adopted.

Mr. P. Burroughs offered the following:

Resolved, That a tender to H. M. Garlick be rendered in tes-
timony of his valuable services in the interest of the club, and
that a committee of three be appointed to collect funds for said
purpose and present same.   Referred to Finance Committee with
power to act.

On motion of W. B. Mills it was

Resolved, That the regular meetings be held on the last Saturday of each month, at 2 o'clock, p. m., on and after November
24, 1888.

At the meeting December 29th, the Finance Committee reported financially, also that Secretary-Treasurer Ackley had
resigned, whereupon Mr. A. H. Morrison offered the following:

WHEREAS, Our Secretary and Treasurer has resigned, therefore be it

Resolved, That this club now proceed to an election of their successors.

Whereupon H. M. Garlick was unanimously elected Secretary and Albert Soper unanimously elected Treasurer. Mr. Soper offered the following resolution:

Resolved, That a committee of five be appointed whose duties shall be to draft a preface or historical account of the times, and biographic history of Chicago's Old Tippecanoes from 1836, 1840, to 1888, the same to be placed in fore part of the register belonging to the club, Carried. Judge C. M. Hawley, Henry Sayrs, Albert Soper, W. H. Bradley, and Wm. S. Elliott were appointed said committee.

The following letter from Gov.-elect Fifer was received and ordered spread upon the minutes:

BLOOMINGTON, ILL., Dec. 1, 1888.

H. M. Garlick, Secretary:

MY DEAR FRIEND. Your recent letter conveying to me the action of the Old Tippecanoe Club of Chicago is before me. It is indeed touching to be so kindly remembered by gentlemen who bear the years and honor that the members of your club carry. I appreciate highly the compliment you extended and ask you to carry to the members of your club, for me, my thanks for their kind remembrance and my sincere wishes for their personal prosperity. Yours most truly,

J. W. FIFER.

Mr. Bennett offered the following resolution:

Resolved, That the chair appoint a committee of five to be known as a committee of political action and that all measures, motions, resolutions, etc., contemplating the political course or endorsement of this club, shall be reported to said committee. Carried.

The chair appointed R. J. Bennett, Albert Soper, Thomas F. Mitchell and William H. Bradley, said committee; when on motion Enos Slosson was added thereto.

On motion of Thomas F. Mitchell, the by-laws were so amended as to read: The regular meetings of this club shall be on the second and fourth Saturdays of each month until further orders

Mrs. Minerva K. Elliott favored the club with an able address for which she received a vote of thanks. She was then voted an honorary member of the club, presented with a badge of the club and $10.

Mrs. Mary M. Hopkins, president of the Sycamore Tippecanoe Club delivered a brief address, was made an honorary member and presented with a badge.

At the meeting January 12, 1889, the First Vice-President presided. Henry Sayrs offered the following:

Resolved, That it is not the province or policy of this club to advocate or promote the nomination or appointment of anyone to office.

Mr. Prince moved that the resolution be referred to committee on political action. After considerable discussion Mr. Sayrs withdrew the resolution rather than have it referred to said committee and then moved that the resolution passed at the last meeting, appointing a committee on political action be re-considered, which motion was laid over until the next meeting.

Mr. Holmes moved that speeches on resolutions be confined to five minutes. Carried.

L. W. Garlick reported the death of one of the members.

Mr. J. H. Bellfield and Mr. Mills announced the serious illness of Luther Lafflin Mills.

On motion of Mr. Garlick a visiting committee of eight members was appointed to look after sick and disabled members, viz: For Hyde Park, L. W. Garlick and Judge C. M. Hawley. For the north division, Colonel R. J. Bennett, and for the west division, Messrs Blodgett and Burrows; for the south division, Henry Sayrs and Colonel R. M. Hough.

On motion of A. H. Morrison it was:

Resolved, That the secretary be, and hereby is, requested to cause to be printed the names of every member of the club, with his residence, the same to be distributed to the members at our next meeting. Carried.

Colonel Clement offered the following:

Resolved, That the club take immediate action to enlarge its membership by adding all names eligible to become members, so that we can take strong action in the coming spring election. Carried.

On January 26, president Smith called the meeting to order and stated his pleasure at being once again permitted to be at his post.

Mr. Burroughs, chairman committee on necrology, reported the death of•Luther L. Mills.   It was therefore:

Resolved, That a committee of three be appointed to draft suitable letter of condolence to the family of diseased and that a copy of said letter be spread upon the minutes, and that similar action be taken with reference to other members of the club who have died.   Reported to committee on necrology.

Judge Hawley then submitted the following:

WHEREAS, The secretary of the Tippecanoe Veterans of 1840, has received from Mr. Calel A. Wall, president of the Tippecanoe Club of Worcester, Massachusetts, a large photograph of the members in group—of 66—and other historical reminiscences, therefore be it:

Resolved, That this club extend to Mr. Wall their hearty thanks and the secretary be requested to forward a copy of this resolution to him.   Carried.

On motion of Mr. Bennett, Mr. Wall's letter was placed on file.

Mr. W. B. Mills moved that a vote of thanks be extended to the Commercial and Traveling Mens' Clubs in behalf of the old veterans, who wished to avail themselves of the low rate of fare etc., to visit Washington on the occasion of General Harrison's inauguration.   Adopted.

Judge C. M. Hawley, chairman committee on preparing preface to the book about to be published, submitted the preface to the consideration of the club.   It was approved.   Given to the press and the author thanked.

A motion by Mr. Albert Soper, to take the sense of the club regarding the publication of the proposed book, its size, cost, etc., caused some discussion and was referred to the revising committee with power to act.   So ordered.

On motion of Mr. H. M. Garlick a vote of thanks was tendered I. A. Fleming for 500 printed catalogues of membership.

Judge Bradley addressed the meeting, when after a song by Mr. Mills it adjourned.

The meeting of February 9, was opened with prayer by Rev. W. Holmes. Committee on necrology announced the death of C. W. Munger and W. F. Myrick; members of the club attending funeral of brother members were requested to wear the club badges.   •

Henry Sayrs called up a resolution which was laid on the table four weeks ago, to reconsider the following resolution, adopted December 29, viz:

Resolved, That the chair appoint a committee of five to be known as a committee of political action and that ALL measures, motions, resolutions, etc., contemplating the political course or endorsement of this club, SHALL be referred to said committee. After considerable discussion the motion was indefinitely postponed, whereupon Colonel Morrison moved, that said resolution of December 29 be so altered by striking out the word SHALL and inserting the word MAY in lieu thereof, as to make it read: That all measures, motions, resolutions, etc., MAY be referred to said committee.   Carried.

Resolved, That a standing committee of three be appointed, of which the president shall be chairman, whose duty shall be to secure speakers to address the club and report same to the secretary, giving names, subject and date, that same may be published with notice of meeting, said notices only authorized when signed by the president, or if president is absent, the vice-president or secretary.   Carried.

Mr. G. S. Knapp came forward and said he had made for the president, Dr. David S. Smith, and now took pleasure in presenting it—a gavel.   The mallet head was of hickory from Missionary Ridge.   In the head was a piece of black walnut from the table used in the convention at which president-elect Benjamin Harrison was nominated, a hickory shoot from Shiloh for the handle; plugged in the end of the handle was a piece of the celebrated black walnut rail which Abraham Lincoln split.   Affidavits from Charles A. Stone attested the genuineness of the hickory.   The splinter from Lincoln's rail came direct from the Chicago Historical Society, to which it was presented by the venerable Dennis F. Hanks.

The president expressed his gratitude and high appreciation of the souvenir and said the gavel would not only call the Old Tippecanoes to order but arouse their most patriotic memories.

On motion of Mr. Slosson a vote of thanks was tendered Mr. Knapp for his gavel.

Mrs. Thomas Collins read an excellent poem of which she was authoress in honor of the Old Tippecanoes, for which on motion of Mr. Mills she received a vote of thanks. It was

Resolved, That the secretary be authorized to have postal cards printed and mailed to the members, asking them to designate the number of books they would take at a cost of 50c. each, and to report same to him. Also, to have such as have not done so, to hand in their biographical history. Adopted.

Judge Hawley and Colonel Clement addressed the meeting and after a song, "The Sword of Bunker Hill," by A. H. Williams, adjourned.

At the meeting February 23, the committee on necrology reported the deaths of William Brace, aged 75 years, and J. G. Doddridge, aged 83 years. The revising committee reported progress. Mrs. B. Remington and Miss Fleming favored the club with recitations, for which they were thanked. The political situation was discussed by Colonel Morrison, George P. Harris, W. S. Elliott, Colonel Clement, Colonel R. M. Hough, R. J. Bennett and J. R. Magee. The course of Mayor John A. Roche was approved. Adjourned.

The regular meeting was held March 9, the first Vice-President, Enos Slosson, in the chair. Rev. Geo. S. Moore opened the meeting with prayer. Minutes of last meeting read and approved. Committee on necrology reported through L. W. Garlick the death of Bro. Wm. Patterson.

W. H. Bradley moved that all manuscript or other matter intended for publication in proposed biographical history of the club, be referred to Mr. I. A. Fleming to prepare, and when so done to submit such revision to the committee for their approval. Carried.

On motion of W. B. Mills the secretary was instructed to invite Hon. David G. Lyon and G. J. Patterson to address the club
at its next meeting.

The secretary stated that he would be pleased to give one of
his pictures from a pen-sketch made by himself from an old oil
painting in the possesssion of Gen. Benj. Harrison of his birthplace,
being the old homestead of Old Tippecanoe in North Bend,
Ohio, providing the club would have the same framed and presented to John B. Drake, Esq., whereupon R. J. Bennett moved
that the secretary be and is hereby instructed to have said picture
properly framed and ready at our next meeting, and that an
order be drawn on the treasury to pay for same. Carried unanimously. Addresses were made by J. K. Magee and Judges
Hawley and Bradley.

At the regular meeting on March 23, the committee on necrol-
ogy, through Mr. Burroughs, reported the death of Bro. Grant
Goodrich. Addresses were made by Mayor John A. Roche, S.
A. Douglas and Mrs. M. K. Elliott. On motion of the secretary,
John A. Roche was made an honorary member of the club, and
the Vice-President presented his honor with a badge of the club.

Representing the club, Henry Sayrs presented to John B.
Drake, the proprietor of the Grand Pacific Hotel, a lithograph of
Gen. Benjamin Harrison's birthplace at North Bend, Ohio, a pen-
sketch by the secretary, H. M. Garlick, from an oil painting made
in 1840. Mr. Drake expressed his gratitude and surprise in his
ever-genial manner, declaring himself a Republican all over and
in full sympathy with the cause, whereupon three welcome
cheers were given him. After an address by Judge Hawley, he
moved, that when the meeting adjourned it should be for one
week. Carried.

Here it was suggested that an entertainment be given under
the auspices of the club at Central Music Hall at an early
date, the proceeds of which, after all expenses were paid,
to be turned into the treasury of the club to be used in the interest of preparing for publication and the publishing of the book
of biographical sketches of the members, and other matter of
interest pertaining to the club's history; therefore be it

Resolved, that said entertainment be had and that a committee of fifteen or more be appointed to perfect the necessary arrangement. Carried.

The following committee was appointed:　R. J. Bennett, P. Burroughs, A. H. Williams, A. H. Morrison, C. M. Hawley, H. M. Garlick, G. S. Knapp, C. R. Vandercook, W. S. Elliott, I. A. Fleming, L. W. Garlick, Mrs. M. K. Elliott, Mrs. S. C. Hair, Mrs. L. W. Garlick, Mrs. G. S. Knapp, Miss Kate Burroughs and Miss Dewey.

The adjourned meeting of the club was held March 30. Committee on necrology reported the death of J. H. Gill at Topeka, Kan. on March 13, whereupon R. J. Bennett moved, that the committee on necrology draft and report suitable resolutions commemorative to the departed brother. Carried.

Henry Sayrs offered the following:

Resolved, that the Old Tippecanoe Club of Chicago, heartily congratulates the President of the United States on the appointment of Robert T. Lincoln, Envoy Extraordinary and Minister Plenipotentiary of the United States to Great Britain.

Resolved, that the secretary be, and hereby is, requested to transmit a copy of the foregoing resolution to Benjamin Harrison, President of the United States.　Carried.

After some discussion on way and manner of the club, proper action on application of its members for endorsement for political positions, the following resolution was offered by Henry Sayrs:　·

Resolved, that for the benefit of persons, NOW MEMBERS of this club, who may be applicants for official positions of the Federal government or the City of Chicago, the president, first and second vice-presidents, treasurer and secretary, or a majority of them concurring each in his official capacity, may upon request, in their discretion and in behalf of this club, duly certify as to the honesty, ability and patriotism of such applicants. Carried.

Mr. A. H. Williams moved, that a vote of thanks be tendered the Marquette Club for favors shown this club during the trip to to Washington and also to G. S. Knapp, who represented the club on the excursion to the inauguration of Benjamin Harrison. Adopted.

R. J. Bennett, chairman, reported that the committee had about completed arrangements for the entertainment and had selected their sub-committee—the committee on program being I. A. Fleming, H. M. Garlick and G. S. Knapp. H M. Garlick being made treasurer of committee. Accepted.

On motion of Mr. Bennett, Phillip Burroughs was appointed to act as Marshall and John King, Jr., as aid for the veterans on the march to the hall of entertainment.

Mr. L. W. Garlick moved, that the members of the club meet at the Grand Pacific Hotel on the evening of April 4, and proceed in a body to Central Music Hall to the music of fife and drum, each member wearing the club badge. Carried.

On motion of Mr. Pierce adjourned for one week.

The meeting of April 6 was called to order by the First Vice-President. Prayer was offered by the Rev. Mr. Severance.

Mr. R. J. Bennett, chairman of committee on arrangement for the entertainment had at Central Music Hall, reported that the committee had not finished so as to enable them to make a definate report; they had done good and successful work, however, and asked for more time to report. Further time was granted and the committee thanked by the club for the able manner they had thus far discharged their duties.

It was then determined that all unsettled business connected with the late entertainment be left for settlement in the hands of the original committee.

Mr. Bennett stated that in consequence of continued absence of the president and treasurer, two other members should be appointed in their stead in signing petitions for applicants of the club for official positions, whereupon Judge C. M. Hawley and Phillip Burroughs were chosen to temporarily fill those vacancies.

Mr. I. A. Fleming moved a vote of thanks be tendered the Hon. Thos. B. Bryan, Rev. Dr. Withrow and Eugene J. Hall, for their valued services at the entertainment given by veterans of 1836, 1840-1888 on April 4 in Central Music Hall, and that the secretary be requested to transmit same to each. Carried unanimously.

Mr. L. W. Garlick moved a vote of thanks to all others who assisted the committee or rendered service towards the advancement of the entertainment. Carried.

Col. Thos. Mitchell moved, that a committee of five be appointed to make necessarry arrangements, in the interest of the club, for the celebration of the centennial of Washington's inaugural, April 30. The chair named as such committee: Thos. Mitchell, John King, Jr., G. S. Knapp, P. Burroughs and Michael McAuley.

Adjourned for one week.

The regular meeting of the club was called to order by President David Smith, M. D., April 13. The president acknowledged his thankfulness and pleasure in being spared to again be at his post after an absence of several weeks in Washington, and was delighted to see so many of the "Boys" ready for duty.

Col. Bennett, chairman of committee on arrangements for entertainment, reported that the committee had not yet been able to get affairs in shape for a complete report and asked that the time to report be extended to the next meeting of the club, which was granted.

The president stated he had received two letters which he requested the secretary to read:

SPRINGFIELD, MARCH 27, 1889.

David S. Smith, Esq., Pres. Old Tippecanoe Club, Chicago, Ill.:

My Dear Sir:

I am in receipt of your letter of March 27 and notice your kind invitation to be with your club on the 4th of April at Central Music Hall. I appreciate your kindness in remembering me, and regret that the pressure of public duties here will prevent my accepting the same. Please convey to the members of your club my kindest regards.

Yours very truly,

JOSEPH W. FIFER.

EXECUTIVE MANSION, WASHINGTON, APRIL 4, 1889.
David S. Smith, M. D., Chicago, Ill:

The president directes me to acknowledge the receipt of your letter of the 30th of March conveying the congratulations of the Old Tippecanoe Club, and to express to you and to the members of the club his sincere thanks for this evidence of friendly regard.   Very truly yours,

E. W. HALFORD, *Private Secretary.*

On motion of the second vice-president said letters were ordered to be spread upon the records.

Mr. Henry Sayrs, in behalf of the club, warmly welcomed president Smith home and to duty, and after humorously reporting to his honor as requested and as in duty bound, how gay the "boys" had been in his absence, especially on the evening on the fourth instant, submitted the following:

CONGRATULATORY. In view of the general and complete gratification expressed by individual members of our club and others who were so fortunate as to be present and partake of the grand literary and musical entertainment given under the auspices of the Old Tippecanoe Club, at Central Music Hall, on the evening of the fourth instant, our hearty congratulations are extended to the committee which had the affair in charge, their "program committee," Messrs I. A. Fleming, H. M. Garlick and G. S. Knapp, for their able indefatigable and successful co-operation are entitled to the highest praise. To Mr. I. A. Fleming is to be accorded the credit of suggesting a public entertainment for the benefit of the club, and to also give our fellow citizens an opportunity to become better acquainted with the veterans, and at the same time, at a merely nominal cost, devote an evening to unalloyed pleasure. Adopted by the unanimous voice of the club.

Colonel Mitchell, chairman of committee on centennial arrangements, reported that no general program had been mapped out, but that arrangements had been made for clubs to march to Central Music Hall, and he asked if it was the wish of this club to do so. Mr. Williams, Mr. McAuley and Mr. Prince thought it the proper thing to do—and be it

Resolved, That we meet at these headquarters on April 30, at two o'clock P. M., and proceed in a body to Central Music Hall, and that the secretary notify the chairman of the centennial committee of this proposed action and ask that 100 to 150 seats be reserved for us. Carried.

Mr. Henry Sayrs presented and read the following:

To the Old Tippecanoe Club, the committee on publication beg leave to report as follows: The forthcoming club history will, in our opinion, be valuable as a record of the principles and doctrines of the whig and republican parties, as illustrated in the biographical and autograph album of the "Old Tippecanoes." You can believe that the general public understand that the "Old Tippecanoe Club" is composed of veterans of the political campaigns of 1836–40—when General William Henry Harrison (Old Tippecanoe) was the standard bearer of the whig party and that in order to be an "Old Tippecanoe" it was necessary for one to be not less than 69 years of age at the time of our last presidential election. While your committee have the highest regard for our younger members, we nevertheless believe that the personality of the "Old Tippecanoes" should be rigidly maintained in both the biographical and autographic collection, as by so doing the value of the work as a souvenir of the political campaigns of 1836–40 and 1888 and of the "Old Tippecanoe Club" would be greatly enhanced. Your committee would therefore respectfully ask the adoption of the following resolution:

Resolved, That the committee on publication be, and hereby is, authorized to insert in the club history the biographical sketches and authograph signatures of such members only who voted for or assisted in the election of William Henry Harrison for president and such other matter as in their judgment they consider proper. Carried.

H. M. GARLICK, Secretary.

Campaign Poem.

BY CLARA HOWARD.

We're nearly all beyond the age
 Of three score years and ten,
But we voted once for Harrison,
 And we'll vote that way again.

Yes, forty years and more ago
 (We all were young men then),
We voted straight for Tippecanoe,
 And we'll vote that way again.

'Twas then we built log cabins,
 Baked Johnny cake for the men
Who helped elect old Tippecanoe
 And we'll "take the cake" again.

Each year our ranks are thinning
 To make way for younger men,
We soon will join old Tippecanoe;
 We may never vote again.

But we'll uphold no free-trade banner,
 And we want no free-trade men;
We've ever voted for the right,
 And we'll vote that way again.

Here's to the health of our candidate,
 Please pass the cider again,
We drank it then to Tippecanoe,
 Now we'll drink to General Ben.

He comes of freedom-loving stock,
One signed the Declaration;
His grandsire fought in eighteen twelve
And he fought to save our nation.

Then give three cheers and a tiger, too,
Join in, all the brave old men,
As we voted once for Tippecanoe
We'll shout for his grandson, Ben.

For Harrison, then, and Morton, too,
Let us give three cheers again;
We'll vote once more for Harrison
Just as we voted then.

Tippecanoe Trip to Indianapolis.

The Old Tippecanoe Club of Chicago, accompanied by the La Salle Club and the John A. Logan Club, in all about 1,100, visited General Harrison at Indianapolis, on September 29, George M. Pullman Esq., generously furnishing the Old Tippecanoes with his best and most elegant palace car. Every large town reached, thousands had gathered to see and greet us. Short speeches were made by our president, cheers upon cheers were returned, the bands playing patriotic airs; the cars moving off amid the most wild and enthusiastic cheers. A splendid time all along the entire route of two-hundred miles. Starting at Chicago at eight A. M., and reaching Indianapolis at four P. M., where we were met by a large gathering, which swelled to one of the greatest. The First Regiment Band preceded us from the depot along the streets of the city, amid the continued cheers of the crowds and the boom of an elevated cannon between the ranks of the patriotic veterans, every one of whom wore an elegantly wrought appropriate silk badge, the civil and military under presented arms, on either side along the entire distance to the ample grounds of the university, provided with a large stand for our reception, to which General Harrison was escorted amid ringing cheers. Judge Green, who accompanied us, delivered a short speech and was followed by our Tippecanoe president, who delivered the following address:

" GENERAL HARRISON: The Old Tippecanoe Club, which hails from Chicago, and which comprises nearly three hundred members, has commissioned those of us who represent them here today, to convey to you the warmest expressions of their confidence and esteem.

In the discharge of that pleasant duty, it is incumbent upon us to take into consideration the almost incessant drafts upon your time and attention, confident that you will not undervalue our assurances of regard because of the brevity of their utterance. Suffice it to say that many of our members shared with you the trials and dangers of the battlefield, in the ever-memorable conflict for the preservation of the Union, and all of us are united in the ardent desire for your triumphant election to the presidency of the United States.

That desire is founded upon our convictions, that the continued ascendancy of true patriotic loyalty to the Union, is opposed by the ideas and practices of the so-called "Solid South," that the supreme court of the United States has already full enough of Democratic flavor.

That there is also an excess of the late disloyal element in our diplomatic service; that the paramount issue of the campaign challenges the championship of us all in continuing that protection of American industry which has so signally advanced the growth and greatness of our Nation; and finally, that all these, and other attendant interests of our common country, can best be fostered and secured by your elevation as the successful standard-bearer of Republican principles. You have our best wishes now, as you shall have our ballots in November, and as we once cast them for your illustrious grandsire."

Then General Harrison stepped forward, hat in hand, and delivered a most elegant, happy welcoming speech to the city of Indianapolis; then turning partly around and facing the vast crowd, extemporized another short, impressive speech to them, amid deafening cheers, after which the personal introductions took place — the president of our club first introducing the first vice-president, following which each member had the pleasure of taking the General by the hand and wishing him God speed. The General was much pleased with the flag borne by us, in the hands of William Slosson, son of the vice-president. It was an old silken flag, beautifully wrought by ladies forty-eight years ago in the most exquisite style throughout, with many colored silks, and was in the convention which nominated the grandfather of the General in 1840. Waiving the General adieu, we were escorted with the music to the New Dennison Hotel. Satisfying the inner man we were soon charmingly serenaded for our amusement by the same Regimental Band from the porch above, while the streets were brilliantly illuminated with the marvelous natural gas. After adieus once again the band marched us back to our awaiting Pullman palace train for our city, reaching home in time for church services.

Grand Popular Demonstration

OF

REPUBLICANS IN CHICAGO, NOVEMBER 3, 1888.

———

The most magnificent of all Chicago parades in the last presidential campaign was that of November 3, of which so many
graphic and detailed accounts appeared in the press of this and
other cities as to render it wholly unnecessary to reproduce them
here.

There seemed to be a representation of every trade or human
industry of any consequence and a significant fact was noticed
that scarcely one of the fifteen thousand men in line was not a
voter—all good men and true, with General Harrison's name
inscribed in their hearts and on their banners.

It was conceded by the press, as well as by observers, not far
from a million of people that had congregated to witness the
superb pageant, that the most impressive feature of the mighty
demonstration was the array in the front rank of the procession
of the members of the Old Tippecanoe Club.

The president, vice-president and treasurer, with one or two
invited guests, occupied the first carriage, followed by a long
train of other open carriages. One of the briefest notices of the
many that appeared in the press read thus, as extracted: "The
carriages are filled with white-headed veterans and there is a tre-
mendous cheer up and down the street, that is taken up and
repeated by people in the windows. The white-beards are the
Tippecanoe veterans of 1840. Their withered cheeks look almost

young again. **They forget the lapse of fifty years.** They are back with **Tippecanoe** and are happy."

A most enthusiastic reception was accorded the veterans during the entire march of the procession and they were greeted with inspiring shouts, many of special significance such as: "We shall follow your glorious example" etc.

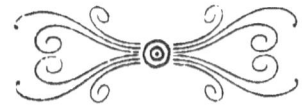

The Old Tippecanoe Guard.

EXTRACT FROM THE EDITORIAL COLUMN OF THE CHICAGO TRIBUNE
OF NOVEMBER 12, 1888.

While the "first voters" performed their work gallantly last Tuesday, full praise and recognition must be made for the splendid services of the Old Tippecanoe voters. The old men over sixty-nine who infused into the recent campaign something of the spirit of 1840, contributed in a great degree to the election of General Harrison. At a moderate estimate at least 50,000 men who voted in 1840 survived to cast their ballots last Tuesday. The old Harrison men were solid for young Tippecanoe, and they brought into line thousands of their old associates who voted for Van Buren in 1840, but made amends in 1888 by throwing their ballots for the second Harrison. As the *Tribune* predicted at the beginning of the campaign, there was a magic in the name of Harrison for the old voters who passed through the famous campaign of 1840, and in innumerable homes the incidents of that campaign were recalled in the last five months, and it is plain that such reminiscent influences did not tend to prejudice the republican party or the republican candidate.

The Old Tippecanoe voters gave to the recent campaign many of the most interesting features—they introduced again into the political field the log cabin, the historic coon, the cider barrel, and some of the old songs of 1840. Most of the Tippecanoe veterans have passed the age for active electioneering, but they had great influence, and they used it well.

These old men were the founders of families—big old fashioned families—and they could appeal to sons, sons-in-law, and grandsons as no one else could. Shouldering a crutch to show how fields were won, they would point out the untimely death of "Old Tip,' which cheated them of their victory and caused the whig party to be Tylerized, and for this reason they begged the younger men to help them put in "Young Tip," so that a Harrison might yet fill out a presidential term, and the veterans could depart in peace after their eyes had seen the salvation of the Lord. The appeal of the old men was a telling one, and they influenced thousands of doubtful and even democratic votes. Many of these old men will live to see another republican adminstration, and some of them probably two or three more. They know that old Whig principles, such as the protection of home industry and the nationalization of the currency, for which they struggled in their youth, are now firmly established and will be steadily maintained by the Republican party. While the Tippecanoe veterans are to be complimented and congratulated warmly on their part in the recent campaign, the grandmothers should not be forgotten. As girls in 1840 they took almost as much interest as their brothers and lovers in the success of "Old Tip," and in 1888 they put in many a quiet, but effective word that influenced sons, sons-in-law, and grandsons to vote for "Young Tippecanoe."

Biographical Sketches

OF THE

Members of the Old Tippecanoe Club,

WHO VOTED FOR, OR ASSISTED IN THE ELECTION OF,
"OLD TIP" IN 1836-40.

JAMES ACKERMAN.

Born in Poughkeepsie, Dutches county, N. Y., on the 21st of August 1815. His parents were natives of the State of New York. He followed the business of merchandising in the city of Yonkers and the city of New York. In 1877 he came west and first settled in Milwaukee. In 1881 he came to Illinois and settled in Hyde Park, where he now resides. He voted for General William Harrison in 1836 and 1840, and for General Benjamin Harrison in 1888.

CHENEY AMES

Was born in Mexico, Oswego county, N. Y., June 19th, 1808. His father, Leonard Ames, was one of the sturdy pioneers of that county. At an early age he was apprenticed to the "hatting" trade, in Cortland, N. Y. His aspirations led to newer fields and a desire for increased knowledge of the world. In 1837 he removed to Oswego, N. Y., and identified himself closely with the commercial interests until 1886, when he removed to Chicago. He was frequently a member of the New York Legislature, and in 1857 was elected to the Senate of that state, serving as Chairman of Commerce and Navigation Committees; and again in 1857 was returned to the Senate. On the breaking out of the war he was appointed member of the War Committee by Gov. Morgan, and from that time until peace was declared he gave his entire attention to his duties in that capacity. His oldest son was killed in the war. Mr. Ames entered very zealously into the campaign of 1840, and from that time to the present has been identified with the Whig and Republican parties, casting his last vote for Gen. Benjamin Harrison in 1888.

ROBERT Y. ASKIN.

Cast his first vote for "William Henry Harrison" in 1840. He has also voted for every Whig and Republican candidate for president up to the present, having voted for Benjamin Harrison in November to succeed "Cleveland." He has a good war record, having fought through seven hard-fought battles and several skirmishes. Being too old to be subject to draft, it was of course voluntary, as he was not in favor of the dissolution of our glorious union and bitterly opposed to slavery.

CAPT. HENRY ASHBURY

Was born in Hansen county, Kentucky, August 10, 1810; moved to Quincy, Illinois in 1834 and has resided in that city for fifty-one years. Was admitted to the Bar, March 1837 and to the Circuit court of the United States, August 4, 1859, and has also held a number of offices by the suffrages of the people, and appointment by presidents of the United States. Voted for Henry Clay in 1832 and has voted with the Whig and Republican candidates ever since. Captain Ashbury was Provert Marshall of the Fourth Congressional District during the war with the rank and pay of Captain of Cavalry, and is now known as "Old Captain" Ashbury.

W. B. AYERS

Was born March 2, 1822 at Utica, New York and secured not only the benefits of a common school education but attended some of the best academies of the day and commenced the study of

medicine in 1840 at Fairfield Medical School, the only one west
of New York. He took an active part in the campaign of 1840
and listened to such eloquent speakers as Clay, Spencer and
Seward, marching in log cabin processions to the detriment of
his studies and the final abandonment of thoroughly learning the
medical profession. He landed in Chicago in 1849, doing various
work till the opening of the Michigan Southern Railway, when
he became purser of the steamer Golden Gate, the property of
that company. Later he deserted Chicago for Buffalo, where he
sunk his savings of years, and after various changes again returned
to Chicago in 1868, and has since been successful and happy. A
strong Republican, he voted "straight in '88."

LEONIDAS V. BADGER,

Another son of New England, born at the town of Portsmouth,
N. H., June 25th, 1806, and now in his eighty-third year. He
sagely, and with respect of truth, says: "I have not yet been able
to see any advantage in voting with the Democratic party," from
which it may readily be inferred that Mr. Badger is, and has ever
been, a Whig or Republican. His first vote for president was in
1832, his first Harrisonian vote in 1836, his second, with better
success, in 1840, and his last for the grandson in 1888. Mr. Badger was one of the original members of the association—a modest,
earnest gentleman.

HENRY BALDWIN

Was born September 19th, 1817, on Greenfield Hill, town of Fairfield, Fairfield county, Connecticut. He attended the common
schools of Connecticut, and he says: "They were pretty common
too." He used to get thrashed two and three times a day, and
was politically a Whig until the origin of the Republican party.
He voted for General William H. Harrison in 1840 in the town of
Fairfield, and voted for General Benjamin Harrison at Riverside,
Cook county, Illinois, 1888.

WILLIAM G. BALDWIN

Was born the 27th of April, 1807, at Bedford, Hillsboro county, N. H., moving to Hopkinston, St. Lawrence county, N. Y., where he remained until 1837. In 1840, at Bristol, Vt., he cast his first vote for Gen. William Henry Harrison. In 1852 Mr. Baldwin removed to Illinois, living in Woodstock for three years, after which time he lived in Chicago, casting his last vote for General Benjamin Harrison.

LILIBRIDGE BARBER,

Son of Col. Edward Barber, a soldier of the war of 1812, was born in Hopkinton, Washington county, R. I., August 31, 1815; working at home on a large farm and at carpentering until 1837. He cast his first vote for Martin Van Buren in 1836, but changed for the better in 1840, when he voted for Harrison. In 1858 Mr. Barber removed to Edgerton, Wis., where he remained until 1867, when he moved to Janesville, and in 1868 to Chicago, where he has since resided, intending to prosecute the carpenter business; but finding times dull, he entered the elevator of Munn & Scott as carpenter foreman, going into real estate after the big fire, which is still his calling. Mr. and Mrs. Barber celebrated their golden wedding December 25th, 1886, and is still blessed with the company of his companion.

JOSEPH PULSIFER BARTLETT,

Born in Campton, Grafton county, New Hampshire, January 16, 1810; voted in 1832, at Meredith, N. H., for Henry Clay; in 1836, at Hanover, N. H., for William Wirt; in 1840 for William Henry Harrison, at Rockford, Winnebago county, Ill.; in 1888 voted for General Benjamin Harrison, at Campton, Kane county, Ill.

JARED BASSETT,

One of Chicago's oldest residents, having removed here in 1816, from Montpelier, Washington county, Vermont, where he was born January 26th., 1814. In 1836, and again in 1840, he voted for General Harrison at Montpelier, Vt., voting for General Harrison—the grandson in 1888. Mr. Bassett is a well known citizen and has ever held fast to the Whig principles of his ancestor.

A. T. BATES.

Born in Westfield, Mass., 1813; removed with parents to Trumbull county, Ohio, in the year 1829; voted for General William Henry Harrison in 1836; removed from Trumbull county to Portage county, Ohio, in 1838; voted for General William Henry Harrison in 1840; came to Chicago in 1866, and has resided here most of the time since. He now resides at 154 Oakley Ave.

WILLIAM HENRY BEECHER,

Eldest son of Lyman Beecher, D. D., and Roxana Foote, his wife, was born at East Hampton, L. I., January 15, 1802.

Delicate in early youth he was not sent to college, but studied at home; he received the degree of M. A., from Yale College, though never connected in any other way with that institution. He studied Theology at Andover, and with his father, then in Boston. In 1835 he went to Ohio and was for twenty years an active home missionary in the new state. By his clear common sense, energy and enthusiasm for the work, he was able to securely found a number of churches and schools, still flourishing.

He possessed in a large degree that clear insight and good judgment which results in what is called "common sense;" his critical ability was of the highest order; his uprightness unquestioned. Anti-slavery, Free-soil, Republican, the sequence was a natural one.

He is living at the family residence, 108 Honore Street, Chicago, crippled and enfeebled in body; but awaiting the summons to go forth, in perfect self-possession. Aged eighty-seven.

Being an anti-slavery man his interest in politics was always deep—the election of the right man a thing of vast importance. He remembers the enthusiasm of the campaign of William Henry

Harrison—its songs and the political issue; took part in it to some extent—voting for him.

His enfeebled condition prevented him from voting for General Benjamin Harrison; but his interest was unabated and profound, his confidence in ultimate success unshaken and his satisfaction in the result is in proportion.

REZIN J. BENNETT.

My grandfather Bennett was a native of Maryland his family being one of the first to land where the city of Baltimore now is. He served through the Revolutionary War, as a soldier under General Washington.

My father, Samuel Bennett, was born and raised on a farm in Baltimore county. In 1794 he married Rebecca Borham, who was born and raised near Mt. Vernon, Va., and was well acquainted with General George Washington and his wife, Martha.

My parents settled on a farm in Frederick county, Maryland, where I was born August 7, 1815. I was the youngest of ten children, being the seventh son. In 1817 my father, with his family, emigrated west in a common road wagon. Hotels and farm houses were few and far between. This fact made it necessary for them to cook their own meals by the roadside and sleep in and under the wagon much of the time. After their long and wearisome journey, we crossed the Ohio river and located in Jefferson county, Ohio; took up quarters in a log cabin, where a clearing had been made. We immediately proceeded to build a hewed log house. After completing this we proceeded to make preparation to put in a spring crop.

In 1818 my father died, leaving my mother with her ten children in a new country, with few neighbors and very few schools, the latter ranging in distance from five to ten miles, and being presided over by such teachers as could be had in such a country. The extent of the years schooling was three months, making it very difficult to obtain even a common school education.

All of the members of a farmer's family had hard labor to perform. At the age of twelve I could perform the work of a full grown man on the farm. At that time we **had** no such farming implements as are now used. We had to use wooden plows, and harrows with wooden teeth. Our small grain was cut with a reap hook and then thrashed out with a frail, out doors on the ground—the grain being separated from the chaff by shaking it through a wooden sieve and using a common bed sheet for a wind-mill.

I remained on the farm until about 1837. I then went to Cadiz the county seat of Harrison county, Ohio, and entered a genera store as clerk for an elder brother, and remained with him unti 1844. He at that time removed to St. Louis, Mo., I remaining in Cadiz, carrying on the same business. In 1847 I was electec Mayor of that town, serving two terms, refusing to serve longer I afterward served as Sheriff and Treasurer of my county. I was for twenty years a member of the Whig County Centra Committee, being also a member of the State Central Committee during a portion of that time, and well remember the campaign of 1824, although only a boy of nine years. John Quincy Adams General Jackson and W. H. Crawford, were the leading candi dates for the presidency—no one receiving a majority of the electoral votes, John Quincy Adams was elected President by the House of Representatives. I felt quite an interest in the elec tion of 1828. Adams and Jackson were the candidates. Jackson was elected—to my great sorrow—and re-elected in 1832. In 1836 I cast my first vote for General William Henry Harrison, a Mt. Pleasant, Jefferson county, Ohio. I took a deep interest in this campaign. Although he was defeated by Martin Van Buren I had great hope that at the next election the Whig party could elect General Harrison. The Whigs called a national convention and nominated him the candidate for the party. When the cam paign opened I organized a singing club of twelve boys. We rigged a canoe on wheels—with a buckeye bush in front, with a live coon chained to the top of it. We traveled over the country singing for "Tippecanoe and Tyler, too," and for Tom Corwin the wagoner boy, who was a candidate for Governor. We also formed a log cabin club in Cadiz. I was elected Secretary and Treasurer. We built a large log cabin in the town for holding

R. J. BENNETT, Second Vice-President.

meetings—it was also used as a reading room—the citizens leav
ing their papers etc., there for the use of the public. During th(
campaign General Harrison, in passing through the state, called
A meeting was held to hear him speak at Cadiz. On Monday ;
committee was appointed to invite and convey him to Cadiz
These gentlemen chartered a new four horse coach and me
the General at Wooster. They arrived on Saturday. A large com
pany of people on horseback met them about six miles ou
and escorted them to the town. The General stopped at m)
brother's house, staying there until Tuesday, attending the Pres
byterian church on Sunday. We all esteemed it a great pleasur(
to entertain so great and good a man. I will never forget th(
pride I took in sitting and breaking bread at the same table an(
walking to and from church with the man I so much admired.

Horace Greeley, of New York, started a paper called *Th*
Log Cabin. I was instructed to subscribe for one hundred copie:
for distribution. The paper was continued through the campaigr
until after the inauguration. The last number gave a full accoun
of the inauguration and address, with a return of the votes o
each state by counties. The last page contained a prospectus o
the New York *Tribune*, to be published by Horace Greeley. :
succeeded in getting a number of subscribers for the first number
Three years ago, on a visit to my old home in Ohio, I foun(
families still taking the New York *Tribune*.

After the defeat of General Scott, the Whig candidate in 1852
there was no permanent organized party to oppose the Demo
cratic party, leaving a large number at sea, not knowing how t(
concentrate their power in opposition to the slave party. In 185!
the friends of freedom and an honest government called a con
vention at Columbus, Ohio, inviting all persons opposed to th(
extension of slavery and the doctrine of the so-called Democrati(
party. I was a delegate to that convention that formed th(
Republican party. The convention was organized by electing
Hon. John Sherman, President, forming the first platform of th(
Republican party in the state, and nominating Salmon P. Chase
for Governor. He was elected, serving two terms. I was dele
gate to the National Convention held in Chicago in 1860, nomi-

nating Lincoln for President; was also delegate to convention held in Baltimore in 1864, when Lincoln was renominated; was also a delegate when General Grant was nominated in 1868. I attended the convention when Garfield was nominated in 1880, and in the convention when Blaine was nominated in 1884, and General Harrison in 1888. Have personally known all the Presidents, commencing with John Quincy Adams, up to the present, excepting Martin Van Buren and General Pierce. As I have already stated, my first vote for President was for General Harrison in 1836; for Harrison in '40; Clay in '44; Zach. Taylor in '48; General Scott in '52; General Fremont in '56; Lincoln in '60 and '64; Grant in '68 and '72; Hayes in '76; Garfield in '80; Blaine in '84, and General Ben. Harrison in '88. Have cast my vote at every election, City, County, State and National, since '36. In '60 I was holding a position in the House of Representatives, under Col. John W. Forney, then Clerk of the House. I belonged to a company of Home Guards in Washington, Col. Forney being the commanding officer of the company. Being home on a vacation when Sumpter was fired on by the rebels, was telegraphed by Forney to report in Washington, to shoulder my musket to defend the government. I immediately left Ohio and received my musket, and retained the same until the close of the war, being in the field much of the time. In '64 I was appointed paymaster in the Regular Army, by President Lincoln, grade of Major; received my commission; was breveted Colonel; resigned in '66 on account of sickness in my family, much against the will of Secretary Stanton. Soon after I was appointed Internal Revenue Inspector, stationed at Cadiz; held my position until the office was abolished by act of Congress. I was then appointed Inspector of Customs at the Port of New York; remained there two years, resigned and retired to Ohio. I was then appointed and commissioned Treasury Agent, located at Chicago, spent some time at Topeka, Kansas, on duty. I then returned to Chicago and was transferred to the position of Inspector of Customs, Port of Chicago, remaining in that position until after the election of Grover Cleveland, who appointed Mr. Seeberger Collector of the Port of Chicago. Soon after I was requested

by Mr. Seeberger to hand in my resignation on account of
my known Republicanism, and the further fact that my place
was wanted for a Democrat. I promptly did as requested and
made way for a hungry Democrat. I was too good a Republican
to serve under a Democratic administration, and here I am a
member of the Old Tippecanoe Club of Chicago, consisting of
five hundred members, and being honored by the club as one of
its vice-presidents.

I herewith give you a fac-simile of the badge I wore in '40. I
also have a fine silk badge worn in '44 that takes me back to the
days when my interest and enthusiasm was younger, but not
greater than in '88.

PHINEAS M. BLODGETT

Was born November 18th, 1809, at Groton, N. Y. His father was
a soldier of the Revolution, and was at one time a prisoner of H.
R. M. George III; confined in the old sugar house in New York
City, but was smart enough to escape, and again joined the patriot
army. Mr. P. M. Blodgett cast his first vote in 1832 for Henry
Clay; in 1836 for Wm. H. Harrison and for every Whig and
Republican candidate since that date, including his latest vote for
General B. Harrison. In 1840 he joined an enthusiastic party of
young voters who went from Ithica to Syracuse, N. Y., to attend
a glorious mass meeting for "Tippecanoe and Tyler, too," and
forty-eight years later, older, wiser, more sedate, but not less
enthusiastic, he joined the grey beards of 1888, in their call on
General Benjamin Harrison and their subsequent rejoicing at his
success. Was commissioned Captain, Ind. Rifle Co., in 1840.

JAMES WOODBURY BOYDEN

Was born May 18, 1822, at Beverly Farms, near the north shore
of Massachusetts Bay—an hour's ride from Boston.

His mother was an only daughter of James Woodbury, whose
grandfather Robert Woodbury was Beverly's second town clerk.
As early as 1630, John and William Woodbury—from whom the
Woodburys of New England descended—emigrated from Somer-
setshire, England, and settled permanently in Beverly, Mass.

James Woodbury died in his eighty-ninth year (1842) and devised one of the picturesque and beautiful Beverly farms to his grand children—of whom James Woodbury Boyden, of Chicago, and Albert Woodbury Boyden, of Sheffield, Illinois, survive.

Dr. Wyatt Clark Boyden, their father, was son of Dr. Joseph Boyden, of Sturbridge, Mass.—who married Mary Heywood, of Gardner, Mass., and practiced medicine in Tamworth, New Hampshire. Dr. Wyatt C. Boyden was a Dartmouth College graduate (1819), and classmate of brilliant and genial Rufus Choate—the superior in talent and acquirement over all his college mates. Not far from Mr. Choate's native place (Essex), his classmate, Boyden, taught school at Beverly Farms. He married Elizabeth Woodbury, was a successful physician, and died in his eighty-fifth year (1879). He outlived the wife of his youth, and second wife—Lydia Leavitt Lincoln, of Boston, mother of Mary Boyden—of Martha, wife of Rev. Stephen W. Webb, and William Cowper Boyden, of Beverly.

Mrs. James Woodbury was niece of Nathan Dane, of Beverly, the eminent member of the Continental Congress from Massachusetts, who drafted the Ordinance of 1787 for the government of the territory north west of the river Ohio. Rev. Manassah Cutler, a leading member of the New England Colony at Marietta, Ohio, was one of Dane's constituents, and active in securing for this ordinance the unanimous approval of Congress. By it the fundamental principles of civil and religious liberty, morality and knowledge were forever established as the basis of all laws, constitutions and governments of the five states of Ohio, Indiana, Illinois, Michigan and Wisconsin. The Sixth Article—"That there shall be neither slavery nor involuntary servitude in the said territory"—was proposed by Nathan Dane, as an amendment, on the second reading of the ordinance—and this amendment was unanimously adopted by Congress. Mr. Dane subsequently published an Abridgment of American Law—donated the profits to Harvard University, as the foundation of a Law Professorship, and secured the services of Mr. Justice Story of the U. S. Supreme Court, as Dane Professor of Law from 1829 till 1845. When Mr. Dane died, his last words were to his executor,

Henry Larcom—"I wish you to see my last letter to Judge Story executed"—and so the copyright of Dane's Abridgment was donated to Harvard University.

James Woodbury Boyden, and the other children of Dr. W. C. Boyden, were faithfully educated by their father at home—and at schools. James began to attend school, when four years old; recited Latin to his father at eight; and at fifteen left Beverly Academy to assist his uncle, Joseph Boyden, principal of Charlestown Academy, near Harper's Ferry, in Jefferson county, Virginia. He was employed as private tutor in Smithfield, in the same county, by Dr. Samuel Scollay, a Harvard graduate (1808), who delighted to recite this last verse of a Harvard commencement valedictory:

> "Valete, Senes—cœlum visuri!
> Valete, Juvenes—viribus ornati!
> Valete, Virgines—luce blandiores!
> Valete atque Plebs."

In May, 1838, he visited the city of Washington. Young Boyden walked to Harper's Ferry and took passage on a canal boat of the Chesapeake and Ohio canal to Georgetown. He gladly improved his opportunity to see and hear Henry Clay, Daniel Webster, John Quincy Adams, John C. Calhoun, Silas Wright, and other eminent statesmen, in Congress assembled.

Boyden in August, 1838 entered Harvard College. He was awarded Aiken's British Poets, under Hopkins' legacy *"pro insigni in studiis diligentia."* The second year, he was an active member of "The Institute of 1770"—one of the literary and debating clubs—and prepared a history of the Institute.

During the Tippecanoe presidential campaign of 1840, he assisted friends of the successful candidate—General William Henry Harrison. He addressed political meetings, marched in processions, wrote articles for the Salem *Register* and did all that he could lawfully in behalf of the hero of Tippecanoe.

In December, 1840, he went to Accomac county, Virginia—then represented in Congress by Hon. Henry A. Wise—and was Principal of the Academy near Belle Haven, until his return north

JAMES W. BOYDEN.

to complete college studies. He joined the junior class, at Dartmouth, during the winter of 1841-2.

Love for fair Harvard brought him again to Alma Mater in the spring of 1842. She inspired him to make the best use of junior and senior class privileges. He was graduated in August, 1843, with the honor of distinction in Political Economy the department of Professor Jared Sparks. The theme of his Commencement Disquisition was "The Attraction of Literary Eccentricity." He was awarded one of the Boylston prizes for a Latin declaration. In addition to the usual diploma, he had diplomas for special courses in Latin and Greek, for those who intended to teach. The oldest Harvard alumni, in point of class graduation, now living in Chicago—are James Woodbury Boyden of the class of 1843 and Samuel Sewall Greeley of the class of 1844.

Mr. Boyden next resided with his father at home, teaching school about seventeen months. During this time he read Blackstone's Commentaries, under the direction of Hon. Robert Rantoul, Jr.

In February, 1845, he returned to Cambridge, and attended Justice Story's and Prof. Greenleaf's lectures at the Law School eighteen months. Among his fellow students were Thomas B. Bryan, Lewis H. Boutelle, John Borden, Cyrus Bentley, Sanford B. Perry and Ira Scott, well known members of the Chicago bar: —also, R. B. Hayes, ex-president of the United States; William A. Richardson, Chief Justice of the U. S. Court of Claims; Walter S. Cox, the Washington Judge who tried and sentenced Guiteau for murder of Garfield; John Lowell, U. S. Judge in Boston—and the eloquent Anson Burlingame, Representative in Congress and U. S. Minister to China and Russia. After Judge Story's death (September 1845), the Law students chose a committee (of which Boyden was a member) to select an artist to paint the portrait of the honored Justice, Professor and Author, which was placed in the lecture room, near that of Nathan Dane, in perpetuam memoriam.

In July, 1846, on application to Professor Greenleaf by Hon. Edward Dickinson of Amherst, Mass., for a law student and future partner, Mr. Boyden was recommended. After six months' study in Mr. Dickinson's office, he was admitted to the bar. He practiced law in Hampshire and Franklin counties—(Western Massachusetts)—thirteen years; and was elected to many offices of trust and responsibility. In this fertile and fruitful valley, watered by Connecticut river, he assisted in organizing and making a success of Hampshire Agricultural Society, and was its secretary and treasurer ten years. He was five years treasurer and clerk of the town of Amherst, and was one of the school committee. At the organization of an artillery company, he was first sergeant and subsequently third, second and first-lieutenant. He was promoted major and colonel, and resigned command of the regiment (3rd Mass. artillery), when reorganized as infantry. He was one of the secretaries of the state convention of June 4th, 1856, at Worcester, which nominated delegates to the first National Convention of the Republicans in Philadelphia. In November, 1857, he was elected to the legislature by the people of Hampshire and Franklin Senatorial District. He served on the joint committees on Probate, Chancery and Military Affairs.

The Hampshire and Franklin *Express* (Nov. 4, 1859), refering to Mr. Boyden's removal to Chicago, said: "The well known secretary of the Hampshire Agricultural Society has left this town to locate in Chicago. To his exertions is the Agricultural Society indebted for its flourishing condition. He represented this county at the Senate Board with great credit. He has also been honored by the people with many other tokens of their appreciation, and leaves behind him many warm friends, who regret his removal, but wish his continued success in his new field."

Col. Boyden came to Chicago in November, 1859. For two years (1862-1864), he was United States Agent for paying army and navy pensions to Northern Illinois pensioners. Several years after the war, he was employed to obtain pensions for invalids and for widows and children of men who died in defense of the Union.

In domestic relations, he has been highly favored. He was first married May 18, 1847 (25th birth day), to Miss Eliza Otis Taylor Dickinson, youngest daughter of Hon. John Dickinson Probate Judge (1820 to 1837) for Washington County, Maine. Mrs. Eliza O. T. Boyden died March 24, 1857, the mother of Mary—now widow of Rev. Edgar Foster of Calais, Maine:—of Lillie, wife of George H. Eaton, of Calais:—and of John Dickinson Boyden, who represented Tamworth, in the New Hampshire Legislature of 1887-1888.

He was married June 19, 1861 to Miss Frances S. Kingsbury, daughter of Major Lawson Kingsbury, of Framingham, Mass.—an officer in the war of 1812. Mrs. Frances S. Boyden, after the Chicago fire of 1871, was in charge of a department of the Chicago Relief and Aid Society, and has been prominent in church and charitable work. Their children were Charles Kingsbury, who died young;—Annie Kingsbury Boyden—and Frederick Kingsbury Boyden, paying-teller of Reid, Murdoch & Co.—who died April 2, 1889, from the effects of a bycicle collision on Ashland Avenue, corner of Jackson street.

Five years (1878—1883), Col. Boyden practiced law in the State of Nevada. He was employed by Chicago parties, interested in the construction of the Nevada Central Railway—which connects the Central Pacific, at Battle Mountain, with Austin and the Reese River Mining District. After a pleasant residence West of the Rocky Mountains, he returned to Chicago in May, 1883, for the improvement of Mrs. Boyden's health and their children's education in Chicago schools.

He has since been identified with real estate, and was four years (1883-'87) with S. H. Kerfoot & Co.—the oldest and one of the most prominent offices in the real estate business.

Mr. Boyden has been a member of the Chicago Historical Society, of the Independent Order of Odd Fellows, Knights of Pythias, Good Templars and the Chicago Young Men's Christian Association.

JOSEPH W. BRACKETT

Was born January 19th, 1815, at Cherry Valley, Otsego county, New York, and was appointed midshipman in U. S. Navy in 1831, serving three years on the U. S. Sloop of War, " Falmouth." He studied for and was admitted to the bar in New York City, and was subsequently a partner of Hon. T. C. Chettenden. In '48 he rounded Cape Horn, *en route* to California, where he aided in the organization of the free State of California. Since 1850 he has resided at Rock Island, Illinois. In politics he has ever been a Whig and Repuplican, voting for Gen. Wm. II. Harrison in Cherry Valley, New York, in 1836; again at same place in 1840; for Lincoln in 1860, and for Harrison in 1888. He served through the war of the Rebellion, and is now a Past Post Commander of Bedford Post, 243, G. A. R. Mr. Brackett was secretary of the Cherry Valley Tippecanoe Club in 1840, and has in his possession the records thereof. We are indebted to Mr. Brackett for the copy of congratulatory address sent to Gen. Wm. H. Harrison by the Cherry Valley Club, November 12th, 1840, which appears elsewhere.

WILLIAM HENRY BRADLEY.

William Henry Bradley was born in Ridgefield, Fairfield county, Connecticut, November 29, 1816. His grandfather, Philip Burr Bradley, was also a native of Ridgefield, a lawyer by profession, and a graduate of Yale. During the war of the Revolution he was a colonel in active service, and his commission is still preserved. He was a warm and trusted friend of Washington, and was appointed by him, when president, Marshal for the District of Connecticut, an appointment renewed in Washington's second term, and also under President Adams. His son, and the father of the subject of this sketch, Jesse Smith Bradley, was also a graduate of Yale, and highly esteemed as a classical scholar. He was elected by the legislature one of the Judges of Fairfield county, an office which he retained until his death, in May, 1833. His wife, Elizabeth Baker, was also a native of Ridgefield, the daughter of a physician of note—Dr. Amos Baker. The fifth son of these parents, William Henry Bradley, pursued his studies at home in Ridgefield Academy, and at the time of his father's death was prepared to enter Yale College. Soon after that event he went to New Haven, and was employed as teller in the City Bank. At the end of four years, in the fall of 1837, he removed, at the suggestion of an elder brother, to

Galena, Ill., then the most considerable town of the northwest. There he was offered the position of Clerk of the County Court. He accepted the appointment, and thus decided his future—for since that time he has been almost constantly connected with courts in a clerical capacity. In 1840, while discharging the duties of his position, and studying law in the office of Hon. Thomas Drummond, then a prominent lawyer in Galena, he was appointed Clerk of the Circuit Court of Jo Daviess county. On the adoption of the new constitution of Illinois, in 1848, he was elected to the same office, and again re-elected in 1852. The large majorities by which he was successively elected, notwithstanding the intensity of partisan feeling occasioned by a presidential campaign, and the nearly equal political division of the county between the two parties, and his active identification with one of them, sufficiently attest the public appreciation of him as a man and a faithful and efficient officer.

In politics Mr. Bradley was early identified with the Whig party. He entered actively in the presidential campaign of 1840, preparing occasional papers which were read before the Jo Daviess County Tippecanoe Club, some of which were printed in the Galena *Gazette* of that year. On the formation of the Republican party in 1860 he heartily endorsed its principles, and was at the Decatur convention of that year, which witnessed the exciting triangular contest for the gubernatorial nomination between the friends of Messrs. Swett, Judd and Yates, finally resulting in the nomination of Richard Yates. Mr. Lincoln was first prominently named for the presidency with great enthusiasm in that convention.

Mr. Bradley has been a consistent, uniform and earnest supporter of the Whig and Republican parties, and of their candidates from 1838 to, and including the recent triumphant presidential canvass of 1888. When congress created a Second Judicial District in Illinois, the Hon. Thomas Drummond, then Judge of the United States District Court for Illinois, having been assigned to the Northern District, with the concurrence of Justice McLean, called Mr. Bradley to be clerk of the new ·courts. He accepted, and resigning his clerkship at Galena, re-

WILLIAM HENRY BRADLEY.

moved to Chicago, and entered upon his duties March 22, 1855.
He was, upon the usual examination, admitted to the bar, but
has never been actively engaged in the practice of his profession.
For about thirty-four years he has performed the duties of his
position as clerk with quiet and unfailing industry and exem-
plary fidelity, winning in this, as in other previous connections
with the courts, a rare and honorable measure of respect and
trust for readiness and accuracy, as well as efficiency and skill in
discharging the large and increasing business that has employed
his energies and occupied his time. Still he has never been indifferent to other public interests, having taken an active part in
the Young Men's Association of Chicago, and being elected its
president in 1860. Of the West Side Railway Company he was
a director for twenty-five years; was vice-president several years,
and president for six years, which last position he resigned in
1875, owing to the laborious and exacting duties incident to the
position.

In June, A. D., 1871, he was appointed, under the will of the
late Walter L. Newberry (deceased), one of the trustees of said
estate, to fill the vacancy occasioned by the resignation of the
Hon. Mark Skinner, and with his associate, E. W. Blatchford, Esq.,
continues to discharge the duties of that trust.

WILLIAM BRACE.

This gentleman is a living exponent of the principles involved in the old-time axiom "a rolling stone gathers no moss."
He was born January 17th, 1814, in the town of Victor, Ontario
county, New York State. He resided there, pursuing the even
tenor of his way for "nigh on to sixty years," when Chicago became his home. He voted for the Harrison's in 1836—'40—'88.

JONATHAN W. BROOKS, M. D.,

Was born of parents of Waldense Welch and Hugenot descent
in that part of Norwich, New London county, Connecticut, now

known as Hanover, November 3rd, 1811. Spent his youth, till sixteen years of age, at work on his fathers farm; aided himself to a classical education in Connecticut. Was first a pupil in medicine, of the late Willard S. Parker, of New York, after that of the late William P. Dewes, George and Samuel McClellan and John Revere, of Philadelphia, Pa.,—graduating from the Jefferson Medical College, Philadelphia, under the presidency of Dr. Ashbel Green, then of Nassau Hall (now Princeton), March 4th. A. D., 1835, entering immediately upon the active practice of medicine, in the then village of Brooklyn (now city), of New York. Voted for General William Henry Harrison there in 1836. In 1837 removed to Norwich Town, Connecticut, and succeeded to the business of Drs. Philerson Tracy and John Turner, who deceased about that time. Voted in Norwich for General Harrison again in 1840 for President. Remained in Norwich sixteen years—was then invited to College Hill, Hamilton county, Ohio, to succeed the lamented M. M. Williams, M. D., where he remained actively engaged until 1861, when by invitation of Dr. Boone and others, he removed to Chicago, settling on Adams street, near the lake, and has continued in the active practice of his profession to this writing, February 22d, 1889, voting for General Benjamin Harrison, in November 1888, the grandson of General William Henry Harrison.

ISAAC W. BRAYTON,

Born March 9, 1811, in the town of Chesine, Berkshire county, Mass.; moved to Albany, State of New York, 1816; used logs to help build log cabin at Albany in 1840; voted for William Henry Harrison in 1836, also 1840; also for Benjamin Harrison in 1888, and is now in the seventy-ninth year of his age.

GEORGE S. BRISTOL.

Born September 3, 1821, in Lima, Livingston county, State of New York; came to western Michigan in 1836, following milling and merchandising for twenty years; served five years as Deputy

U. S. Marshal in Western Michigan; was commissioned by Gov. Blair, February, 1862, as First-Lieutenant and Regimental Quartermaster of the Twelfth Michigan Infantry; participated in the battle of Pittsburg Landing on the 6th and 7th of April, 1862, lost my health and was obliged to return home the last of June, and then served as Marshal until the close of the war; has resided in Chicago the last seventeen years.

PHILLIP BURROUGHS

Was born in the town of Warrick, Orange county, N. Y., 24th of January, 1811. Mr. Burroughs and his father were both born in the same house, which was built by the grandfather prior to the Revolutionary War, when his parents located in Orange county, and the nearest store was twenty-five miles distant, nor was there "highway," "by-way" or "turnpike," other than a bridle-path.

Washington's headquarters were located but twenty-two miles distant. The father of Mr. Burroughs frequently saw General Washington pass to and fro. Mr. Burroughs voted for General William Henry Harrison in 1836 in New York City, but lost his vote in 1840, which year he came west, locating in Chicago, where he has ever since resided, casting his vote, with the rest of the Tippecanoe Club, for Gen. Benj. Harrison, and from that time up to the present working hard and earnestly for the best interests of "our club."

THOMAS B. CARTER

Was born in Norristown, Norris county, N. J., March 26th, 1819. His first recollection of a political campaign or election was connected with John Quincy Adams' unsuccessful canvass in 1828, when his father cast his first vote for that candidate. Mr. Carter commenced his business career in a general store in Morristown, N. J., in the fall of 1832, from whence he came to Chicago in 1838 with a stock of dry goods and groceries, reaching here the fifteenth of September, the journey requiring twelve days. Before

PHILIP BURROUGHS.

leaving Elizabethtown, N. J., the firm of F. B. Carter & Co., was organized, and continued in busines on their arrival until 1861. In the fall of 1861 he was elected Clerk of the Superior Court of Chicago, which office he held for six years, afterwards serving as one of the general agents of the Equitable Life Insurance Association. In 1840 he cast his first vote for Gen. William Henry Harrison, taking an active part in the campaign and attending the big Whig convention at Springfield, on behalf of the election, fulfilling his duty in every respect except the "drinking of hard cider." Mr. Carter closes his sketch by saying: "I shall probably never cast another vote, but should my life be spared another four years, I shall vote for the candidate of the honest old Republican party."

COL. EDWARD H. CASTLE.

I, Edward H. Castle, was born in Amenia, Dutchess county, N. Y., August 5th, 1811. My grandfather, Gideon Castle, served under General Washington in the Revolutionary War; my father, Wm. Castle, was a Dutchess county farmer. In the winter of 1838 I purchased a stock of merchandise in Philadelphia, transporting it over the Allegheny mountains with the old style six and eight horse teams. Reaching Pittsburg, on the Ohio River, I chartered a small steamer, and completing my stock with the great staple produce of that then thriving town—nails and hardware—proceeded down the Ohio River to its mouth, over 1,200 miles, thence up the Mississippi to the Illinois River, and up the Illinois to Peru, Illinois. Stopping at St. Louis, Mo., I again made additions to my stock. After opening my store at Peru, I went to Joliet, Ill., where I established another store in what was then the " Old Stone Store," belonging to Dick Wilson, editor of the Chicago *Journal.* I also engaged with Gov. Matteson and Hiram Blanchard in the construction of the Illinois and Michigan canal. After remaining in business a year, I sold my interest in the Peru and Joliet stores, and left for Chicago, arriving there on the first day of May, 1839, where I immediately opened a stock of general merchandise, and also engaged in commercial purchasing, shipping by boat and canal to New York ("The Old Settlers' History" gives me the credit of shipping the first one hundred thousand bushels of wheat from Chicago to New York), at the same time buying and selling real estate for six or eight years. In 1840 or '41, I entered six thousand acres of swamp land, in the Illinois valley, at ten cents per acre, a portion of which I sold for fifty dollars per acre. Entering a section at the town of Wheeling, Cook county, I engaged in farming, and established a fine dairy of fifty cows, finding a ready sale for all the milk at the hotels and private residences of Chicago. During this time, still dealing in real estate up to '47, I assisted in the construction of the first railroads to the city. I voted for William Henry Harrison for president in 1840, as in 1888 I voted for Benjamin Harrison for that high office.

Starting for the California gold fields in November, 1849, I took passage on the canal packet, Capt. Connett, by Illinois canal to Peru; steamer Atlantic, by Illinois river, to St. Louis; steamer James Hewitt, by Mississippi river, to New Orleans; there taking the mate's position on the bark Florida to Chagres; then crossing the Isthmus by walking over the mountain, after being transported up the Chagres river forty miles in a pearug, poled by the natives, clothed in the garb that nature gave them, the climate requiring no more expensive apparel. A pearug is a mahogany tree dug-out, about four feet wide and twelve feet long, and will carry twelve persons and baggage. After leaving the river, we reached Panama in two days, with blistered feet and tired out. Here I was offered one of the Aspinwall steamers to take to San Francisco. Taking command of the ship Unicorn, a four-decker, three hundred feet long, drawing twenty-eight feet of water, we sailed for Toboga island. After cleaning, painting, watering and coaling, we returned to Panama, and, provisioning her for the voyage to San Francisco, took on board seven hundred passengers and their baggage, which, with the crew and others, made nearly one thousand persons on board. Going ashore for my passport, I met Commodore Porter, who had just arrived, being in command of the Pacific Department, and invited him to make the trip with us and relieve me of a part of

the responsibility, which he consented to do. Sailing on the 28th
day of November, on a voyage of over 4,000 miles, we stopped
at the fine harbor of Acapulco, one of the state capitals, on the
west coast of Mexico, where we took a ship load of coal and two
hundred head of fat cattle, for the purpose of supplying fresh
meat, and, purchasing all the vegetables we could obtain in that
market, and a fresh supply of provisions and water, again put to
sea—nothing occurring to disturb the usual monotony of a sea
voyage. The weather being fine and the evenings warm and
pleasant, they were passed in dancing and other social amuse-
ments, and we arrived at the mud and cloth town of San Francisco on the 5th day of January, 1850.

The Unicorn being laid up and used as a store ship, I took
command of the new steamer, Eldorado, which had been brought
in sections as freight from Philadelphia, and designed for the
river trade between San Francisco and Sacramento, making three
trips weekly between these two points (it being about the same
distance as from New York to Albany, and the scenery very fine
and quite as interesting). By purchasing goods at auction at
San Francisco and transporting them to Sacramento, where they
were disposed of at auction, I was enabled to add considerable
to my store of wealth. After being several weeks thus engaged
I left the water and rented a hotel at Clark's Point, San Francisco, christening it the Illinois House. Help being scarce and
high, I purchased a half dozen girls, that were sold for their
passage on a British ship from Sidney, as dining-room waiters.
In those days there was no scarcity of patronage. John H. Collins, having just completed the building of the first and only
warehouse in that port, furnished a spacious apartment with ele-
gance, comfort and attractiveness, as a rendezvous or headquarters for the large number of officers always found at this port,
engaged me to take charge of the same. By keeping a man
stationed on Telegraph Hill, with a good glass, to notify me of
any ship in sight, and furnishing me a man and boat, I was enabled to be the first man aboard, and never failed to purchase or
get consignment of the cargo, taking the passengers to the Illinois House, of course. During the year's engagement I boarded

EDWARD H. CASTLE.

over four hundred vessels, and had the reputation of being the most successful manager of both hotel and warehouse to be found.

On account of failing health, I closed up my business, and in the fall of 1851 left on the steamer Columbus for Panama. My health having somewhat improved, I continued my journey, crossing the mountains from the latter place on that ever faithful animal, the mule. Shipped on the steamer Falcon to the mouth of the Chagres River, for Cuba, there being transferred to the steamer Ohio, for New York; we lost thirty-seven passengers on the voyage from cholera.

Arriving at New York, I met my wife and little daughter, all rejoicing that the home circle was complete. While here I received the appointment, from Chas. Minot, Superintendent of the Erie Railroad, as General Freight and Passenger Agent of that road for the entire northwest, with headquarters at Chicago. Emigration pouring into the new country very fast, I established a line of steamers between Chicago and Dunkirk, securing a large amount of new traffic for the road, and soon received the appointment as General Agent for the entire Mississippi valley, with a salary accordingly.

In the fall of 1858–9 I secured the passage of a charter through the Missouri legislature for a line of railroad through the northern tier of counties of that state—from Canton to the mouth of the Platte, on the Missouri river, two hundred miles. The charter provided for a stock subscription by these counties, in a corporative capacity, to the amount of $500,000. Taking the contract to build and equip said road for $7,000,000, and receiving the stock in part payment, I was to control the first mortgage bonds, and retain possession of the road until the balance was paid. Lecturing through these counties, I very soon succeeded in securing a subscription of double the amount of stock required, from counties and individual subscriptions of farmers.

When the Rebellion broke out, in 1861, having the road about half built, my operations were very speedily interfered with, the rebel Gen. Green taking possession of my stores, stock, location, iron and cars, amounting to some $2,000,000. Enlisting my men in the service of Uncle Sam, I chartered a steamer, and taking them to St. Louis, reported to Maj.-Gen. Fremont, receiving the appointment of Colonel on his staff and Superintendent of Railroads for the Western Department—comprising twenty-seven roads—with headquarters at St. Louis. I very soon connected the different lines of railroad in St. Louis, and with 4,000 men I was kept very busy repairing the roads and bridges as fast as they were interfered with or destroyed by the rebels. I was instructed by the War Department to get up a scale of rates to be used as a standard in transporting all government stores, which, when completed, was immediately indorsed by all the proper officers of the government, and became a law for the government business of the United States, as the "Castle rates," during the rebellion.

Being transferred to the Mountain Department, with General Fremont, I was placed in charge of the Pontoon brigade with the army in the Shenandoah Valley, where I was kept busy until after Sheridan's raid up the valley, when I was ordered to Washington to do some special service for President Lincoln. After the surrender of Vicksburg, I was detailed to supply Gen. Grant's army with ice. Chartering four steamers and twenty-nine barges, I ascended the Mississippi River 1,500 miles, to Lake Pepin, where I purchased 28,000 tons of ice, transporting it to the army at Vicksburg, where, on my arrival with the ice cargo, the boys in blue illuminated the town. President Lincoln and Gov. Chase desired me to proceed to New Orleans, to advise with Gen. Banks in regard to the Red River expedition, but my suggestions not meeting with favor from Gen. Banks, I soon returned to Washington, and after the surrender of Richmond by Lee, I returned home. Both houses of Congress joined in paying me a vote of thanks, and President Lincoln gave me the appointment of Chief Engineer to build the Pacific Railroad, which was a great surprise, as I had never asked for any appointment during my service with the army.

I gladly returned home, but before reaching New York the Lord was pleased to cause me to think how many a good man I had left in a soldier's grave, much better than myself. Arriving at New York, I stopped at the Astor House, and on Sunday went to hear Henry Ward Beecher preach. Being convinced of my sins, and feeling the need of a Saviour, I commenced to ask the Lord Jesus to forgive my sins and grant me His pardoning love in my heart. I left immediately for home, praying every breath for peace to my soul. After arriving at home, and praying many days, and, with my good wife, reading God's promises to poor sinners, the Lord was pleased to show me a bright light, and great peace came to my soul, and joy came to my heart. Praise God! I went from house to house for three years, telling my neighbors of Christ's precious love to my heart, and I feel Christ precious, and his great love has attended me. Praise the Lórd! the fear of death has been taken away, and he is still willing to hear my poor prayers. Oh! that I could tell all my acquaintances what great things the Lord has done for me, and is willing to do for all those that ask, believing on Him

When General Grant captured Vicksburg, he telegraphed Captain David White, of Cincinnati, and Colonel E. H. Castle, of Chicago, to report forthwith to him at Vicksburg, and we happened to meet on the same train before arriving at Vicksburg, where we reported within forty-eight hours. Upon meeting Gen. Grant he informed us that the wounded and sick were suffering and dying, and commissioned us and ordered us to proceed forthwith to furnish the army with ice for the use of the hospitals; and within six hours we had chartered four steamboats and twenty-nine barges and shipped one hundred men, and commenced receiving fuel and stores for a trip of fifteen hundred miles to Lake Pepin, and by sun-up the next morning we had the barges shipped to the steamers and bid General Grant good-bye; Colonel Castle taking charge of the leading steamer—Captain White following—stopping only on account of darkness and to obtain pilots, arriving at Lake Pepin in seven days, and within four hours purchased twenty-eight thousand tons of ice—starting immediately thirty or forty wagons into the adjacent country for straw to pack the ice. Within three days we had seven barges and one steamer loaded, and Col. Castle left for Vicksburg, telegraphing General Grant he was "Making Vicksburg as fast as the weather and circumstances would admit," arriving in Vicksburg inside of ten days—General Grant meeting him in tears, and the boys in blue illuminating the town, and there was a general rejoicing. General Grant and Captain David White soon after followed our fathers and hosts of soldiers and officers in the sleep that has no end, where the battles are over and peace reigns triumphant. I am left behind; ninety-nine per cent of my comrades are at rest.

And now, after reaching nearly four score years, enjoying the blessing of a comfortable and pleasant home, as my life's journey nears the end, and memory turns back the leaves in the book of time, it seems like a dream or panorama, and after wondering, I can only give praise to that Supreme Ruler who watches and guides our every footstep. Thankful from my inmost soul for His many mercies vouchsafed to me, and the loving care of our beloved Saviour, I pray daily that I may be able in some manner to become worthy of that love, and in my humble way aid others to know that love and enjoy its blessing. Having been a member of Park Avenue M. E. church for many years, I only wish that I could tell to one and all of my youthful associates the comfort and enjoyment it has been to me—the peace and quiet after the turbulent and exciting life of my younger days, taking the fear of death from me.

STEPHEN HENRY CLEMENT

Was born at Newburyport, Mass., September 15, 1823, the seventh child of Joseph Warren Clement and Mary Fitz Clement. His ancestors came early from England. Moses Clement landed at Plymouth Rock, Mass., in 1628, and settled in Boston, Massachusetts, then a colony of Great Britain, and in 1652 he was appointed Privy Councellor to Governor Winthrop. A few years later, other members of his family came (also) to America. Among these were Robert Fawne Clement (who arrived in 1632), and Job Clement (who came in 1638), the latter of whom became a resident of Haverhill, Mass. It was here that Job received from the provincial government, a grant of land as a premium for building and operating the first tannery in the province of Massachusetts.

At that early period the ancestors of Stephen H. appear to have been prominent in the history of the commonwealth. Several of them held important positions, both in the colonies and after they had become independent States. Joseph Warren Clement (father of the subject of this sketch) was, by profession, an architect and builder, and carried on his business at Newburyport, Mass. On the 8th of November, 1807, he was married to Miss Mary Fitz, to them were born six boys and five girls. Mary Fitz Clement was a lineal descendant of Robert Fitz, Esq., who immigrated from " Fitzford," England, to Virginia in 1614, where he owned and cultivated a tobacco plantation. In tracing the genealogy of the Fitz family, it is noticeable that Daniel Webster, of New Hampshire, the celebrated orator and statesman, and Stephen H. Clement, were cousins.

About the year 1835, Joseph Warren Clement, accompanied by his son Charles, came to Alton, Ill., and engaged as contractor in the construction of many houses and stores, and while there became an unwilling witness to the murder of Elijah Lovejoy, in 1837, and the destruction of his printing office by riotous slave-holders and border ruffians from Missouri. These incidents, so disgraceful and barbarous, soon caused the senior Clement to return to his home in Massachusetts, where he often related the story of the Alton outrages to his eagerly listening boys. Henceforth he became imbued with the spirit of Abolition; and the perusal of the *Boston Emancipator*, and other kindred journals, did much to inspire his children with an intense ardor for political liberty and the personal freedom of the slave.

In 1838 Stephen H. entered upon his apprenticeship in the watch-making and repairing business at 82 Washington street, Boston; and in 1842 he began his journey to the West, to "grow up with the country." By stage, railway, canal and steamboat he reached Buffalo, N. Y. There he secured a passage up the great lakes on the steamer " Great Western," commanded by Captain Walker—both the boat and her commander being then

STEPHEN HENRY CLEMENT.

the best and most popular afloat—and after a few days he landed at the village of Southport (now the city of Kenosha), in the Territory of Wisconsin. Here he opened a watch and jewelry store, and prospered in his business.

It was while thus engaged, owing to the aggressions of the Southern slave-holders and the supineness of the Northern "dough-faces," that he was led to manifest much interest in Abolition and Free Soil discussions, and when the Republican party was formed he became a "stalwart" among them, and was ever afterwards within the picket-lines of that political organization, to which, in the meantime, all his relatives by blood and marriage, including his five sons, have belonged.

While he lived at Southport it is worthy of note that Mr. Clement erected the first public hall in that place; and at the dedication of it to liberty and equality under the law, the event was made memorable by the liberty-loving citizens in a glorious celebration. Among the speakers on that occasion was Colonel Charles Clement, who soon rose to distinction. He was soon called to positions of responsibility and honor. In 1848 he was a member of the first State Constitutional Convention of Wisconsin, and afterwards a State Senator from Racine county, besides holding other important offices in the gift of the people and the government. Under such gratifying auspices Clement's Hall became the rallying wigwam of the liberty-loving advocates of our Republican institutions.

After several years Stephen H. found that his close attention to business was injuring his health, and an opportunity soon occurring, he sold his establishment, and for a season retired from active pursuits. Rest and recreation having eventually restored his physical energies, he removed to Beloit, Rock county, Wis., and there again engaged in the jewelry business.

An interesting incident added its zest to his quiet life in 1855, when he was happily married to Miss Rachel Fullager, of Catskill, N. Y. A few months after this event, his brother George, then living in Texas, made him a visit, and so highly recommended the climate of that State that Stephen H. was induced to dispose of his business and emigrate to that southern paradise.

There he invested his means in live-stock, and at once engaged in the business with such energy and prudence that his labors were soon crowned with complete success, as his large droves of horses and cattle, and flocks of sheep on the hills and in the valleys of the "Lone Star State" sufficiently attested.

Every picture has its lights and shades, and every life its vicissitudes. The tide of prosperity which had hitherto borne him upon its top wave, soon began to turn and recede. And this was when the first distant mutterings of the Southern Rebellion and the threatened intestinal disruption of the American Union fell upon his ear. The weak administrations of Pierce and Buchanan had paved the way for southern insolence to declare itself in favor of secession. Buchanan's easy good nature had furnished the opportunity for Floyd, the Secretary of the Navy, and Jefferson Davis, the whilom Secretary of War, to attempt the disruption of the country by bringing the conspiracy of the slaveholders to the arbitrament of arms.

The "Knights of the Golden Circle," all over this fair land, North and South, under the command of General Bickley, of Kentucky, organized bands of assassins, and robbery and murder became rampart throughout the South. On every hand Southern conspirators and their minions continually sought out Northern men who had settled in the South. If these were possessed of lands, money or live-stock, they were despoiled of all they had, and in many instances murder was added to the crimes committed upon those Northern residents who had no sympathy with the rebellious spirit that brought on the war of the Rebellion. Every sort of annoyance and outrage characterized the conduct of the slavocracy toward the Northern men in the South who dared to cling to their loyal principles. The mails were kept under constant espoignage, and letters and packages by mail addressed to Northerners were broken open and read, in order to obtain the sentiments of the writers regarding slavery and the Southern policy, with a view of persecuting and expelling (those who opposed) them from the South at any sacrifice.

At that time Stephen H. Clement's brother Charles was publishing the *Advocate*, and subsequently the *Journal*, at Racine,

Wis., and very freely expressing his sentiments in favor of suppressing slavery and Southern methods—for Charles was thoroughly imbued with the Republican, Free Soil, Abolition spirit, and aggressive in everything that related to the Southern policy. Every week his paper was mailed to his brother in Texas, and the Southerners were not long in finding out that Stephen H. was no friend of their political principles.

Before the first gun had been fired at Fort Sumpter, the "Knights of the Golden Circle" sent notices to all Northern sympathizers to leave the South. One of these missives reached Stephen H. on the 6th of January, 1861, giving him twelve hours in which to leave the State. Not heeding their threats, he made no preparation for such a sudden leave-taking of his home and family; but, soon afterward, another similar demand came from sixty armed men, prepared for immediate action. Death or flight was the only alternative. By the advice of friends he was induced to accept the situation, mount his horse, turn his face northward, and leave behind him wife and children, and all that he had accumulated during years of industry. Fortunately he escaped all threatened perils on his way, and as soon as possible gained the free soil of Illinois, where the stars and stripes insured free thought and speech to every citizen.

Not long after his arrival he entered the service of the United States government as enrolling officer, under the District Provost Marshal. Capt. James, who, with the Hon. Isaac L. Milliken and Dr. L. C. Paine Freer, constituted the United States Board of Enrollment, and attended faithfully to the duties of his position until the close of the war.

Since the war ended, Stephen H. has traveled extensively throughout the northern and extreme southern States, including Old and New Mexico; and at the present writing is engaged in the wholesale jewelry business in Chicago. With his early training and predilections, he has always been an active participant in Republican campaigns, and in that of 1888 was an earnest and vigorous speaker in behalf of Harrison and Morton.

Well acquainted with the inside working of the Southern policy before the war, Mr. Clement will soon embody his views in a brief history of the Slaveholder's Rebellion, including numerous interesting facts not yet made public,

HENRY L. CHAPIN

Was born in Hartford, Connecticut, March 7th, 1817. He espoused the political principles of the Whig party, and co-operated with that party at all elections. Voted and worked for the election of William Henry Harrison in 1840. When the Republican party was organized he sympathized and co-operated with it and always voted for its candidate on every election, including the triumphant election of Gen. Benjamin Harrison, on the 6th of November, 1888.

ISAAC COALE

Was born about four miles west of the Junction on the Susquehanna River, August 15th, 1803; remaining on the homestead until 1820, when he went to Baltimore and obtained employment there, engaging in the mercantile business—afterwards removing to Boston in 1825. Mr. Coale's first child was born in Boston, and now resides in Washington, aged sixty years. In 1836 and 1840 Mr. Coale was engaged in farming in Virginia, and voted for William Henry Harrison. In 1850 he removed to New York, and subsequently to Chicago, where he is at present living, and where he voted for Gen. Benjamin Harrison in 1888. Mr. Coale was the father of the 1st-Lieutenant, one John H. Coale, who was well known in army circles, and was connected with Gen. Custer's brigade, and who recently died at Ft. Madison. Although retired from active business, Mr. Coale is still an active republican, and ready at all times to vote for the Republican party, to whom he has ever been loyal.

FRED. W. COFFIN

Was born at Boscamin, State of New Hampshire, county of Merrimac, May 28th, 1815, where he resided for some years, subsequently removing to Rockingham, in the same state. Mr. Coffin came to Chicago in 1860, and has resided here ever since. He voted for Gen. William Henry Harrison in 1836 and 1840, both votes being cast at the place of his nativity, and in 1888 he voted in Chicago for the younger Harrison.

HENRY CONVERSE

Was born August 22d, 1815, in New Brainton, Worcester county, Massachusetts, and was one of six boys. Henry was the third son, and at the age of fourteen he was anxious to learn some trade, so his father put him to learn the tanning trade, where he remained one year, when his health failed him so he had to leave it, and was then sent to school for two years; then he went into the office of Dr. I. N. Bates, of Barise. In 1836 he concluded to go west, where he arrived at Sandusky, Ohio. In 1840 he took a lively interest in the election of General William Henry Harrison —was one of the committee to receive and escort the General to Fort Meigs celebration. The General remained one night at Sandusky, and the following morning they all went aboard the Steamer Sandusky, and before they started a fleet of six steamers sailed into the Sandusky Bay. When they reached Toledo, they got Captain Wilkinson (who sailed the Steamer Commodore Perry) to pilot the fleet up the Merrimac river. But before he would start he said he must have the General in his boat. Well, as long as he had a log cabin on the deck of his boat, it was decided to put the General aboard of his boat. They reached Perrysburg safe, and had a two days' celebration at Fort Meigs just above Perrysburg. Was appointed Port Master by General Taylor; held it through that administration. In 1877 moved with his wife to Chicago, where they are both living. They are now on their fifty-third year that they have lived together,— having six grandchildren and two great-grand-children.

ASAHEL T. CROSS

Was born in Freetown, Cortland county, N. Y., May 21st, 1815. Resided in N. Y., until 1883, at which date he removed to Chicago

HENRY CONVERSE.

He inherited a hatred for slavery from both his parents, and recollects that in the year 1825 two slave boys came to his father's house, and were by him fed and helped to Canada. In 1836 he cast his first vote for William Henry Harrison, and again in 1840 for the same party, being so thoroughly disgusted with John Tyler that he vowed never again to vote for a slave-holder. In 1844 he voted for James G. Binney; in '48 for Martin Van-Buren; in '52 for John P. Hall; in '56 for John C. Fremont. Was active in the Lincoln campaign, and has always voted for the Republican candidate, casting his vote for Gen. Benjamin Harrison, in whose honesty and ability he has entire confidence.

CAPT. JOHN DAME

Was born in the town of Barnstead, county of Strafford, State of New Hampshire, March 10th, 1799. His father was of Welch descent. His education was obtained around the family altar, in a country school house, and the church. The school house afforded him about twelve weeks of winter schooling in a year—his home training constituted a rigid discipline in the habits of honesty and frugality. Early in life lessons were given in the rudiments of useful and productive industry, and the principles which were believed to be essential for a self-relying, independent and successful manhood. What he lacked in opportunities he sought to make up by diligence, economy and perseverance. In his boyhood there was a premium on honest and efficient labor, and a penalty against idleness and prodigality. He moved from Barnstead, N. H., in 1843 to Wisconsin, and settled on a farm in the town of Spring Prairie, where he has resided forty-six years. He cast his first vote in 1820 for John Q. Adams for president. He voted in 1836–'40 for William Henry Harrison for president, and in 1888 for his grandson, Benjamin Harrison, for president. At all other elections he voted the Whig ticket until 1856, when he voted the Republican ticket, and has done so ever since. He has participated in eighteen presidential elections, and voted in them all except two. He is now in very good health, and but for the loss of his sight could walk several miles a day with little trouble.

WASHINGTON DEWEY

Was born in Middlebury, Vt., on the 10th day of September, 1818, and moved to Detroit, Mich., in 1829. This trip from New York State to Detroit was all made by water from Northwest Bay, on Lake Champlain, to Whitehall, and from thence by canal to Buffalo. He lived in Detroit two years, and then moved to Malden, Canada; lived there one year and went to Sandusky, Ohio, in 1833, where he made his home until he came to Chicago in March, 1869. On coming through Chicago in 1839 he landed at the light-house, and walked up to Rush street on planks laid in the grass along the river, and was ferried across by two men in a scow boat, and a rope stretched across the river. Chicago had then about 4,000 inhabitants. He and a brother two years his senior are all that remain of twelve children— seven daughters and five sons. In July, 1840, he went to Fort Wayne, Ind., by stage, and from there to Farmer's Creek on horseback, over four hundred miles, but got back to Sandusky in time to vote for Gen. William Henry Harrison, and in 1888 rejoiced to be again permitted to vote for Gen. Benjamin Harrison.

---- ----

MADISON DURLEY

Was born on the 5th day of August, 1817, in Colwell county, Kentucky. His father moved to Illinois in October, 1819, on a pack-horse, and settled near Sugar Creek, twenty-five miles south of Springfield. His nearest neighbor was twenty-five miles, except Indians—they were plenty. In 1840 he lived at Hennepin; went to Springfield in June of that year to attend the demonstration; went south ten miles among his old friends, and was appointed marshal of the Sugar Creek Stone Quarry Delegation. Of what followed Mr. Durley says: "We mounted a cabin on wheels, attached twenty-four yoke of oxen to it, and drove to town. Upon our arrival we were more than welcomed—in fact we were taken by storm—people climbing on the cabin until our team was stalled. Mr. Lincoln happened by, and I said to him: 'Abe, won't you take a whip and drive the lead cattle?' He did, and his voice could be distinctly heard above the din and applause from thousands of throats. We had a big demonstration—about fifty thousand." Mr. Durley voted for Old Tippecanoe at Hennepin, on the Illinois River, and for his grandson in 1888.

SHERMAN W. EDWARDS,

Born on September 14th, 1819, in the town of Conneaut, Ashtabula county, Ohio; from whence he removed at the age of seven years to Plymouth, Ashtabula county, and engaged in business there until his twenty-fifth year, when he removed to Fairfield, Huron county, Ohio, where he remained, engaged in various business capacities till 1869, taking no active part in the late war on account of physical disqualifications. In 1860–61 served as sergeant-at-arms in the House of Representatives of the State of Ohio, and prior to that time was for three years commissioner of Huron county, Ohio. In 1869 Mr. Edwards came to Chicago, where he has since resided; entered the grain business, and became a member of the Board of Trade in 1875, with which body he has since been identified. Mr. Edwards was a strong " Whig " in the days of that party, and at Plymouth, Ohio, in 1840, he cast his first vote for the "Whig" presidential candidate—William Henry Harrison. From the date of its organization, Mr. Edwards has been a member of the Republican party, and has supported with enthusiasm all its presidential candidates, and especially the last one—Benjamin Harrison.

WILLIAM SIDNEY ELLIOTT,

A native of the "Empire State," having been born in North Hampton, Montgomery county, January 18th, 1813. In 1819 his parents removed to Balston Spa, Saratoga county, New York, and remained there until 1836. During these years the elder Elliott followed agricultural pursuits. W. S. Elliott attended school in winter and worked on farm in the summer until 1833, when he engaged in teaching in Rochester, in a free school, supported by Gen Riley. At this time the slavery agitation became the question of the day. The first anti-slavery convention ever held in New York State met in 1835 at Utica, and the subject of

W. S. ELLIOTT.

this sketch was a delegate to that historical meeting. In speaking of this convention Mr. Elliott says: " On assembling great opposition was manifested to the movement—and the president was barely elected before we were driven from the hall, and later from the city. But by the good hand of God upon us, the great colonizationist and Christian, Garrett Smith, of Peterborough, arose in the confusion and said: 'Gentlemen, the cause that subjects you to this treatment, subjects me to the same, and the same cause I here and today espouse, and invite you to my house and city to finish your deliberations.' We left Utica at once, any way we could, and as the sun arose the next morning we quietly rested our weary limbs under the protection of one of America's greatest philanthropists. If I had wanted anything in enthusiasm in this cause of the abolition of slavery, I and we all were now equipped, as the meeting showed. We were girded with the subject, and we parted to our homes and fields of labor— vowing vengeance upon the giant sin, the giant inconsistency of a self-styled home of the free."

After this Mr. Elliott returned to his home, fully imbued with the idea that the great West was the place for the full fruition of free thoughts and actions, and where the death of slavery would be worked out. He soon after removed to Michigan, locating one hundred miles east of Chicago. Here he became familiar with the fact that the negroes were helping themselves to freedom, and he lent a helping hand on every opportunity, so that two hundred escaped bondsmen, via. the Indiana, Ohio and Michigan Underground Railway, had to thank Mr. Elliott, whose section of the road covered a distance of twenty miles. About the time the war broke out he removed to Chicago, and later to Quincy, Ill., where he aided in equipping men of younger years for the great struggle. A few years after the close of the war he again returned to Chicago, where he still resides, an honored and respected citizen. An underground conductor had no politics but Whig and Republican—his first vote being for William Henry Harrison in 1840; later for J. G. Birney, and his vote in 1888 was with the rest of our brand, a solid unit for General Benjamin Harrison and Levi P. Morton.

FRANKLIN EMORY,

Born March 9th, 1827, in the manufacturing village of Dover, New Hampshire, his father being a machinist by trade—working for the Dover Manufacturing Company. At the age of one year his parents moved from there to Exeter, New Hampshire, his father being employed to build and put up the machinery in the cotton factory in that village. In the course of the year following his father bought a small farm in Stratham, N. H., a town adjoining Exeter on the north. Here he lived until he was eighteen years of age. At the age of thirteen years his father died, having been sick for two years. At the age of twelve years he was put to work, as best he could, going to school three months each year in the winter, until he was eighteen years old, when he went to a trade in Boston, Mass., working at the carpentering business. After working at this business for three years he went to Lowell, Mass., where he went into the employ of the Merrimac Manufacturing Company, and was in their employ for about five years, two years later coming to Chicago, arriving here on the 17th day of November, 1853. At the time Gen. William Henry Harrison was elected by the Whigs in 1840 he was not old enough to vote, but sung the songs and carried the flag to help the cause along, his father being a very strong party man, and was overjoyed at having a Whig president.

At the age of twenty-three he married Miss Alice Watenhouse, of Portland, Maine. Eight children were the fruit of this marriage, four of whom are living and have families of their own.

When the Republican party was organized, in 1856, in this city, he was one of the first to espouse the cause, and has ever since voted that ticket and worked for it—the last vote cast by him being for General Benjamin Harrison for president. Believing the Republican party is the only one to be trusted to bring about reforms in our national government, he has always stuck very close to it.

DANIEL CAMPBELL FERGUSON

Was born in Argyleshire, in the highlands of Scotland, February 17th, 1819, and came with his parents to America when two and a half years of age. They settled on a farm in the town of Oswegatchie, county of St. Lawrence, and State of New York, near Ogdensburgh. There he spent his boyhood until twenty years old; attended the district schools of the neighborhood; attended the Ogdensburgh Academy, and also the Attica Academy, Wyoming county, N. Y. Taught school and studied law with Hon. Senator Harvey Putnam and Judge Hoyt. Voted for William Henry Harrison in 1840; has voted the republican ticket at every presidential election since. He has four sons and two sons-in-law, all staunch Republicans, who cast their ballot for the man whose personal character and political principles they admire and respect—General Benjamin Harrison—citizen, patriot, jurist, hero.

J. C. FERGUSON

Was born in Bourbon county, Kentucky, October 5, 1810. In 1827 he was sent by his father, Dr. C. Ferguson, to Cincinnati, Ohio, to learn the watch-making and jewelry business. He remained there four years, and then removed to Richmond, Ind., remaining there twelve years. While there he voted in 1836–'40 for William Henry Harrison for president of the United States. He then moved to Indianapolis, Ind., and lived there about thirty-eight years, voting the Whig and Republican ticket. On leaving Indianapolis he came to Chicago, where he now resides, having voted here for Garfield and Harrison—the latter of whom he has known personally for twenty-five years, both being citizens of Indianapolis. Of him Mr. Ferguson says: "I always felt safe when he advised me in law matters; and I believe our country will be safe and prosperous as long as he is president of the United States."

J. D. FOLLETT

Was born in the State of Vermont. His father left Vermont for Ohio in 1832 with his family, but had barely reached there when his father died, leaving the children orphans, the mother having died some years previously, and Mr. Follett cared for his brothers and sisters on his own individual efforts for some eight years thereafter. In 1840 he voted for William Henry Harrison, at Bellevue, Ohio. In 1850 he crossed the plains to California, where he remained until 1854, when he returned home with a fair amount of gold dust, and engaged in the hardware businesss at Alleghan, Michigan. In 1888 he voted for the grandson of W. H. Harrison.

CHARLES GILES FOSTER

Was born in Hammond, St. Lawrence county, N. Y., December 14, 1821. His father, Ozias Foster, was a Connecticut Yankee, from Sharon, Litchfield county. His mother, Margaret Banker Foster, was a native of the Mohawk Valley, N. Y, The parents of C. G. removed from St. Lawrence county to Rochester, N. Y., when he was but an infant, and was made an half-orphan that same year by the sudden demise of his father, from apoplexy. His widowed mother afterward married a Vermonter by the name of Alvin Hulbert, and the boy Charles remained at home until the age of fifteen years, when, in the fall of 1836, he commenced the printing business, as an apprentice, on a weekly Universalist paper, published in Rochester, called *The Herald of Truth*. The publisher failed during the first year of his venture, and the subject of this sketch was soon after employed on the *New York Watchman*, also published in Rochester, by Delazon Smith, afterwards known as " Delusion" Smith, being thus nick-named by George Dawson, editor of the *Albany Evening Journal*. Said Smith (pardon the digression) had been appointed by President Tyler (of " Tippecanoe and Tyler, too," fame) a consul to some obscure point in South America, and although he drew his salary with great regularity, he somehow managed to elude the grasp of the government a year or two after it desired to recall him.

His second employer having also failed during the first year of his enterprise, young Foster worked for a time on the old *Genesee Farmer*, and on the *Rochester Daily Advertiser*, both published by Luther Tucker. Having sold the *Daily Advertiser*, in the spring of 1839, to Thomas H. Hyatt, of Lockport, N. Y., Mr.

Tucker soon after removed to Albany and started the *Cultivator*, which was subsequently consolidated with the *Country Gentleman*. By this change of base on the part of his employer, young Foster was again thrown out of employment, and determined to go east in search of work. He secured a letter of introduction to Rev. A. B. Grosh, editor of the *Evangelical Magazine and Gospel Advocate*, of Utica, N. Y. Here he found employment for two months, and while there became acquainted with several of the leading clergymen of the Universalist denomination, who were regular contributors to the last named publication. From Utica he pushed eastwardly, and found steady employment on the old *Troy Daily Whig*, on which journal he worked for ten consecutive years, from the fall of 1839 to '49. Here he imbibed his political ideas; and during the entire campaign of 1840, being then not quite nineteen years of age, he was actively engaged in a glee club, which nightly made the welkin ring with the praises of

> "Tippecanoe and Tyler, too,
> And with them we'll beat Little Van, Van, Van,
> Van is a used up man;
> And with them we'll beat Little Van."

We sang one song during the campaign which I should very much like to recall, but the title to which has entirely escaped my memory. It represented all the States rigged up as sailing vessels for a grand naval engagement, and I can recall only this verse:

> "Missouri, new rigged, will next hoist her sail,
> Harrisonians will give her a glorious gale:
> At the port which she starts for she proudly will call,
> Leaving tumble-bug Benton rolling his ball.
> > On the shore of Salt River,
> > On the shore of Salt River,
> > On the shore of Salt River,
> > Salt River—I—O!"

In September, 1849, Mr. Foster removed to Beloit, Wis., where he at once entered into a co-partnership with John R. Briggs in the publication of the *Beloit Journal*, a staunch Whig newspaper. In 1853 he purchased Mr. Briggs' interest in the paper, and upon the demise of the Whig party in 1854, Mr. Foster made the *Journal* a Republican paper, and run it until the fall of 1855, when he sold it, and temporarily retired from journalism.

Becoming dissatisfied with the long and severe winters of Wisconsin, he determined to imigrate farther south, and in January, 1858, he removed to St. Louis, and embarked in the book and job printing business. He found a milder clime, but could not become accustomed to the usages and business methods, not to mention the execrable political ideas, of the people of a slave State; and hence, in the spring of 1859 he, metaphorically speaking, "left the world and climbed a tree," bringing up in the State of Arkansas. After floundering about for a year or two, on the 5th of July, 1861, he reached Fort Smith, on the Arkansas river, completely "out o' sorts." The slaveholders' war on the Union was then thoroughly inaugurated, and it being entirely unsafe for him to work his way north into "God's country," he resigned himself to his fate, within the lines of "Dixie." By keeping a close mouth, and by strict attention to his business as a job printer, he managed to replenish his exhausted exchequer sufficiently to maintain himself until Gen. Blunts "Army of the Border" drove off the rebels and took possession of the city and fort. This occurred September 1st, 1863. He was immediately employed by the General commanding as government printer, and from that time on his star was in the ascendant. At the close of the war he located at Kansas City, Mo., in April, 1865, with a new job printing outfit. In April, 1867, he formed a co-partnership with Col. John Wilder, of Boston, and purchased the Kansas City *Daily Journal*, the only newspaper that survived the war at that point. Col. Wilder having been assassinated in April, 1869, Mr. Foster associated with himself in the publication of the *Journal*, Col. R. T. Van Horn and D. K. Abeel. In the fall of 1871 he sold his interest in the *Journal* and removed to Chicago, where he immediately opened a newspaper advertising agency, which, together with newspaper correspondence, has occupied his time almost exclusively down to the present time.

W. P. FRAILEY

I was born in Baltimore, Md., on the 12th of July, 1819, and my few first years were uneventful, as is the case generally with most children. At the age of five years the presidential contest virtually between John Q. Adams and Andrew Jackson—although there were several other candidates in the field took place, and it was of unusual rancorous feeling—manifesting at that day the feeling which characterizes the prominent parties of the present, sound argument and intelligence guiding the Whigs in their conduct of the contest—whilst corruption, whisky and profanity were the potent weapons of the Jackson democracy—and they have so continued down to the present time. Although but five years old at that time, I can remember distinctly the scenes enacted at the polls near my home—and my politics for the time and since may be said to have been formed from that date—as I have continued to be a determined opponent to Jackson Democracy—which is but another name for that of the present day—Jackson being the god-father of it, instead of Jefferson.

I have seldom, if ever, cast a vote for a Democrat, but have at times omitted to cast my vote for candidates put forward by my party when I considered them unworthy. Henry Clay was my idea of a statesman, and my standard and guide in politics whilst the Whig party continued in existence. When it disbanded I attached my fortunes with the opponents to the corrupt *Loco Foco* Democracy, and enrolled my name on the list of the Republican party, and cast my vote for John C. Fremont in 1856, and have had no occasion since to regret my connection with the party of reform—under whose guidance the country has been led to be the foremost nation on earth.

My early life was spent in acquiring the rudiments of an ordinary English education, which ended about my sixteenth year, from which time my life was checkered. In 1839 and part of 1840, up to July of the latter year, I was engaged with the government forces of the Navy Department in connection with the army in driving the Seminole and other Indians out of Florida, and have paddled in a canoe over most of what is known as the Everglades in search of the red-skins. In the spring of 1840 the naval part of the expedition, consisting of one brig and five schooners, were ordered home—and reached Norfolk, Va., early in July—where I resigned my position and returned to my home in Baltimore, where I remained, and in the fall of that year cast my first vote for Wm. H. Harrison for president of the United States. Remaining in Baltimore until 1843, in the fall of which year I visited Ohio, and became so well pleased with western life that my home was made at various times in the several States of Ohio, Indiana, Nebraska, and finally, in 1859, in Illinois, in which latter State I have since resided—nine years at Galesburg and over twenty years last past in Chicago. Thirteen years of the twenty spent in Chicago—from 1869 to 1882—were spent in the employ of the Pennsylvania Co. (R. R.) in its general passenger department—when changes in the head of which resulted in my release.

It gave me unspeakable pleasure to be able to cast my vote in 1888 for Benjamin Harrison for president, that I might be able to say that I had cast my suffrages for two generations of the same family for the most exalted position on earth—both of whom were well fitted by nature and education to fill the place with honor to themselves and benefit to the nation. I regret that my financial condition would not admit of my witnessing the inauguration of the grandson as I did of the grandfather.

S. D. FROST

Born May 16th, A. D., 1816, at Pompey, Onondago county, New York. His early life was more full of vicissitudes than fall to the lot of most boys, by reason of the death of his father; but when nineteen years of age he had mastered the trade of harness-making and the carriage trimmer's art, and later became a professional occulist. He cast his first vote for General William Henry Harrison in 1840, at Pompey, and voted for Clay in 1844, and came west in 1854 to Xenia, Ohio, removing to Chicago in 1871. In the disastrous fire of that year he lost his all, and like many others, was compelled to go back to first principles, again entering the ranks as a journeyman carriage-maker. In his seventy-third year he still follows his trade, when work is to be found, but believes that carriage-makers are "opposed to a gray-bearded administration." His vote in 1888 was cast for "Young Tippecanoe," and he is right proud of the grandson—while duly respecting the memory of his glorious grandsire, whose sudden and untimely death he attributed to partisan treachery.

JOHN GAGE

Was born in Litchfield, Herkimer county, N. Y., 12th day of August, 1802. He remained on his father's farm for eighteen years, where he learned the trade of a moulder in brass. He removed to Watertown, N. Y., in 1823. In 1835, with a large covered spring wagon, he started for Chicago, arriving here August 4th, 1836, with a vowed purpose of building a flouring mill. He was, however, unable to find lumber or materials, but in five months he had overcome these difficulties, and was operating three run of stones, and made flour enough to reduce the price from $17 to $12 per barrel. In 1836–'40 he voted for Gen. William H. Harrison in this city, the polling place being at Scott's planing mill, between Canal street and the river. He was chairman of the Tippecanoe Club of Chicago in 1840, which was continued some time after the election, the meetings being held in the second story of a frame building on the northeast corner of North Water street and State street. We can better imagine than describe the pleasure to Mr. Gage for being allowed to live to see the grandson of the illustrious Whig in the presidential chair; to join the Old Tippecanoe Club of 1888, to parade the streets with it, and to again attend the meetings, this time not in a second story of a frame building, but in the commodious club rooms in the Grand Pacific Hotel.

LEMAN WOOD GARLICK

Was born January 1st, 1815, in the town of Kent, Litchfield county, Connecticut. His parents, Leman and Mary Garlick, that year moved with seven of their children to New Lisbon, Otsego county, N. Y. Leman W. lived with his parents until

L. W. GARLICK.

twelve years of age, and was brought up in strict accordance
with the teachings of the Bible. He then went to live with his
oldest brother, Horatio Garlick, who had settled in Mt. Upton,
Chenango county, N. Y., and remained three years, going to
school and working in the shop with his brother at the tailoring
business. At the age of sixteen, having a strong desire to be a
wood-worker, he, by mutual consent, left his brother and went to
learn the trade of cabinet-making with James B. Frasier, of Harpersville, Broome county, N. Y., where he remained for five years.
At that time all workmen were required to work from six in the
morning until nine at night. During the time of his apprenticeship he formed the acquaintance of the young people of the
place, and was invited in society, and for the first time in his
life was invited to a sleigh-ride. He being almost a stranger, and
but partially acquainted with the young ladies, did not get
around to make his choice soon enough, as the other young men
had engaged them. He did not know what to do. As he was
then attending school he selected a little girl two years his junior
who had never been in company. She accepted, and they went
off in flying colors for the first time—but it was not the last
time—for on December 25th, 1835, in the town of Harpersville,
Broome county, N. Y., they were made man and wife, and have
lived as such over fifty-three years in the true love and affection
that belongs to man and wife. They have been blessed with
four sons, all now living, and one lovely daughter, who died
when she was twenty-two years old.

At the time L. W. G. was married he took his young wife to
Oxford, Chenango county, N. Y., where he was engaged at his
trade. In 1836 he cast his first vote for William Henry Harrison
for president of the United States, and in the same town in 1840
he again voted for William H. Harrison, and he was elected, but
to universal regret, died four weeks after taking the chair. Mr.
Garlick has voted at every subsequent presidential election, and
is thankful today that it has been a Whig and Republican vote,
including that for General Benjamin Harrison.

In 1843 Mr. Garlick left Oxford with his family of wife and
three children, and settled in the village of Tecumche, Michigan,

and lived there nine months, then moved to Adrian, Mich., where he remained for over twelve years; then he moved to Hudson, Mich., remaining two years. His health failing him, he sold out and went to Coldwater, Mich., and remained there three or four years; then to South Bend, Ind. Not being content there he moved to La Porte, Ind., where he went into the furniture business. In 1861 his health entirely gave out, so by the advice of friends he went to traveling in the interest of a life insurance company. In 1871 he came to Chicago and engaged in the same business until fall, when the great fire destroyed all its business prospects for the near future. He then went to Tiffin, Ohio, for two years, and then returned to Chicago, where he has ever since lived with his sons. He is a member of the Old Tippecanoe Club, and hopes to live to vote for a second term of President General Benjamin Harrison, the true representative of his life-long political principles. Mr. Garlick always lived a quiet, peaceful life. In consequence of age and ill-health he was disqualified, and could, therefore, not be accepted to perform military service in the war of the Rebellion, but he did what he could for his country, and with that motive uppermost always worked hard to elect, first Whigs, then Republicans to office.

WILLIAM GARNETT.

I was born at Glasgow, Barron county, Kentucky, on the 27th day of March, 1816, of Virginia parentage. My father was Clerk of Barron Circuit Court from its establishment, some forty years. My educational advantages were quite limited. On the 21st of January, 1840, I was married to Angonia Tompkins, daughter of the Hon. Christopher Tompkins, of Glasgow. He was many years Circuit Court Judge, and for two terms a member of Congress. We raised nine children—six sons and three daughters—all living, except our oldest son Christopher, who, in August, 1862, went into the Union army as a private in the Seventy-Second Illinois Regiment, and on the 23d of May, 1863, was killed in a skirmish around Vicksburg. During all these years of our married life my wife has been a real "home missionary"—having

given her life fully to her husband, children and home.   In the
fall of 1840 I gave my first presidential vote to Gen. William
Henry Harrison, "Tip. and Ty." The "Ty" proved to be very
unsatisfactory.   I have never regretted the Harrison vote,
and was ready in November, 1888, with five sons, one son-
in-law, and one grandson, to vote for General Benjamin Harrison,
with equal success.

In June, 1839, I was appointed Clerk of the Barron Circuit
Court, in which capacity I served until the summer of 1850
(eleven years), after which I resigned and went into the mercantile and manufacturing business in Louisville, Kentucky,
from whence I came to Chicago, and have been a resident of
this city ever since that date. In 1859–60 I was cashier of
Southern Bank of Kentucky, at Louisville.

In my early life I had scruples about slavery, but also possessed an ambition to acquire wealth, and took slaves by gift
and purchase. However, after much reflection and anxiety on
the subject, I became convinced of the fact, and accepted in my
mind that the often forgotten words of the immortal Jefferson,
in the Declaration of Independence, "That all men are erected
free and equal, and entitled to life, liberty, and the pursuit of
happiness," meant exactly what they said, and that slavery was
a sin against God, and in the sight of a large percentage of the
best men and women of the age. So, "believing that slavery
was wrong in principle and practice, and productive of great
evil to both master and slave" (as expressed in deed of emancipation), on the 20th day of October, 1845, I went into the Barron
County Court and duly emancipated eight slaves (all I at that
time possessed), and gave bond for their maintenance, as was required by law, retaining guardianship of them until they were
of age. Among them were three names of national and world-
wide fame, viz:

Daniel Webster, seven years of age,
Henry Clay, five years of age,
John Quincy Adams, three years of age.

For this act there was heaped upon me the wrath of many
old friends, of both political parties; but they neither killed me

nor rode me on a rail. However, I so much expected the latter that I kept a loaded gun to defend the fort, for I did not propose to ride in any such way, and guess it was generally understood that such was my determination, for however many were the threats, they were never carried out, and my life went on in the even tenor of its way.

When Mr. Lincoln was first a candidate for the presidency, my home then being in Louisville, Kentucky, the commercial city of the State, with a population then of some 60,000 (now said to be some 200,000), I was one of one hundred and thirteen in that city who voted for Lincoln, and, with Capt. Hamilton, was placarded up around town as " having voted the Abolition ticket." But that did not disturb me very much, for as far back as 1849, in my own native county, at a public political debate, before a large gathering, one of the speakers from the stand pointed me out " As the king of the Abolitionists." Even this intended insult elicited no reply. Such taunts as these could not move me. I was firm in my convictions then, and nearly half a century has only served to strengthen me in them. While not loving my native State less, but my country more, I think I may lay claim, in all modesty, to the proud title of a " loyal man."

DR. AARON GIBBS

Was born in Litchfield, Conn., the 17th day of April, 1807. His father was a private in the Revolutionary War. He removed to Buffalo, N. Y., practiced dentistry for seven years. He came to Chicago in 1844; he voted for William Henry Harrison in 1840— has been an active Republican, and voted for General Harrison in 1888.

CAPT. GEO. W. GIDRON

Was born in Philadelphia, Pa., on the 31st of May, 1814, of Prussian parentage, and was educated for a physician. He left that city for the then "far west," and arrived in Galena, Jo Davies county, State of Illinois, in April, 1835, and in 1836 was appointed captain of the steamer "Heroine," navigating between Galena and the port of St. Louis, and remained on the Mississippi river commanding and superintending various steamboats until he received the appointment of U. S. Inspector of Steam Vessels of Galena district. He held that position until removed by the Cleveland administration, July, 1885, "without cause," but the real cause was he escorted the late lamented Gen. John A. Logan from Galena, Ill., to Dubuque, Ia., in the campaign of '84. He voted in Galena in 1836–'40 for Gen. W. H. Harrison, and in 1888 for "Young Tip.," Gen. B. Harrison.

J. H. GILL

Was born in Jefferson county, Mt. Pleasant township, Mt. Pleasant town, Virginia, January 31, 1813. His parents were Quakers. They followed banking, milling, stock-raising and farming. His father, two brothers and himself all voted for General Harrison in 1836–40—not one of their family being Democrats. Their Whigism commenced with the Revolution in 1776—his grandfather, William Hana, of Berk county, Va., carrying a musket seven years during that war. Mr. Gill died March 13, 1889.

THOMAS GOODMAN,

Born at Market Harborough, in Leicestershire, England, on February 2, 1816. When I was about five years old the family moved to London, where I was brought up as far as to the age of sixteen. On July 26, 1832, I bade farewell to my father and mother and native home, and sailed on the good ship Columbia, Captain Delano, Mate Morris, 2d-Mate Delacroix, for the United States. Perhaps you smile at my particularity, but let me tell you a sea voyage in 1832 was no insignificant enterprise. I reached New York in good order on September 1832; went up to Albany on a steamer, and then on a canal-boat to Buffalo, thence on a schooner to Ohio. My first stopping place was Cleveland, but it was a little bit of a village—only twelve hundred people. Stayed there about eight months, then went to Canton, which was about double the size. Reached there in May, 1833. The

Clerk of the Court of Common Pleas appointed me his clerk, to make up records, etc. Remained in that office five years. Was naturalized at Ravenna, Portage county, Ohio, on the 26th of September, 1837—less than one month after my five years residence closed. Voted the Whig and Republican tickets. I married June 26, 1838. It was in that same town of Canton I voted for General Harrison. He had been in Massillon a few months before in company with Tom Ewing, Tom Corwin, and Salmon P. Chase. I met him there, shook hands with him, and wished him good luck in the name of the Lord. I helped sing him into the presidency. I have five daughters and three sons, all well— no break in that chain—four girls married, all the boys married. Seven good Republican votes now, and all those seven for Benjamin Harrison; and of the fifteen grandchildren, all in *de bene esse*, there is a prospect of more Republican votes in future.

Last summer I was in Indianapolis, and my friend Carr, the Auditor of State, took me to his house and introduced me to General Harrison. Upon my word he don't look unlike the old General in 1840. I told him I voted for his grandsire, and should vote for him, and I did, here in the Eleventh Ward of Chicago. I think we have been mighty fortunate in getting just that man and no other.

SAMUEL B. HAGGARD

Was born in Winchester, Clark county, Kentucky, November 8, 1814, to which place his father, Dawson, moved with his parents, in 1793, from Virginia. His grandfather, David Haggard, was born in Virginia, and was a near neighbor of Thomas Jefferson. He served in the army during the war of the Revolution, being present at Yorktown at the surrender of Cornwallis. In 1818 S. B. moved to Christian county with his father, and afterward to Trigg county, where he was raised and lived until the age of twenty-one years. From there he went to Bloomington, Ill., making the journey on horseback. Here he learned the carpenter trade. In 1837 he was married to Miss Mary Mason, who was also a native of Kentucky. In the fall of 1843 he removed to Chicago, making the journey in a wagon—occupying about a week's time.   Here he entered the employ of Scoville & Gates, with whom he remained until 1847, at which time he connected himself with McCormick & Gray, setting up the machinery for their reaper works.   In 1850 he left their employ to engage in the pump business, and later in hardware.   In 1887 Mr. and Mrs. Haggard celebrated their golden wedding.   In 1836 he voted for William Henry Harrison and again in 1840.   Since this time he has voted for every Whig and Republican presidential candidate, including Gen. Benjamin Harrison in 1888.

URIAH HAIR

Was born in Washington county, Pa., April 7th, 1812.   His father was a Whig, and in the campaign of 1840 his six sons who had survived him, and the husbands of five of his daughters took a lively interest in the campaign, and cast ten solid votes for "Tippecanoe and Tyler, too."   But two of the Hair family are now living, these two being members of the Tippecanoe Club, and with their descendants—numbering in all thirty-seven—cast a solid vote of thirty-seven ballots for Gen. Benjamin Harrison in 1888.   It will thus be seen that the affections of the Hair family have ever been "solid" for the Harrisons, and the best wishes of the survivors are for the successful administration of the present occupant of the presidential chair for our country's sake.

T. W. HALL

Was born near Richmond, Jefferson county, Ohio, July 12, 1818, residing in the same State till 1839, when, with his family, he removed to Savannah, now in Ashland county, Ohio, where, in 1840, he cast his first vote for the successful candidate.   On the breaking out of the gold fever in '49, Mr. Hall crossed the plains via. the usual route of the day—ox team –and was moderately successful, returning in 1853, when he invested his surplus in Wisconsin farms, but in 1861 Chicago's commercial outlook induced his removal here, where he afterward did a very large business as a wool merchant.   He voted with the "Tippecanoes" in 1888.

S. B. HAGGARD.

M. W. HAMMOND

Was born in 1809. Cast his first vote in Otisco, in 1830; in 1832 his first presidential vote for Andrew Jackson, giving his reason therefor " he was not a Tory Democrat," and Mr. Hammond adds: " I may say, right here, that I do not think there is a Jacksonian Democrat now living who is not a Republican." In 1836 he voted for Gen. William Henry Harrison, and being a musician put his " best wind " into the campaign, and again in 1840, with a little more success, he used the same old instrument for " Old Tippecanoe." In 1888 he cast his vote for the " chip of the old block," being greatly pleased at having " lived to see the day."

JOSEPH WARREN HARMON, M. D.,

A physician and surgeon, was born in Jefferson county, New York, June 20th, 1815. He graduated at the Black River Institute, at Watertown, N. Y., in 1840, and voted for Gen. William Henry Harrison the same year, at Watertown. He graduated from the Albany Medical College in 1845. For twelve years before the war he resided near Cleveland, Ohio, and was a near neighbor and family physician of President Garfield. In 1861, when Garfield was appointed Colonel of the Forty-Second Regiment Ohio Volunteer Infantry, he requested his appointment as surgeon of his regiment. Since the war he has resided in and around Chicago, and voted for Gen. Benjamin Harrison at Blue Island, Ill., in 1888.

GEORGE PAINE HARRIS

Was born in Carlow, Carlow county, Ireland, March 5, 1818. His father was an Episcopalian; his mother a Quaker, descended from one of the oldest Quaker families of Ireland, named Moffit. His father, George Paine, was one of the old Paine stock of Revolutionary times, whose name was Thomas, and who wrote " The Age of Reason," " Common Sense," etc.; a fast friend of Thomas Jefferson, the third president of the United States. The father of the subject of this sketch generously furnished his thirteen children with the best facilities the country afforded for their education.

In 1834 he left his parental roof and became an apprentice to a soap and tallow chandler. The country was in turmoil. Two years latter he became seriously impressed concerning his future life, and on May 28, 1837, when the lightning was flashing, the thunder raving and the rain falling, he made a vow as high as heaven, as deep as hell, as wide as the world is round and as long as his life should last, that he would never use tobacco or liquor, which vow, by the grace of God, he has sacredly kept. In 1838 his minister, Rev. George Vance. was absent, attending a conference, and as he at the same time had an appointment at Castledermes, a Mr. Kerr accompanied Mr. Harris to fill the latter. The Protestants of the village having been notified accordingly, the meeting was largely attended, and was first addressed by Mr. Kerr. Mr. Harris then spoke, when under the influence of the spirit every person in the house fell, except one man — a policeman — and the cries for mercy were like those on the day of Pentecost. In September, 1838, Mr. Harris started for New York, bringing letters of recommendation and certificate of church membership, and united with the M. E. Church — Rev. S. D. Ferguson, in that city — wherein he soon found many congenial Christian, anti-slavery spirits, who with himself became active and enthusiastic workers for the election of William Henry Harrison in 1840. The death of the president in 1841 was deeply lamented. That summer, Mr. Harris and eight confederates, held regular Sunday religious meetings on the wharfs on the North river with good results. Upon urgent solicitation, he was then induced to move to West Flamboro, a country town in Canada, to teach school and preach the gospel. Enroute he addressed a large concourse of people at Utica, N. Y. A Mormon preacher answered him, whereupon Mr. Harris, if the demonstration of the crowd was evidence, handled Mormonism and its advocate to their utter discomforture. Arriving at his destination, Mr. Harris was hospitably welcomed, and on the following Sunday preached to large audiences — most of the congregation had never heard or seen a Methodist before. The next day school opened in the new school house and all went well. He was chosen a class teacher, and held that position until he became

an itinerant minister, preaching acceptably throughout the circuit
— many souls being converted. He continued his itinerant labor,
either as curcuit minister or presiding elder, until 1857, when,
differing from his brethern on articles of Methodist faith separa-
tion ensued, and he continued preaching as a man instead as a
Methodist. Soon thereafter, he purchased a farm. Crops proving poor, he traded the farm for other property, and in 1860 engaged in new business. He was an ardent admirer of Abraham
Lincoln, and on hearing the disastrous results of the Bull Run
battle, raising his hands heavenward he exclaimed, "Thank God!
Now the North will awake, and not only will the rebellion be
crushed, but slavery must die with it." Moving to Minnesota, he
enlisted in Company F, Minnesota Mounted Rangers, which was
sent by the War Department to the frontier against the Indians.
During this service he availed himself of the opportunity to
preach at every visited fort. On the expiration of his term of
enlistment, he entered as a veteran in Company D, Second
Cavalry, by re-enlistment—was commissary of company—and so
continued until promoted to Company Eight, First Infantry;
never wore shoulder straps nor went to the company; was
stationed at Fort Snelling by appointment from Gov. Stephen
Miller, and took charge of the Convalescent Department until the
close of the war, after which he went to Vermillion mines,
St. Louis county, Minnesota, but was never re-imbursed for the
time and money invested there. At that time Duluth's population consisted of seven families. In 1873 he spent from April to
September in the South—preaching at Baltimore and Washington.
Was a delegate to the Young Men's Christian Association of
which John Wannemaker was chairman. Returned to St. Paul—
remaining there during the winter—was employed to go to
Nobles county, western Minnesota. While there he profoundly
realized new impressions, concerning another life. There he met
departed friends face to face, and had positive evidence that
under the eternal, inexorable and unchangable law of the Infinate
Father, he could converse with those whose spirits had departed,
in his native land. In 1876 he came to Chicago, where he has
continued to reside, with the exception of three years in Wheeler,

Porter county, Indiana. He is now connected with a railroad company. Mr. Harris rejoices in unselfishly endeavoring, during a long, eventful life, to perform his duty towards the amelioration of the condition of his fellow-men and lead them in a righteous path. The enforced retirement of Cleveland meets his hearty approval and bids him exclaim:

The dread angel of death spread his wings on the blast,
And breathed in the face of poor Grover as he passed;
The eye of the President waxed death-like and chill,
And his breast heaved but once, then—for ever—kept still.

Politically—Amen.

CYRUS MADISON HAWLEY

Was born in Cortland county, New York, on the 27th day of January, A. D., 1815. His ancestors were from Derbyshire, England, and of Norman blood. Joseph Hawley, the earliest ancestor of whom he has reliable information, emigrated to this country with his brothers Francis and Johnathan, and landed in Boston, Mass., in 1640. Soon after Joseph settled in Stratford, Conn. Maj. Hawley, of the Revolution, was a descendant. Captain Francis Hawley was the father of Joseph Hawley II, the grandfather of the subject of this biography. He settled in Old Huntington, Fairfield county, Conn., and married Aanah Lewis, of the same place; and their son Lewis was born February 5, 1778. He was a cousin of Governor Charles Hawley, of Stanford, Conn., and married Sarah Tanner, of New Port, R. I. The Tanners were relatives of the Hazzards, Hillyers, and Thurstons, of New England.

Cyrus Madison Hawley is the son of Lewis and Sarah Tanner Hawley, and a brother of Hon. Lewis Tanner Hawley, of Syracuse, N. Y., and a relative of Gen. Joseph R. Hawley, now representing the State of Connecticut in the Senate of the United States. His first vote for president was in 1840, when he cast it for Gen. Wm. H. Harrison in the interest of a national currency and a tariff to protect our home industries. In the interests of universal liberty according to the letter and spirit of the constitution of the United States as then existing, in 1846 he was nominated as a candidate for Congress against Judge Duer and Gen. Huff; but came out second in the race—Duer being elected by about three hundred majority over him. In 1847 Mr. Hawley came to Chicago, and was admitted in 1849 to the bar of the State; and in 1862 to the bar of the supreme court of the United States.

Not until 1860 did he take an active part in politics, except to cast his vote for the candidates of the Free Soil and Republican parties from and after their respective organizations. He did so because he loved freedom and hated slavery. Early in 1861 he wrote articles for the press, under the *nom de plume* of "Madison," in which he advocated the right and duty of the government to issue United States Treasury Notes as a circulating medium, and for the use of the government to meet its immediate demands; and in which he antagonized the assumption then put forth by the "Copperheads" at the North, and the rebels of the South, that the States had the right to withdraw from the Union at will. John C. Calhoun was the originator of this treasonable doctrine, and Jeff Davis and Toombs were the leaders in the attempt to put it in practice. He was also an earnest advocate of the proclamation of the President as commander-in-chief of the army and navy, as a war measure, to preserve the Union at the expense of slavery, and the employment of the newly-made freemen as soldiers, and in other helpful ways, and as citizens equal before the law, their endowment with the elective franchise. These principles of freedom being settled, he favored clinching them with the thirteenth, fourteenth and fifteenth amendments of the constitution, and so remove all possible doubts in favor of liberty and justice.

Succeeding his association with Hon. L. and G. Trumbull in the practice of law, in 1869, with the consent of the Senate, he was appointed by President U. S. Grant a Justice of the Supreme Court of Utah Territory, and held the office one judicial term. Soon after his arrival in Salt Lake City he attended the reception given by Mr. and Mrs. F. H. Head to Hon. Wm. H. Seward and party, where he met, for the first time, Brigham Young, who, on

C. M. HAWLEY.

being introduced to Mr. Hawley, assumed an air of importance as he extended his hand, and remarked in measured tones: "Sir, I hope you have not come here, as other Judges have done, to persecute my people." With like deliberation Mr. Hawley replied: "Sir, I have not come to persecute the people of Utah, but to administer the law as I find it." This ended their relations, except in the court of adjudication, where Young was obliged to appear as a party defendant.

Among the earliest judicial opinions of Judge Hawley was the reversal of all former decisions of the District and Supreme Courts, whereby they had conceded the right of the legislature of the Territory to extend the jurisdiction of the Probate Courts to that of common law and chancery. On appeal to the Supreme Court of the United States, his opinions of reversal were sustained. But this in nowise relieved him from the hostility of the Mormon hierarchy, nor from the anathemas of their church paper. Their excited wrath was perhaps greater, when, on information, after arguments, and upon consideration and judgment, he issued the "Writ of Prohibition" against Probate Judge Murdock, restraining him from other jurisdiction than that of Probate and its incidents, which he had resumed in defiance of the Supreme Court. And their wrath was re-enkindled, when, on the application of the Governor, he issued a writ to the United States Marshal for the arrest of the officers of a Mormon regiment, charged with rebellion against the government. Their arrest was the signal for the assembling in and around the court room and in the streets of thousands, whose whispered threats were intended to intimidate, or to postpone judicial action. But in face of the demonstration, those arrested were held to the grand jury, and on their refusal to give bail, were remanded to custody. Another complaint of the hierarchy was by reason of his letter written at the request of Maj.-Gen. Ord, showing the need of a Military Post at Beaver City, near the Mountain Meadow massacre of over one hundred and thirty citizens on their way to settle in southern California, by the Mormons, disguised as Indians, to possess themselves of the property of the emigrants, valued at one million of dollars. The letter was trans-

mitted by Gen. Ord to the Secretary of War, and by him trans-
mitted to Congress, with the approval of the General and of the
Secretary. This letter was construed by the Mormons to be an
attempt to bring to justice those of the Mormons responsible for
this horrible slaughter; and among the disguised Mormons were
leaders in the church. The church paper commented upon the
letter as an atrocious act of hostility to the people, The Post,
notwithstanding, was established, Bishop Lee, the protogee of
Brigham Young, and by his appointment was the Indian Agent
at the time in southern Utah, who lead the murdering slaughter,
was arrested, indicted, convicted, and was executed for his
bloody deed on the identical spot of the massacre.

At the close of his judicial term, notwithstanding the previous
sharp antagonism of the Mormon papers to his judicial acts, they
awarded him both judicial ability and honesty, insisting, however, that he was prejudiced against their religion.

Before leaving the Territory, the bar tendered him a banquet
at the Walker House, which was joined by the officers of Camp
Douglas. He then proceeded to Washington, D. C., and entered
into co-partnership with Hon. A. G. Riddle, under the firm name
of Hawley & Riddle. Their practice was confined to the Supreme Court of the United States and the Departments of State.

His wife is the daughter of Hon. Henry Fellows, of Monroe
county, N. Y., and the grandaughter of Gen. John Fellows, of
the Revolution, who commanded a Brigade near Saratoga
Springs, first under Gen. Schuyler, and afterwards under Gen.
Yates, who succeeded to the command of the American forces
in northern New York in 1777, at the time the British troops,
under Gen. Burgoyne, were threatening our lines in the endeavor
to reach their supplies and re-enforcements, then on the way
from New York City up the North River. Gen. Yates antici-
pating Burgoyne's movement, dispatched Gen. Fellows with fifteen hundred men to the east side of the North River, on the
supposition Burgoyne would attempt to cross over; but in this
Gen. Yates was mistaken, and Gen. Fellows, having ascertained
the mistake, received orders to re-cross the river to the north
side, which he succeeded in doing, and took position on " Batten

Kill," where he was able to hold the British forces in check, and to prevent their re-enforcements and supplies from reaching them. This placed Burgoyne and his command in our hands, and compelled his surrender to Gen. Yates on the 7th of October, 1777. These particulars are recited more fully by Gen. Bullard in his centennial address in Saratoga county in 1876.

Mrs. Hawley inherited from her grandfather—Gen. John Fellows—and has now in her possession, a precious souvenir—the personal general order memorandum book of Gen. George Washington in his own handwriting, from the 5th day of August to the 28th day of September, 1776, inclusive. As to how her grandfather came to possess it is not known.

By reason of impaired health, Judge Hawley retired from professional labor, and in 1879 returned to Chicago, and in 1880 took residence in Hyde Park, Illinois, where he now resides. In the Republican compaign of 1888 he was an active participant, and voted to elect Gen. Benj. Harrison and Levi P. Morton president and vice-president of the United States of America.

WILLIAM P. HEWITT

Was born March 25th, 1816, in Syracuse county, N. Y., moving to Ontario county shortly after, and at sixteen years of age learned the carpenter's trade, which he has followed until within the last few years. Cast his first vote in 1840 for Gen. W. H. Harrison. In 1846 he removed to Chicago, but not "liking the mudhole as it was then," went to Wellington, where he carried on his business for twenty years, returning to Chicago in 1866, and has lived here ever since. Voted for Gen. Harrison in 1888, and has ever voted the straight Republican ticket.

WALTER S. HINKLEY

First saw the light of day in January, 1815, in the town of Buckland, Franklin county, Mass. His father was a descendant of Thomas Hinkley, the last Governor of Plymouth Colony. His mother was of the same stock as James Otis, of Revolutionary

fame.   His early life was spent on his father's farm at Holland
Purchase, N. Y., whither the family had removed in 1816.   In
1834 he studied law and taught school.   In 1872 he removed
with his family to Riverside, Cook county, Illinois.   He has never
sought office, but was appointed by William H. Seward, Ex-
aminer in Chancery and Master in Chancery in 1840, and for several years held the office of Justice of the Peace in the towns
where he resided,   Mr. Hinkley has traveled considerably, having made the tour of the continent of England and Scotland,
and, unlike many Americans, has "done" his own country.   He
voted for William Henry Harrison in the years 1836 and 1840, at
Rochester, New York.   Took an active part in both campaigns,
being marshal of the processions, "sometimes miles in length,"
and attended the Baltimore convention.   In 1888 he was for
Gen. Benjamin Harrison first, last, and all the time, and he adds:
" I think he has made no mistake, but shown remarkable ability
and fitnes for the high office."

REV. DANIEL GARLAND HOLMES

The subject of this sketch was born in the town of Barnstead,
Stafford county, New Hampshire, April 5th, 1812, and is, therefore, in his 77th year of age.   Mr. Holmes comes of good old
Puritan stock—his ancestors being among the earliest emigrants
from old England.   His father, Isaac Holmes, was born and always lived in the town of Farmington, New Hampshire, where
he died at the age of of 78.   Mr. D. G. Holmes had the usual
New England schooling advantages, or disadvantages, as three
months at school in a year might certainly be called, but he was
more fortunate in fitting himself for the ministry, as he had the
advantages of schools and colleges at Lowell, Boston and
Andover, Mass., and Whitestown, N. Y., at which latter place he
graduated.   Mr. Holmes celebrated his first presidential vote on
the wrong side of the fence, voting in 1836 for Van Buren, but he
soon saw the error of his way, and when Van Buren attempted a
second term, Holmes' vote was added to the rousing majority of
William Henry Harrison, and from that time to the present he

has ever been a steadfast, hard-working Republican, and he glories in it. As a reason for his change of heart Mr. Holmes says:

"The great change wrought in my mind in 1840 had a *cause*, and that *cause* was so plainly presented to the people that party lines could not prevent, nor party leaders hold the people from a change. The Democratic party, under the leadership of Presidents Jackson, Van Buren, and others, had manifested a great deal of ability in overthrowing the national bank, and in breaking up the old system of finance; but the people had discovered also that they had not the ability to provide a better system to put in its place, nor did they have wisdom or the power to put limits to the work of destruction they had already caused; for the work of ruin and waste went on until in 1837 every bank in the nation suspended specie payment and failed, and our whole country was in financial ruin. This party did not even suggest a system of banking or finance in which the people had any confidence; nor have they ever been able to gain the people's confidence in this respect. Whenever that party has been in power ruin has followed, as the history of 1837, 1857, and 1860 proves."

In 1888, in our own fair city, Mr. Holmes voted with great pleasure for General Benjamin Harrison, and attended his inauguration. Mr. D. G. Holmes is an ardent worker for the cause of education and reform, and is one of the foremost active workers in every good cause.

GEORGE HOLT,

Born April 16th, 1818, in Milford, Hillsboro county, New Hampshire. His first vote for president was in Lowell, Mass., for Wm. Henry Harrison. The campaign in Lowell was a lively one, and great interest and enthusiasm was manifested by the Whig party for an honest government and tariff protection. A large campaign gathering of Whigs at Concord, Mass., was held July 4th, 1840, and it was estimated that one hundred thousand people were on the old battle-ground. There was a grand parade of military, with bands of music, and Whig clubs from all over the

State participated. Eminent Whigs gave splendid speeches, showing the great benefit of a protective tariff for our manufacturers, and the particular fitness of Wm. Henry Harrison as the standard bearer of the Whig party.

At Lowell the Whig party had a log cabin thirty feet long and twelve feet wide, furnished with steel traps, live coons, and two barrels of hard cider. The cabin was put on trucks and drawn by forty horses to Concord, Mass., seventeen miles from Lowell. It was a clear, pleasant day, and all had a grand good time. He has always voted for the Whig party until it disbanded, or merged into the Republican party, as he loved freedom for all the people—black or white—and liberty of life and the pursuit of happiness in its broadest sense. He joined the Republican party, believing it would carry out all its promises for an honest ballot, and a right to have it counted without fear or intimidation, and has voted for all candidates for president of the Republican party, including Benjamin Harrison.

JOHN D. HOWE,

Born February 11, 1798; removed to York State in 1835, and from there to Iowa, stopping in Illinois on the way one year, but lived in Iowa twenty-four years. He then came to Chicago, and is now living at 53 University Place. His occupation has been a country blacksmith. His age is now ninety-one years, and he is able to take his rations.

THOS. HUBBARD,

One of the oldest members of the Club, born at Brimfield, Hampden county, Mass., June 12th, 1802, casting his first vote in 1824 for John Q. Adams, at Brimfield, and in 1836–'40 for Wm. Henry Harrison at the same place, and for every Whig and Republican candidate to and including Abraham Lincoln in 1860, at the same pretty New England town. In 1864 we found Mr. Hubbard voting for Lincoln in Chicago, and at every presidential election since that date he has voted a straight "Grand Old Party" ticket, voting for Gen. Harrison in 1888, in the Fourth Ward of our own city—an honorable man and a good citizen.

JOHN HUNTINGTON,

A New Englander, who lived in Mobile, Alabama, when he cast
his vote in 1836-'40 for Gen. Harrison. Born in the town of Ben-
ningtown, Hillsborough county, N. H., July 24th, 1813. Naturally
the place of a New Englander from 1856 to 1865 was north of
the Mason and Dixon line, and Mr. Huntington came as far
north as Chicago, where he voted for Gen. Benjamin Harrison in
1888.

H. H. HUSTED.

I was born June 7th, 1813, at Danbury, Fairfield county, Conn.
Having been born during the war, when Gen. Wm. H. Harrison
was well thought of, by my grandfather I was given the name of
Harrison. In April, 1835, I left Connecticut for New York City,
being then about twenty-two years of age. I remained there un-
til June, 1843, when I came to Chicago. In 1836 I voted the
Whig ticket, consequently voted for Gen. Harrison for president.
In 1838 I voted for and helped a little to make W. H. Seward
Governor of the State of New York. In 1840 I voted for Gen.
W. H. Harrison—"Tippecanoe and Tyler, too, and with him we
beat Little Van," and now, forty-eight years later, I have voted
for the grandson, Gen. Benjamin Harrison, with whose election
I am well pleased. I have always voted the Whig or Republican ticket in all national elections. In local elections I may have
scratched sometimes, though I am not quite sure of that.

BRICE VIERS HUSTON

Was born in Londenderry, Guernsey county, Ohio, June 26th,
1821; moved to Illinois in 1831, via. the Keel Boat to Cairo, hence
towed to St. Louis, hence to Hennepin on the steamer "Winnebago." His uncle was United States Senator, and had sent for
young Brice in order that he might attain school advantages, but
being a politician, and presumably desiring to view political
opinions with the youngster, he took him through the campaign
of 1840 in Ohio, Pennsylvania, West Virginia, and "Old" Vir-

ginia. He was at the inauguration of Gen. William Henry Harrison, and was the youngest and best known Whig in that campaign. He did not vote for Gen. Harrison by reason of his age, but has a very distinct remembrance of the "coon skins, hard cider, and log cabins." He voted for Henry Clay, and took active part in the campaign as against Allen G. Thurman and other "free trade" speakers. On the occasion of Gen. La Fayette's visit to the United States he was the guest of the parents of Mr. Huston, as was also Gen. Jackson during a portion of each year of his term as president. He is personally acquainted with Gen. Benjamin Harrison, and worked hard for his election, and was "as happy as a coon over the result."

WILLIAM HYDE.

This gentleman probably ranks as the second oldest man of the Tippecanoe Club, having been born at Portsmouth, N. H., 7th of February, 1799, and was perfectly familiar with the incidents relating to the War of 1812, having worked—in connection with other school boys—on the forts then in construction, and the ladies in the town furnishing their luncheons. As Mr. Hyde remarks: "We were all Revolutionary boys, and were in for the war," subsequently proving his war-like nature by joining the various military companies. In 1824 he voted for John Q. Adams, taking an active part in the campaign. In 1826 he removed to New York, where he voted for Gen. William Henry Harrison in 1836 and 1840, taking part in all the celebrations, parades, and lending his voice in swelling the Tippecanoe songs of the day. Some years after Mr. Hyde removed to Chicago, where he has since resided. He is at present engaged in preparing a history of Boston as it was in 1815, and his former familiarity with the subject will undoubtedly make the work an interesting one. Mr. Hyde cast his last vote in Lake View, Nov. 6th, 1888, for Gen. Benjamin Harrison, informing the Board that "though ninety years of age he had always voted the Whig and Republican ticket; knew the Democracy like a book, and had no use for it."

WM. W. INGRAHAM,

A native of the " Green Mountain State," having first seen the light of day in the town of Essex, Chittenden county, April, 1818, and it was in this same town where, in 1840, he showed his Whig sense by voting for Gen. Wm. H. Harrison. Soon after this election he removed to Burlington, Vt., where he engaged in business as millwright, machinist, and mechanical engineer, coming to Chicago on a visit in 1843, and permanently locating here in 1846, and has resided here ever since, being a voter in 1888 for the grandson of his first choice for president. Mr. Ingraham comes from good old stock—his grandfather, for whom he was named, having been a Continental Volunteer during the Revolutionary War, serving seven years, and his father, Chester Ingraham, doing Uncle Sam good service in the War of 1812. This is nothing very extraordinary, however, for old Vermont has always turned out soldiers and heroes, and there are many whose proudest boast is that they are from the old " Green Mountain State."

FREDRICK INGERSOLL

Was born in the town of Vernon, county of Oneida, State of New York, on the 15th day of December, 1804. He was educated in the common school, but at the age of fourteen, by reason of his love of music, he gave attention to its studies. He changed his residence to the village of Vernon, where he entered upon the mercantile business, which he continued for ten years. For more than twenty years he taught vocal music, and was considered one of the best leaders of church choirs in central New York.

In 1841 he was one of the organizers of the Oneida County Agricultural Society, and for ten years held the office of one of the Directors of the Agricultural County Board of Executive Officers; and for two years was the treasurer of the Society. In association with Hon. Levi T. Marshall, he drafted the by-laws of the County Society, which, afterward, were also adopted by the Agricultural Society of the State. He was chairman of the committee on Devon blooded stock. He was instrumental in organizing the Agricultural Society of the town of Vernon.

Soon after arriving at the age of sixty, he moved to the town of Phelps, where he set out and cultivated a vineyard of over three hundred plants with eminent success, and his example was soon followed by hundreds of farmers living near and around those charming lakes in western New York.

His wife, Susan S. Ingersoll (now deceased), was a highly cultivated lady, and in a moment of surprise, in 1844, was requested to improvise an agricultural song, on the delivery of an agricultural address in the native town of her husband, to be sang by him on the occasion. She at once complied, and in a few moments presented the following:

> " Ye farmers, one and all, raise your standard high
> With one united force;
> Let onward, onward be your cry,
> Though toilsome be your course.
> * * * * * *

> " Bright science on your path shall shine,
> Truth shed her glorious ray,
> And joy, and hope, and love divine
> Lead on to endless day.

CHAS. P. JACKSON

Was born June 4tn, 1820, at Sheldon, Genesee county (now Wyoming), New York. Was not old enough to vote for William H. Harrison in 1840, and was sent as a delegate to the Fort Meigs celebration of the victory of 1840. In 1844 he lived in Wabash county, Indiana, being engaged in the railroad business, the company being known as the "Underground Railroad," in which calling he was most expert, and did splendid service. As a boy his tendencies were toward the Democratic party. In 1838 he was shown a part of the press destroyed by the slavery faction at Alton, Ill., and had previously read of the killing of Mr. Lovejoy. These circumstances influenced and changed his sentiments, and ever after he used every legitimate measure against slavery. Voted for Gen. Benjamin Harrison at Chicago, and feels quite proud of the fact.

JOHN JAMES.

Born in Truxton, on the 13th of July, 1806; removed to Bell-ville, N. J., in 1828, and engaged in mercantile business; moved to Utica, Macomb county, Mich., 1831, and engaged in the same business. In 1848 he moved to Detroit, Mich., and engaged in wholesale grocery trade, and then changed his trade to hardware. In 1877 he moved to Hyde Park, having retired from business, where he still resides. Always a Whig and Republican.

CYRUS JONES

Was born December 15th, 1805, in Genesee county, New York. In politics he has ever been a staunch Whig and Republican, casting his first ballot for Gen. William Henry Harrison in 1836, in Tippecanoe county, Indiana, where he then lived; and again (with more success) in 1840. In 1888 he voted for Gen. Benjamin Harrison, making two out of three successful votes for the Harrisons.

WILLIAM KEELING

Was born May 12, 1814, in Derbay Line, Vermont. Moved from Highgate Vermont to New York City; stayed there several years; moved from New York City to Riverhead, Long Island, and married Eliza Ann Brooks, of Middletown, Connecticut, in 1839. Voted for William Henry Harrison in 1840. Moved from River-head in 1841 to Middletown, Connecticut. His wife died in 1861. They had five children, three boys and two girls—two boys died. Moved to Amboy in 1862; to Chicago in 1866; is a carpenter by trade. He has one son and two daughters—Mary J. Knight, living in Chicago; Alice Ward, living in New York City, and George F. Keeling, living in Council Hill, Ill. His son served four years and a half in the army—Twenty-fourth Massachusetts, Company F. Voted for Benjamin Harrison in 1888—not guilty of having voted the Democratic ticket at any time, and now lives at 215 Hermitage Avenue.

JOHN M. KENNEDY.

In 1836 I became a voter, and one of my neighbors—a school-mate of Martin Van Buren—and I, made a trade. He and one son, then a voter, with another son that would be a voter in 1840, would all vote for the next Whig candidate, no matter who he might be, so in 1840 the three voted with me for William Henry Harrison in Little Rock, now Kendale county, then a part of Kane county; my last vote was cast for Benjamin Harrison. Was a Whig from boyhood till the free soil party, and from that a Republican, dyed in the wool.

JOHN KILE,

The son of the Green Mountain State, having been born in Bennington county, October 28, 1818, removing with his parents in 1819 to Monroe county, N. Y. In 1835' located in Will county, Ill., where, in 1840, he cast his first vote for Gen. William Henry Harrison, subsequently removing to Chicago and performing the same service for the grandson in 1888.

ISAAC C. KILGORE

Was born in Fayette county, Ohio, on the 4th of September, 1817. His parents emigrated from Kentucky to Ohio, when Isaac was six years old. He, with his parents, a few years later, removed to Illinois and settled down to farming in McHenry county. His first vote was cast for Gen. William Henry Harrison in 1840. He was a Whig until that party was merged into the Republican party in 1855-6. Has always been proud to vote and cast with the Republican party, and cast his last vote for Gen. Benjamin Harrison on the 6th of November, 1888.

JOHN KING, Jr.

Was born in Palmer, Massachusetts, April 5, 1805, and resided there till twenty-one years of age; then in Monson, Mass. one year; in North Adams, Berkshire county, seven years; in New

York City five years, and settled in Chicago in 1843 up to the present time, March, 1889. He voted in New York City in 1840 for William Henry Harrison, and attended his inauguration, March 4, 1841, in Washington, D. C.; also his funeral procession in New York City, in April, 1841. Was the son of John King, Sr. and Bessy Brown King, of Palmer, Hampden county, Mass., and was a born federalist and protection Whig to this day.

ISAAC D. KINNE.

I was born at Kirmes Four Corners, town of Hannibal, Oswego county, State of New York. At an early period of my life, I, with my brother and uncle, was put to teaming—about three years in all. In January, 1832, my father, with his family of eight children, moved to Ohio, to settle on land opposite Toledo. We went on runners to Buffalo, then by wagon. The whole country was a muck-hole—snow, mud and clay was our daily treat, arriving at Sandusky at night when it began to rain. We laid by one day, then began our march through that what was then called the Black Swamp—muck eighteen inches deep. Snow ten inches deep made traveling slow—sometimes it seemed as though there was no bottom—often had to double teams. After trials and privations for five days and five nights, we reached Perrysburg, on the Maumee River, thirty miles from Sandusky, then we made one day's journey on the river to the land selected opposite Toledo. Father built a fine log house, intending to make it a home, but changed his mind, and in July moved up the Maumee River twenty miles, and located near Waterville. The family were put on board what was then called a perogue—a large canoe—the teams and goods went the road. A boat-ride of about twenty hours brought us to our distination. Here a house must be built, land cleared, a farm opened; Indians were plenty, but quiet. The hardships of this new venture ot two years, and my father's declining health, he thought best to make one more venture, so we moved to Illinois, having heard much of Illinois prairies. We started late in the fall of '34, with two yoke of oxen, two teams of horses, one saddle horse and two milch cows. We encountered many difficulties, bad roads and no roads, mud ice and snow; many times our rations were short, and we began to turn our eyes towards the land of our birth, and, like the children of Israel, longed for the flesh pots of Egypt, after one difficulty after the other was overcome. We struck sands near Michigan City—a day and night here to recruit, and replenish our stock of provisions. Here R. K. Swift passed us on his way to Chicago—in after years he became banker in Chicago— was prominent in quelling the whisky-riot. Our train left Michigan City at an early hour, making our way along beach and sand hills, and gulches on the lake shore. About three or four o'clock in the afternoon, the king-bolt of one wagon broke and I was sent on horseback to Michigan City for repairs. The smith was out, but came soon and repaired the break, and at twelve o'clock was on my way up along the beach in search of the wagons. It was about sun-rise when I made camp. A little refreshment, and the repairs completed, we commenced anew our fearful journey. This day was dry sand, and slow and hard work for teams. At night we took to the pines for shelter. During the night the wind changed and blew off the lake, and we were obliged to get higher up the sand hills, but left the wagons. In the morning the sand was six inches deep over felloes of the wheels, and water to the box of the wagons. By shoveling and doubling teams, we got liberated, and about noon started again to try the unknown; this day the sand was wet and made fair progress. Thus far, four days and five nights we were tossed to and fro, wet and hungry, and far from friends or home. Fifth day brought us to the Calumet river, where we got the first hay for ten days for our teams. Apparently a large Indian settlement was once here, remnants of huts, etc., a large burying ground, also. Each grave was fenced around with poles, two feet wide and six feet long. Rested one day; crossed the Calumet on a sand bar,--water three feet deep. After crossing the river, the bank was higher, so kept away from the lake. Here was the first view we got of the Illinois prairies. This day was spent in an effort to get some game, as our provisions had given out, and night found us along the shore, some bushes for shelter, and hunger increasing—no house in sight Next day we captured some prairie chickens, and along in the afternoon we passed through what seemed to have been a wheat field; it was the soldier's farm, and belonged to Uncle Sam, at Ft. Dearborn. We called at the fort, but got no relief. We then made our way to the south branch of the river, crossed to the west bank, where there was a log cabin. Near the door stood the lady of the house. It was Mrs. Indian Robinson. She was wrapped in a heavy blue blanket, and wore a large plug-hat with three wide silver bands around it. I could speak a little of her language, and asked her if she could give us a little of anything to eat. She gave us liberally of vension; we camped for the night; it was windy and cold. Next morning, father made the acquaintance of Mr. Robinson, who was a white man; father was well acquainted with his brother at Maumee City. One day in Chicago—a very small town at that time. On the north side of the river lay canoes as thick as they could be; up the north branch, on the west side, was a large tract of land that had been cultivated in corn, by the Indians. After a day's rest, we made another start. After traveling all day in grass to our hips, water ten inches deep, and a little ice, we made Whisky Point. Here we got a little meal and had a feast of corn bread. The next day, at four o'clock in the afternoon, we got to the Desplaines river; here were plenty of Indians, but quiet; we camped for the night. In early morn we started for Meacham's Grove, twelve miles away, which we made late in the evening. Coming to the east end of the grove, we found some hay stacks, and camped along side, remaining two days. In the meantime father visited the two Meacham families, Noah Stevens, Harry Woodworth, and Elias Maynard. Father took a claim along Salt Creek, with a grove of about one hundred acres. Mr. Maynard offered us home with him until we could build, which we gladly accepted. Father and myself went to work chopping logs the second day. A man and three nearly grown boys came and ordered us off, saying, we could not jump his claim, and if we did not want to get hurt, to leave at once. Father knowing it to be a dangerous business, left, going to the settlers and reporting. They advised him to go ahead, that the man was claiming all the county and scaring settlers out. Father commenced cutting logs again, and again appeared the man and his boys, each armed with a gun, and warned father off his alleged claim, or he would shoot him. Father had his ax in his hand, and told me to get my gun. I did so. Father walked up to him and told him the settlers were with him and he would not leave, and he must go away or he would get hurt, and after little parlying for a little money, they left, and we were troubled no more. Many hardships had to be encountered in settling the prairies of Illinois.

Politics had little place at first in people's mind. But when the campaign of 1840 opened, people began to divide and get warmed up. Long John Wentworth was the Democratic shining light. He traveled long and late. Democratic whisky was plenty and cheap. The Democrats at the east end of Meachan's grove, at Alansing Watson's Hotel, got a large hickory tree and set it up naming it "Old Hickory," pickled it in whisky and named "Old Hickory Forever." To be a Democrat then was popular. My people were all Democrats. To be a Whig was to be despised, insulted, abused and humiliated. The hickory pole was surrounded, sung to, praised, etc. They marched around it, yelling with fury for the hero of Democracy. A few Whigs had the log cabin and hard cider songs. Some of my choice acquaintances were Whigs. William Henry Harrison was an Indian fighter. His many victories over the Indians was then a great honor to the man.

My sympathies rather increased than diminished in favor of the Whigs. The Kansas move to extend slavery I was strongly opposed to—all this belittled Democracy in my view. Then came the Lovejoy calamity, which so imbittered me against slavery and Democracy—its twin brother—I have left them to their idols—whiskey and office! Then the John Brown affair had its influence. I was active in the campaign for Fremont; then Lincoln. Was at the wigwam when he was nominated, and rejoiced; and also mourned when he was killed. I have participated in all the campaigns since 1856—have seen all of the presidents except Arthur and our Ben. Harrison. Since the formation of the Republican party I have never failed to improve the opportunity of voting the full Republican ticket. Having heard Blaine speak many times I admired him. When he was a candidate I went my whole strength for him—was always marching in line. When it became a fact that Blaine could not get, or did not want the nomination, and Harrison was the man, then I gave him up. I was at the convention when Harrison was nominated, and such a howl was never before known,

My first vote was cast for William Henry Harrison, of Tippecanoe fame, with log cabins and hard cider—the grandfather of Ben. Harrison. My last vote, and the votes of my five sons, were cast for Ben. Harrison. We all belonged and marched with the several clubs of the city. We all enjoyed it, and I felt as though I was doing God's service. Now I hope I, or my children, will never have cause to regret the interest we took and felt in the campaign which elected Ben. Harrison—hoping he will rule in the fear of God, give equal justice to all, guard our shores from foreign paupers and uncongenial emigration, command the nations of the earth to honor and respect our nation, our people, and our flag.

_____

CAPT. JAMES LANING,

Late U. S. Navy, was born May 19th, A. D., 1821, in the village of Bridgeport, Fayette county, Penn. Educated in the village school. His father, John Laning, being a practical mechanic, engaged in cabinet-making, house carpentering, and at a later period built and operated the first steam saw-mill (above Pittsburgh, Pa.,) on the Monongahela river, thus affording the son an opportunity to acquire a thorough knowledge of these trades. Being a natural born mechanic, he had by the time he reached the age of eighteen years, mastered the details of business as developed in a country village, and was placed by his father as an indentured apprentice in a large cabinet shop in the city of Pittsburgh, Pa., where he served until he was nearly twenty-one years of age in completing his education as a cabinet-maker. During this period, viz. 1839 till 1842, the Tippecanoe campaign of 1840 occurred. Being only nineteen years old of course he could not

vote, but inheriting from his father a strong feeling of antagonism to so-called Democracy, and thoroughly trained in the school
of Clay and Webster, he threw his whole soul into the political
cauldron, and helped with youthful ardor to build log cabins,
sing campaign songs, and roll the ball for Old Tippecanoe, and
afterward had the extreme pleasure of standing near General
William Henry Harrison and listening to and applauding his address delivered from the steps in front of the Pittsburgh Hotel,
when on his way from his home in North Bend to Washington,
to be inaugurated president of the United States. It was during
the campaign of 1840 that the shot-gun policy was first introduced into politics (but for a very different purpose than that
which has characterized its use in late years), the subject of this
sketch being in an humble way a party concerned, a brief description of which may prove interesting. A member of Congress
from the Cumberland district of Maryland, whose name was
"Shriver," in a Whig speech gave an allegorical representation
of the Whig party as a rolling ball, which was rolling with irre-
sistable velocity over all the States, crushing out Democracy and
Loco Focoism, and arousing the people to a sense of duty, and
leading them to vote for Old Tippecanoe. His father being a
zealous Whig, as well as a decided anti-slavery advocate, conceived the idea of typifying Mr. Shrivers' allegory, by building a
rolling ball to be used in the campaign. It was about fourteen
feet in diameter, and had a long pole or axle passing through its
centre, and projecting several feet on either side, with which to
roll it, and a rim like a tuyere around the other centre, on which
it was rolled. It was frame-work covered with canvas, on which
was painted the names of the presidential candidates, extracts
from Whig principles as embodied in the platform of the party,
amongst which were "Protection to Home Industry," "A Sound
National Currency," "No More Slave Territory," "Slavery is
Sectional," "Freedom is National," and prominent among the
mottos was a tribute to "Shriver," of Cumberland, who first conceived the notion of putting this great ball in motion. This ball
was a decided success, and its appearance created the wildest
enthusiasm. It was rolled all 'round in Fayette and Green coun-

JAMES LANING.

ties, and ferried across the Monongahela river to Washington
county, and on one occasion it was placed on a flat-boat and
poled and towed up the river fifty miles to Morgantown, Virginia, and rolled at a convention there. Amongst the prominent
speakers in that campaign was the Hon. Andrew Stewart (known
as Tariff Andy), of Uniontown, Pa., and the Hon. Thomas M. T.
McKennan, of Washington, Pa. (afterward a member of President Fillmore's cabinet), and the Hon. Walter Forward, of Pittsburgh, Pa. The national turnpike road extending from Wheeling, Virginia, to Cumberland, Md., passed through Brownsville,
Pa., and members of Congress from the South took that route by
stage-coach to and from the capitol at Washington, D. C. Upon
the adjournment of Congress that summer, the southern members, amongst whom were Clay and Crittenden, of Ky., Grundy
of Tenn., and Benton, of Mo., were passing through Brownsville
on their way South one day when the "ball was in motion"
through the village, and the "boys," in a freak of fun, took after
the stage in which the august Senator Benton, from Missouri,
was riding. The Senator did not relish the joke, and told the
driver to whip up his team and run away from the d——d thing,
and a lively race ensued for a time, but the horses proved too
long winded for the "boys," and so the chase had to be given up;
but serious results were threatened, for the Democrats felt themselves insulted by the action of the Whigs in singling out Senator Benton for their fun, and swore they would destroy the ball.
It was kept, when not in use, in a close shed built for its protection by his father, who owned the land on which it stood, and
the ball was his own property, and he determined to defend it, if
needs be, with his life. So he loaded up his double-barrelled
shot-gun, and some small arms he had, and with his sons kept
watch, and waited the attack of the Democracy. But they, knowing well the character of the man they had to deal with, concluded that an attempt to destroy the ball might lead to some
"unpleasantness," and so abandoned the attempt, and the old
ball rolled on till the campaign was over and President Harrison
duly installed in the White House.

    Ephraim L. Blaine, Esq., (father of our most distinguished

statesman, James G. Blaine) who lived just across the river, was one of the prominent Whigs who helped to roll the ball, and little James G., then nine years old, was one of the boys who ran after and "whooped her up from behind." The subject of this sketch, also on a visit at his old home, took an active part in rolling and guarding the ball.

On completing his term of apprenticeship in Pittsburgh, he again returned to his old home in Brownsville, Pa. His health being somewhat impaired from hard work and close confinement in a shop, the working hours those days being from 7 A. M. to 9 P. M.,—by candle-light in winter. As a change of vocation he took a position as clerk in a general merchandise store for a year, and in the fall of 1843 went to Cincinnati, Ohio, with the view of making that city his permanent home, taking with him his chest of tools to fall back on in case of necessity. He made an effort to secure employment in a mercantile business, but though having good letters of recommendation, was not successful, and so went to work at his trade, with good prospects of success; but unfortunately, then, as now, a few designing men were agitating the subject of "more pay and less work," and soon succeeded in bringing on a strike for higher wages. As winter was approaching, and no good results from such a course probable, he opposed a strike with all his might, and thus incurred the enmity of the ringleaders, who threatened him with violence. The steamer "Lehigh" happening to pass Cincinnati about this time, with the officers of which boat he was well acquainted, he went on board, and the captain, on learning the situation, offered him the position of 2d clerk, at a salary of $50 per month, which he gladly accepted, and so bid adieu to the strikers, and engaged in a more lucrative employment, and learned on his return from St. Louis that they had suffered an inglorious defeat, and were glad to resume work at ten per cent discount from former wages. On the arrival of the "Lehigh" at Pittsburgh he was promoted to 1st clerk, at $75 per month, and continued to fill that position until September 9th, A. D., 1845, when he was married to Katharine Emma Jones, only daughter of Rees R. Jones, Esq., of Brownsville, Pa., and settled down to business on shore in the grocery and tobacco trades. Soon after resuming residence in Brownsville again he became an active member of Brownsville Lodge and Encampment of I. O. of O. F., passing through the chairs and representing both branches of the order in the Grand Lodge and Encampments of Pennsylvania in the sessions of 1848-9, held in the city of Philadelphia, Pa. He continued in the grocery and tobacco trade until the fall of 1848, when he was offered 1st clerkship of the steamer "John Quincy Adams," and again took to river life, but the cholera breaking out that winter, and proving so destructive to life as well as river business, he again settled on shore and engaged in steamboat cabin building, house carpentering, and saw and planing mill business, under the firm of Laning, Johnston & Co. He continued in this business until 1854, when he again changed to river life, taking an interest and 1st clerkship on the steamer "W. A. Eaves," which he super-intended the building of for the Green River trade, as a weekly packet between Louisville and Bowling Green, Kentucky, closing up his business and removing to Bowling Green, Ky. Remained in this trade one year only, when he sold out his interest in the " W. A. Eaves " and removed to La Salle, Ill., in April, 1855, and engaged in the iron and hardware trade until 1859, when he de-cided to remove to St. Louis, Mo., for the purpose of forming a co-partnership with his uncle, Mr. Paul Laning, in the iron busi-ness; but unfortunately for him, before he was fairly settled, his wife took sick and died, leaving him three little daughters, aged five, ten and fourteen, who are at this writing all living. With these daughters and their husbands and families he now resides, alternately. The loss of his wife again changed his plans, and he again took to river life as 1st clerk of steamers " Dr. Kane " and " Harmonia," plying in the upper Mississippi trade, from St. Louis to St. Paul, and was thus engaged when the war broke out. In the spring of 1861 his boat, the " Dr. Kane," was sent to Nashville, Tenn., loaded with bacon, corn, etc., supplies for the Southern Confederacy, then about to organize—the news of Jeff Davis' election to the presidency thereof reaching the boat on the way up the Cumberland river, at Dover, and causing great excitement on board, as most of the passengers were rebels, and the boat being then in the Confederacy, they let themselves loose and had a regular jollification over it, whilst the Unionists had to keep quiet, especially the officers, as they had a cargo on board which must be delivered and freights collected before they could feel safe to avow their principles.   As clerk of the boat it was his special duty to look out for that.   He had secured the friendship of Mr. B——, a rebel passenger, and owner of part of the cargo, who kindly aided him, on arrival at Nashville, to get the steamboat agency to receive the cargo and pay the freights. After a good deal of delay and financiering he succeeded in getting rid of the cargo and securing the money for the freights, and was very glad to save the steamer, which was allowed to return in safety to St. Louis.   Whilst in Nashville he was walking the streets with his rebel friend B—— (afterward a prominent rebel officer), where he saw the first rebel badge—a rosette of *white* and *red*, the blue left out—one of which B—— procured and pinned on his own lappel, but was kind enough not to offer one to the clerk.   On his return to St. Louis he found the excitement running high, and the rebel camp Jackson creating a good deal of uneasiness, which culminated a few days after in its capture by Gen. Lyon (then in command of the U. S. arsenal near St. Louis), with United States troops.   The subject of this sketch was not long in deciding to offer his services to help maintain the Union, and naturally chose the gunboat service, where he could be most useful, and accordingly, as soon as the Western Flotilla was organized, presented himself to Commander Wm. D. Porter, then in temporary command (a few days previous to the arrival of Capt. A. H. Foote), and his services were accepted, and he had the honor of being the second officer appointed—his brother-in-law, Capt. Robert K. Riley, of St. Louis, Mo., being the first appointment made.   These appointments were promptly approved by Flag Officer Foote on his arrival, and Riley and Laning were selected by Commander Porter for First and Second Masters of his vessel—the iron-clad " Essex "—which afterward made a glorious record in the Mississippi squadron.   The naval career thus began by the subject of this sketch was, by a singular combination of circumstances, perhaps the most varied

and peculiar of any other officer in the volunteer service of the
United States inland navy, a brief synopsis of which may be interesting, and is herewith appended:

   Volunteered September 23d, A. D., 1861, as Second Master in
the Western Gunboat Flotilla; was assigned to duty on board the
U. S. iron-clad gunboat "Essex," Commander Wm. D. Porter,
U. S. N.; had command of her battery in the battle of Fort
Henry, February 6, 1862, and had the honor of firing the first
shot which entered the breastworks. Received such injuries from
concussion, caused by the rapid firing of the nine inch guns
under casements, as to seriously impair his hearing, and disqual-
ify him for the duties of a watch officer. Was promoted First
Master for meritorious services in the battle, and assigned to
shore duty in the Construction Department at St. Louis, being a
practical builder and navigator. Assisted Commander Porter in
designing the iron-clad ram gunboats "Lafayette" and "Choctaw," and was placed in charge of their construction. The su-
perintendence of this work involved immense labor and extraordinary responsibilities, the exigences of the service requiring
prosecution of the work (with relays of men) day and night and
Sundays for a period of seven months. He completed both these
vessels, mounted their batteries, took on board their supplies and
outfit, hoisted their flag when they went into commission, and
delivered both at Cairo, the "Lafayette" in January, and the
"Choctaw" in April, 1863. They were amongst the best and
most formidable vessels in the squadron, taking prominent part
in all the heavy engagements on the lower Mississippi, without
the loss of a man killed in action. Their cost was about $500,-
000 for both—a much less sum than was expended on other iron-
clads built by contract, which proved much inferior in service.
In the prosecution of this work he had the entire confidence of
the army department, through Quartermaster-General M. C.
Meigs, U. S. A., in the prompt remission of all funds asked for,
notwithstanding that owing to the exigies of the war the cost of
the vessels was much beyond original estimates. He received,
also, the commendations of Admiral D. D. Porter, commanding
the squadron, and the honorable Secretary of the Navy, who again

promoted him to the rank of Act. Vol. Lieut. Having completed and delivered both vessels to the Admiral at Cairo, Ill., he was ordered to return to St. Louis and settle his accounts, after which he was assigned to the command of the U. S. steamer "Rattler" (tin clad), stationed at Rodney, Miss., with command of the river from Grand Gulf to the foot of Rodney Island. Served in this district until 1864, when his vessel was ordered to Davis Bend, Miss., to guard the "Indianola," one of our most formidable iron-clads, which had run the gauntlet of the Vicksburg batteries in the spring of 1863, and was captured by the enemy and sunk at high water on the main land, just outside the levee, on Joe Davis' plantation, where she had lain high and dry for fifteen months, carefully guarded and preserved, being very valuable, and worth about $180,000 for service again. She lay just one mile from the channel of the river at low water, and seven hundred feet from the river at an ordinary stage of high water. Her weight was over eleven hundred tons. Having made a survey of the vessel and surroundings, he decided that she could be launched and restored to the service, and at little cash outlay, and at once submitted to the Admiral plans and estimates, and volunteered to do the work. His services were promptly accepted by Admiral Porter, who gave him *carte blanc* orders. He prepared a set of launching ways at Mound City navy yard, and with a gang of carpenters and caulkers, and a full supply of all needed materials, loaded on barges, with a towboat, ran the gauntlet, five hundred and thirty-five miles through the enemy's country, arrived safely at the scene of action, raised the vessel from the ground with jack-screws, repaired, caulked, and placed her on cradles, dug a basin in the sand bar and laid launching ways, and when the river rose sufficient to fill the basin, launched her into the basin, and floated her out over the bar, and anchored her safely in the stream. This work was prosecuted and successfully accomplished under many difficulties, and at an actual cash outlay of less than seven thousand dollars, and the "Indianola" was safely delivered at Mound City navy yard on the 17th of January, 1865, being just three months and seventeen days from the date of his departure to perform the work. For

this service he was highly commended by both Admirals Porter
and S. P. Lee, who succeeded Porter in command of the squadron whilst the work was in progress, and was highly recommended to the honorable Secretary of the Navy for promotion
to the highest grade of rank in the volunteer naval service.

It will thus be seen that his services were not only varied, but
most valuable to the government.   He served on five different
iron-clads, building two of them (viz. " Lafayette " and " Choctaw ") and launching the " Indianola." When the Western Flotilla was transferred, Oct. 1st, A. D., 1862, from the Army Department (under which it was organized) to the Regular Navy, the
" Lafayette " and " Choctaw " being in an unfinished condition,
were, by act of Congress (in order to avoid confusion in accounts), exempted from transfer until entirely finished—so that
whilst being Superintendent of Construction under the Army, he
was Lieutenant in command of both vessels under the Navy, on
special service, until both vessels were finished and delivered to
the Admiral at Cairo

At the close of the war, in the spring of 1865, he was offered
a clerkship in the Northern Line Packet Co. of steamers, plying
between St. Louis and St. Paul, and assigned to duty as 1st clerk
of the steamer " Canada," and continued in that vocation until
August, 1866, when the dreadful scourge of cholera again drove
him from river life, the first case on the upper Mississippi that
year having occurred on board the " Canada " at Rock Island,
and before reaching St. Paul no less than twenty-two cases had
occurred on board, every one of which proved fatal.   On arrival
at St. Paul the infected steamer discharged her cargo and left
immediately for St. Louis, without either freight or passengers.
Her commander was so frightened that he left the boat at
Keokuk on her way down, leaving him to deliver her to the
owners at St. Louis, who at once sent her to Alton Slough to be
laid up for the balance of the season, whilst he went to his home
in La Salle, and bid a final adieu to river life, after a chequered
experience off and on for twenty-three years.   He was not long
idle, but immediately commenced the erection of a planing mill
and box factory, and secured a contract for supplying the win-

dow glass factory with their packing boxes, and in 1870 became the principal stockholder in the Phœnix Glass Co., which he organized, and was elected superintendent and treasurer, and took charge of that business also, which he carried on extensively until 1877, when his health became so much impaired by reason of his arduous labors, and the physical disabilities contracted during the war, resulting in total deafness and nervous debility, and general prostration, he was compelled to retire, and removed to Hot Springs, Arkansas, for the benefit of his health, where he erected a large boarding house, known as the "Laning Mansion," a very handsome location in the north end of the valley, where he spent most of his time until 1885, and partially regained his health (but not his hearing, as he is now, and has been for years, totally deaf in both ears). His property in Hot Springs was destroyed by fire in 1885, when he sold his lots and again removed to Illinois. He spent the summer of 1880 in Chicago, and as a member of the Union Veteran Club took an active part in the Garfield campaign.

In 1884 he also attempted to speak at a ratification meeting for Blaine and Logan, held in front of the Sumpter House, Hot Springs, Ark., but was compelled, by the howls of the Democrats, who surrounded the little band of Republicans, to desist, and was followed by Hon. Powell Clayton, who succeeded in restoring order. Finding it entirely useless to made any further efforts in that bourbon-ridden State, he went to Chicago and gave his humble efforts for Blaine and Logan—returning to Hot Springs in time to vote, for the mere sake of voting.

In the glorious campaign of 1888 he was unable, by reason of advancing years, declining health, and total deafness, to take a very active part—making only one little speech -"The Rolling Ball"—at Hyde Park Centre, early in the campaign, and attending one or two meetings of the Old Tippecanoe Club, of which he is very proud to be a member, and having the extreme pleasure of casting his vote at Woodlawn Park precinct for the entire Republican ticket, containing fifty-one names, without a scratch, and this has been his course for forty-six years past—having never, in the whole course of his life, voted (as such) the Demo-

cratic ticket. His first vote for president was for Henry Clay—
though his first work was for Old Tippecanoe. He is a Master
Mason since 1859; an Odd Fellow since 1844; a member of Chicago Union Veteran Club since 1880; a charter member of
Warren Stewart Post, No. 533, G. A. R., of Cairo, Ill.; a member
of the Farragut Naval Association of Chicago.

M. A. LAWRENCE

Was born in Otsego county, New York, June 12th, 1820, removing in 1837 to Girard, Erie county, Pa., where he took part in the
campaign of 1840. The excitement of this campaign in Pennsylvania was so intense that it has never been equaled. Mr.
Lawrence had an election wagon fitted out to attend conventions
with. One of his wagons had five big " K's," which, being inter-
preted, meant: " Kinderhook's Kandidate Kant Kome it Kwite."
These features were the cause of many contests, in which the
Republicans generally came out best. For some years past Mr.
Lawrence has resided in Chicago, where he cast his vote last
November for "Young Tippecanoe."

M. LOVEJOY,

Born September 1st, 1815, at Weston, Windsor county, Vermont,
where he remained until 1832, when he removed to Boston, subsequently returning to his native town, where, in 1840, he cam-
paigned and voted for Gen. William H. Harrison, naming his
only son after the illustrious Whig. His grandfather was a soldier in the Continental Army in the Revolutionary War, of which
fact Mr. Lovejoy is quite proud. He never lost a valid opportunity to cast his vote for " our " candidate. In 1854 the gentleman
came west, settling in Illinois in 1855. He served two years in
the Army of the Potomac, and has lived in Chicago twenty-four
years. Mr. Lovejoy has been engaged in various mercantile pursuits; his patriotism has never waned, and his interest in the
election of Gen. B. Harrison was intense, although in his eighty-
fourth year. Mr. Lovejoy joined the rest of the boys in the

parade of the town. He "hopes that the remainder of his days may be passed under a Republican administration," which laudable ambition will, without doubt, be realized, as the Harrisons are good for a number of years more in the presidential chair.

CARLETON G. McCULLOCH

Was born in Sherburne, Chenango county, New York, April 10, 1818. At seven years of age he removed with his parents to Erie, Pa., and when fifteen years of age he went to Buffalo, N. Y., and learned the drug business, with C. C. Bristol. When twenty-one years of age he settled in Lower Sandusky (now Fremont), Ohio, remaining there eight or ten years—subsequently living in Newark and Sandusky City, Ohio, and Portage City, Wis. When the war of the Rebellion broke out he went to Springfield, Ill.— the home of Abraham Lincoln—where he kept a drug store for five years; then came to Chicago and went into the manufacturing business, the firm being Gillet, McCulloch & Co., with which house he was connected some fifteen years. He now resides in Chicago, is in vigorous health, and is pleasantly surrounded. He voted for Gen. Harrison for president of the United States in 1840, and for the second Gen. Harrison in 1888.

CAPT. HIRAM McHENRY

Was born in the town of Westfield, Chautauqua county, State of New York, December 31st, 1818, and lived there until thirty years of age. In the year 1840 he cast his first vote for General William Henry Harrison; in 1844 voted for Henry Clay, in Buffalo, N. Y., and all the other Whig and Republican nominees for the presidency, including Benjamin Harrison, in Chicago, the 6th of November, 1888. Capt. McHenry's grandfather moved into Chautauqua county when the nearest white inhabitant was twenty-eight miles distant, viz. at Erie, Pa., and Catasagus Creek, in Catasagus county, east thirty miles. His uncle was the first white child born in Chautauqua county, N. Y. In the year 1825 he met with Gen. La Fayette the last time he visited the United

Stares.   The first time he came to Chicago was in the year 1836 (in July), as "Royal Boy" on board the ship " Julia Palmer." He sailed on the lakes forty-three years.

JAMES A. MARSHALL

Was born in London, England, June 12, 1809. Son of Major John Marshall, of the British Army, who came to America in 1816; was Commandant of the barracks at Perth, Canada, but finding the place so unfitted for education of his children, he re-signed his commission and removed to the United States, locat-ing in Ogdensburgh, St. Lawrence county, New York.   His son James received his academic education at the Bellville Academy, New York, afterward attended the University of Maryland, a medical institute at Baltimore, and graduated in the class of 1831.   Came west, and arrived in Chicago April 20, 1832.   Visited Navarino (Green Bay), returned to Chicago and engaged in the real estate, auction and commission business.   Has resided in Chicago since that time, voting for William Henry Harrison in 1840, and has voted the Whig and Republican ticket fifty-nine years, his last vote being for Benjamin Harrison.   He is the oldest settler in Chicago at the present day — and carries the gold medal for being the same.   He has a wife, one son (James F. Marshall), and one daughter (Mrs. P. C. Hanford), now living-- all residents of Chicago at the present time.

ISAAC MARSH

Was born in Victor, Ontario county, N. Y., in the year 1809. Voted for William Henry Harrison in the year 1836, and also voted for the same gentleman in Lockport, N. Y., in 1840; voted for Benjamin Harrison for president in the fall of 1888, taking an active part with the great Republican party in the defeat of a wicked and incompetent administration—an administration that had sought through the Democratic party the destruction of the best government in the world—through a rebellious war of four years, in the destruction and murder of 300,000 of our people, and at a cost of $4,000,000,000.

JAMES A. MARSHALL.

J. C. MEARS.

This gentleman, now in his ninety-third year, is the oldest member of the Old Tippecanoe Club having been born March 22d, 1797, in Milton, Chittenden county, Vt. thus lacking but seven years of being a centenarian. Mr. Mears cast his first vote for James Monroe at his second election. He was also one of the only two voters in Switzerland, Ind., for the first anti-slavery candidate—the other voter being Mr. Morris, a Presbyterian Divine, of Rising Sun, Indiana. In concluding a short biographical sketch of himself, Mr. Mears says: "I voted for William Henry Harrison in 1840, and for my crowning and probably last vote, for his grandson in 1888." Let us hope that Mr. Mears may be spared to cast one more vote for Gen. Harrison.

NATHAN MEARS

Was born at Billerica, Massachusetts, December 30th, 1815. His parents were Nathan and Lucy Levistone Mears, who both died before he was twelve years old. He was educated at the Billerica and Westford Academies. At seventeen years he secured a position with Nichols & Leeder, wholesale and retail dry goods, in Boston, and continued with them until 1836, when he formed a co-partnership with his two older brothers, Edwin and Charles, and with a stock of general merchandise removed to Paw Paw, Michigan, and opened a store, the firm being E. & C. Mears & Co. In 1839 he bought out his brothers, continuing until 1850, when he removed to Chicago and commenced the lumber business with his brother Charles, the firm being C. Mears & Co. In 1861 his brother retired, Eli Bates succeeding him, under the firm name of Mears, Bates & Co. This firm for a number of years handled more lumber than any firm in the world, and owned a large fleet of vessels on the lakes, until Mr. Bates' death, in 1881. He was succeeded by Mr. Mears' son Charles H., the firm being Nathan & Charles H. Mears, until the spring of 1889, when Nathan retired from the firm. In 1867 the Oconto Co. was incorporated, Geo. Farnsworth and the firm of Mears, Bates & Co., (then including Nathan Mears, Eli Bates, James C. Brooks, and

NATHAN MEARS.

Geo. H. Ambrose), being the owners. Mr. Farnsworth was elected president, and Nathan Mears vice-president, which office he has held continuously to this time. This company has lumbered extensively since its organization, and owns a large amount of standing timber, and upwards of one hundred thousand acres of land on the Oconto river in Wisconsin. In 1881 the Bay De Noquet Co., of Nahina, Delta county, Michigan, was organized, the Oconto Co., being owners— Geo. Farnsworth, president, and Nathan Mears, vice-president. This company has a large amount of standing timber, and upwards of seventy-five thousand acres of land on the Sturgeon river that flows into Big Bay De Noquet, at the north end of Green Bay, in the northern peninsular of Michigan. The mills of these two companies are manufacturing at this time over four hundred thousand feet of lumber a day. Mr. Mears was married to Ann Elizabeth Gilbert, of Battle Creek, Mich., February 6th, 1840. They had four children—two sons and two daughters. Their youngest son, Nathan, died in infancy, in 1858. Their oldest daughter, Lucy A., married Mr. Johnathan Slade; Sarah Elizabeth married Mr. James R. McKay; and Chas. H. married Miss Harriett Wright, all of Chicago, where they now reside. Mr. Mears voted for William Henry Harrison at Paw Paw, Mich., in 1840, and for Benjamin Harrison in Chicago in 1888, and was joined by his son, two sons-in-law, and his oldest grandson, Mr. Gilbert L. Slade, who all voted the straight Republican ticket.

Mr. Mears was brought up a Unitarian—one of the organizers of Unity Church in this city—has contributed toward its support over $40,000, and is still hale, hearty and generous.

N. F. MERRILL

Was born August 27, 1816,. in the town of New Boston, New Hampshire removed to Boston, Mass., in 1833 where he remained till 1839, when he made a six-year-stay in Macon, Ga., later returning to his native state, as the South contained almost too many Democrats for healthy climatic surroundings—to Republicans. Mr. Merrill came to Chicago in 1852, and has resided here

N. F. MERRILL.

ever since, being actively engaged in mercantile, railroad and real
estate business. He voted for Harrison in 1840 at Macon, Ga.,
and in Chicago for all the presidents of the Republican platform,
including the late campaign of the "Old Tippecanoes," and his
highest ambition is to be able to "do it again;" his health bids
fair to permit. Residence, 1401 Washington boulevard.

WILLIAM MENDSEN,

Born near Cherryville, Northampton county, Pa., September
11th, 1817. He was a descendant of German parentage—his
father being a clergyman of the Lutheran church, and voting for
Gen. William Henry Harrison at both elections—1836 and 1840.
Mr. Mendsen cast his first vote for Gen. William Henry Harrison
in 1840, at Triedsville, Pa. Has been engaged in business in
Chicago ever since 1851, the year of his arrival, enjoying good
health, and among the more important events of his later life
was his vote cast for Gen. Benjamin Harrison, and the celebration of the fiftieth anniversary of his marriage, which occurred
in 1888.

JOHN MILLER,

Born January 16, 1816, in Turin, Lewis county, New York. His
parents were of Massachusetts Puritan descent. In 1824 his
parents removed to Louisville, St. Lawrence county, N. Y., on
the St. Lawrence river, where he was reared. His father, Rev.
Levi Miller, was a Methodist clergyman, and a leader of the
work of that pioneer church in this then newly settled region.
He was also the representative of James McVicker, one of the
original proprietors of a large portion of that county.

The subject of this sketch was admitted to the bar at Ogdens-
burg, and practiced his profession at Canton, N. Y. He voted
for William Henry Harrison for president in 1840, and for the
Whig and Republican candidates for president at every presidential election since he arrived at majority. He has always
taken an active interest in political matters. He was in charge

of the office of the County Clerk and Recorder, and Clerk of Court of St. Lawrence county, N. Y., for sixteen years, and was County Clerk of that county from 1868 to 1871. In 1884 he came to Chicago, where he has two sons living, and since that time he has been with his son, John S. Miller, of the law firm of Miller, Leman & Chase, of Chicago.

WM. BRUCE MILLS

Was born in the town of Charlestown, Clark county, Indiana, on the 22d day of May, 1818. In 1820 his father moved to the adjoining county of Washington, and settled down at Salem, the county-seat. His father was a great admirer of Henry Clay, the original protectionist, and founder of the Whig party, and W. B. imbibed the principles of this great leader, and has followed them out by voice and vote during his long lifetime. In 1840 he cast his first vote for president and vice-president of the United States, in the town of Greencastle, Putnam county, Indiana, to which place he removed in 1837. William Henry Harrison was his candidate in 1840, and Benjamin Harrison in 1888.

GEORGE S. MOORE

Son of Philip and Sarah Moore, was born April 14, 1809, in Tinicum township, Bucks county Penn. His father was a blacksmith by trade, and had five sons and one daughter. He enlisted in the year 1812 in the second war with Great Britain. When George S. reached twenty-one years of age he voted the Whig ticket, voting in 1840 for Gen. William Henry Harrison, and having long borne the heat and burden of the day, he felt thankful to have lived and seen, and helped elect in 1888 his grandson, the present president of the United States.

LUTHER LAFLIN MILLS

Was born in Canton, Hartford county, Conn., in 1819. His early years were passed in commercial pursuits with good success, when, in 1849, the fame of young Chicago induced him to come

west, where he resided up to the time of his decease, which occurred at the Gault House, in this city, January 14, 1889. In
politics Mr. Mills was originally a Whig, being a delegate to the
young Whig ratification at Baltimore in 1840. From 1856 to the
time of his death he was a constant, earnest Republican—a man
of strong resolute character, scholarly in his tastes, kind to everybody, a model of perfect old school gentleman. Mr. Mills' relatives number many of our most worthy and prominent citizens.

THOMAS C. MOORE

Was born near Shelbyville, in the State of Tennessee, November
26th, 1817; removed to Clark county in 1821, and settled near the
Wabash river; then removed to Coles county in 1826, settling
near the present location of Mattoon (at that time Coles county
had not been organized, nor had Charlestown, the county-seat,
been located), and labored as a farm hand until 1837. Attended
the Academy in Marshall, Clark county, and studied law in the
office of Judge Harland. Was admitted to the bar in Marshall,
May, 1843. Removed to Chicago in June, 1845, and from thence
to Batavia, Ill., in August, 1848, where he has since resided, engaged in the practice of law. He had been a Whig in politics
until the formation of the Republican party in 1854, which he
helped to organize, and was a delegate to the first Congressional
Convention ever held under the name of "Republican." That
convention was held in Aurora, Kane county, Ill., on the 19th day
of September, 1854. He was a member of the Committee on
Platform at that convention, and assisted the late Judge Ma-
nierre, of Chicago, in drafting the platform. The committee
recommended to the convention the name of "Republican" for
the new party, which was adopted. He voted for Gen. William
Henry Harrison in 1840, and joined the Tippecanoe Club, of Chicago, during the presidential in 1888, voting for Gen. Benjamin
Harrison.

COL. ALEX. H. MORRISON,

Of St. Joseph, Michigan, was born in Quebec, Canada, February
21, 1822, of Scotch and American parentage. Came to Chicago

L. L. MILLS.

in October, 1839; was employed in a canal office at what is now called Lemont, Cook county, Ill., and labored with assiduity before and on election day in 1840 for Gen. Wm. Henry Harrison for president. In the fifty years of residence in the northwest, thirty-eight years have been spent in St. Joseph, Michigan; was chairman of the Board of Supervisors in 1851; candidate for Presidential elector on the Whig ticket in 1852; elected State Senator in 1856, and supported Zack Chandler for Senator In 1860 was elected to the Assembly, and was chairman of the Committee on State Affairs in the Legislature for three sessions, and was on the staff of Gov. Bingham, and also on that of Gov. Wisner, with rank of Colonel; was a member of Republican State Central Committee from 1862 to 1866; was Collector of Internal Revenue, appointed by Abraham Lincoln, for Second Congressional District of Michigan. The last position held was member of Republican National Convention in 1880, and voted upon every ballot, as did Benjamin Harrison, our present president. His Chicago address is 4322 Berkley Avenue.

CHARLES H. MORTON,

Born on the 11th day of June, A. D., 1816, near Lexington, Fayette county, Ky. (in the neighborhood of "Ashland," the residence of the immortal Henry Clay). In the year 1831, at the age of fifteen years, emigrated to Clark (now Coles) county, Ill., settled in Charlestown, the county-seat; in the year 1868 removed to Chicago; followed the occupation of a retail dry goods merchant, then a private banker, then president of a national bank, and finally a manufacturer and wholesale dealer in ready-made clothing, in the city of Chicago. Gave first presidential vote in 1840 for Wm. Henry Harrison; in 1844 for Henry Clay; 1848 for Gen. Taylor; 1852 for Gen. Scott; 1856 for Gen. Fremont; 1860 and '64 for Abraham Lincoln; 1868 and '72 for Gen. Grant; 1876 for Gen. Hayes; 1880 for Gen. Garfield; 1884 for James G. Blaine; 1888 for Gen. Benjamin Harrison—never cast a Democratic vote for even the smallest office when there was a Whig or Republican candidate.

C. W. MUNGER

Was born in the village of Herkimer, Herkimer county, N. Y., but was raised in Auburn, where he resided until 1838, when he moved to Chicago, and with the exception of an interval of three years spent at his former home in Auburn, has been a resident of this State.

In June, 1840, he was a delegate to the Whig State Convention at Springfield, and at the close of the convention he visited Chicago, then a town of 4,500 inhabitants, and cast his first vote where he also cast his last vote, for "Tippecanoe."

In 1852 he located in Peru. At this date the C., R. I. & P. R. R. had commenced grading and laying track from Chicago to the head of navigation on the Illinois river. He remained in Peru until June, 1886, when he made his final residence in Chicago.

Mr. Munger was an attendant at the Tippecanoe Club meetings until confined to his house by sickness. He died on the 9th of February, at his residence in Hyde Park, and was buried February 11th. The funeral was largely attended by the members of this club.

JOHN NOURSE

Was born January 7th, 1812, in the town of Hampden, county of Penobscot, State of Maine. He attended school until he was fourteen years old, acquiring a fair English education. He then entered a store as clerk, remaining in that capacity eleven years, then commenced, in conjunction with a partner, and continued fourteen years, then on his own account continued in the same business until the year 1853, when he went to Lower Canada, and remained in business there four years. He then, with his family, moved to Michigan, and connected himself with a railroad. Here he remained until 1865, when he came to Chicago, where he has continued in the railroad business. He voted in 1840 for Gen. Wm. Henry Harrison for president of the United States. In conclusion Mr. Nourse says: ".\ltogether I have voted for seven or eight presidents, the last one being Gen. Benjamin Harrison. As a coincidence I will state the fact that I was town clerk in my native town for seventeen years consecutively, and

as such had to make up a certificate whenever there was an election, and forward it to the capitol, showing who the town voted
for. Being clerk in 1840, when Harrison was elected, of course I
had to make up the certificate of election and forward it. Forty-
eight years afterward, on Nov. 6, 1888, as one of the Judges of
election in Chicago, I assisted in making up the returns for the
election of Gen. Benjamin Harrison. I am now seventy-seven
years old, in the enjoyment of perfect health, and retain all my
faculties—mental and physical—and am happy in the thought
that I have been a Christian man for about sixty years, and expect in due time to change this for a better world."

FRANCIS NOURSE

Was born in Merrimack, N. H., April 17th, 1817, and traces his
geneology back six generations, to Francis Nourse, born in 1618,
and the original emigrant of the Nourse family from Yarmouth,
England, A. D., 1634. Mr. Nourse has been a resident of Chicago
for many years, and had two sons in the " Board of Trade Battery " during the war of the Rebellion. Mr. Nourse voted for
Gen. Harrison in the year 1840, at Cambridge, Massachusetts,
and for Benjamin Harrison in 1888, and all Whig and Republican
candidates in the interim.

THOMAS PARKER

Was born in the town of Indiana, Pa., on the 12th day of Dec.,
1814. In 1836 he removed to the town of Butler, Pa., where he
voted the Democratic ticket till the spring of 1840, when they
had a town Democratic meeting in the court house, at which he
offered a tariff resolution, but it was voted down as a disturbing
element in the party, and he then and there declared he was no
longer a Democrat—voting the Whig and Republican ticket ever
since. At the election of 1840 he voted for Gen. William Henry
Harrison, and at the election last fall voted for Gen. Benjamin
Harrison for president, on the same issues of the campaign of
1840.

ORVILLE OLCOTT.

In the year of 1814, Orville Olcott, the subject of this sketch, was born at the town of Lenox, Madison county, N. Y. When but six weeks old his father died, leaving himself, mother and an older sister, to battle with the world on a pioneer York State farm. Subsequently, however, his mother married again, and although other children were born, it devolved upon young Orville as the oldest, to give the most aid to his step-father in reclaiming an uncultivated and rugged farm into a prosperous and valuable property. This was not done without years of toil, unaided by the labor-saving farm machinery of today, which makes farming comparatively an easy task. In the meantime, and until he attained the age of fourteen, his schooling was confined to the meagre advantages of a common school education, obtained during the winter sessions. Just such an experience as many of the old time New England and York State settlers, now prosperous citizens of the western states, can look back to—an experience which laid the foundation of their characters, and made possibly their latter day successes. When at this age, he moved to Utica, N. Y., at the instance of his uncle, to learn the business of canal boat building on the Erie Canal—about this time just completed—and to secure the advantages of a better education. He continued in this business until 1835, when, at the age of twenty-one, his uncle relinquished the business to him in order to go west. In those days the Erie Canal was the great thoroughfare for passenger and freight traffic, and for thirteen years he carried on a prosperous business in building and repairing canal boats. He constructed many of the passenger and mail service packets which plied between Albany and Buffalo, and in those days were regarded as elegant and rapid means of transit. During this period of his life in Utica, he took an active interest in politics and all matters of local concern, and served in every capacity—from a volunteer fireman to a seat in the common council of the city. He was thrice elected as alderman, and took a prominent part in the campaign of 1836, of Harrison against Van Buren—his first vote being recorded in that year for the former in his unsuccessful candidacy for the presidential chair.

Again, in the campaign of 1840, he worked and voted for Harrison, and this time, while more successful, it was rendered more the less futile by the untimely and much lamented death of Gen. Harrison, soon after being installed in office.

In 1848, the advent of the railroad having cut an inroad into, and depressed the business of the canal, he made a trip to the then far western town of Chicago, at the instigation of a canal boat company, to report upon the prospects of the Illinois and Michigan canal, then being built. The result was the obtaining of a contract to build a line of packet boats there. From that time to the present, Mr. Olcott has lived in Chicago, and witnessed its marvelous growth. For almost thirty years he was engaged actively in business. Of the five dry docks built here, he, with his partners, were instrumental in building three of them, and some of the oldest boats now sailing the great lakes, were built under his supervision.

He was one of the original members of the Board of Trade, but has confined himself during all these latter years, stictly to business, ignoring any active participation in politics, except to be a constant and consistent voter of the Republican ticket, both at local and national elections. Throughout he has endeavored to be an honest and law-abiding citizen. He has recorded three votes for the Harrison family—in 1836, 1840 and 1888—and hopes to live to vote many more Republican tickets.

He has been twice married, and has had six sons, who lived to vote the same ticket, four of whom are still living—two having served through the war for the Union — and all honor their father's political predilictions, by being staunch Republicans.

JAMES M. PERRY

Was born in Chelsea, Orange county, N. Y., March 20th, 1811. When some ten years of age his father moved to the town of Ira, Rutland county, Vt., where, in 1836, he cast his first vote for Wm. Henry Harrison. In 1839 he emigrated to Illinois, and voted again for William Henry Harrison for president, at Bourbonnais Grove, being then in Will county. In 1888 he voted for Gen. Benjamin Harrison, and is proud of it.

R. P. POTE.

ROBERT P. POTE

Was born in Belfast, Maine, in 1817. He attained his majority in the same town, and cast his first vote for William Henry Harrison in 1840, and moved to Chicago in 1855, and has ever been a staunch and true supporter of the Whig and Republican nominees during his life, casting his vote in 1888 for Gen. Benjamin Harrison, and sincerely trusting that he may be allowed to poll one more vote for the Harrison family.

AMOS H. POWERS

Was born September 1st, 1819, in Phillipston, Worcester county, Mass. He passed his early boyhood days on his father's farm, with the usual New England district-school privileges, and later moved to Worcester and learned the trade of a tailor. In September, 1840, he moved from Worcester to Boston, thereby losing the opportunity of casting his first ballot for Gen. William Henry Harrison, although working for his election by marching in torch-light processions and shouting Tippecanoe songs, etc. In 1845 he formed a co-partnership as merchant tailor with George Lyon, which continued until the year 1856, when his health became impaired by too close application to business, and he, removing to Chicago, engaged in more active out-door pursuits. His wife is of the seventh generation from Deacon Simon Stone, of Watertown, Mass., 1635. In the year 1883 he compiled and published a history of Walter Powers, who settled in Concord "village," Mass., in 1660, and some of his descendants to the ninth generation. Mr. Powers' vote in 1888 was cast for the " Young Tippecanoe."

LUCIAN PRINCE

Was born March 31, 1819, in Dudley, Mass. I cast my first vote in Holliston, Mass., in 1840 for " Tippecanoe and Tyler, too."

An exigency arose within two years that caused me to loose faith in the then acting President of these United States, John Tyler, because of his interference in the legitimate manner the inhabitants of Rhode Island were endeavoring to become a State in accordance with the constitution of these United United States, by adopting a Republican form of government, it having existed up to this time under a charter granted by the King of Great Britain early in the sixteenth century. In 1842, President Tyler ordered the garrison at Fort Adams, at Newport, to be strengthened. He dispatched his Secretary of War to that State, with instructions and authority, to call upon the Governors of Massachusetts and Connecticut in concert with the U. S. troops at Fort Adams, for the purpose, if found necessary (as he says), " to uphold the rights of the charter State government." He was opposed to the people's movement to establish a " Free Constitution," as he in his special message to Congress, April, 1844, when called upon to explain his official action toward the State of Rhode Island, said virtually in that message that he would use all necessary means in his power to overthrow the People's Constitution. In his conduct toward the party which elected him to office he proved recreant, and forfeited their confidence. Finding himself ostracised and condemned, he sloughed off into the Calhoun Democracy of the South, and went into political oblivion—drinking the health of the Southern Confederacy. His action heightened the indignation of very many of the Whig party in Massachusetts who opposed the election of Gov. Davis, because of his personal sympathy with Tyler, and it caused Davis' defeat by a majority of one on a popular vote—and elected the Democratic candidate, Marcus Morton. As I was the only voter who changed from Whig to Democrat in Holliston in 1842, I claim his election, having acted from a sense of duty I owed myself—the government which my grandfather shed his blood at the battle of Bunker Hill to establish—and the national spirit underlying the government under which we live. Whenever I could, by voice or vote, advance the cause of human freedom and liberty, in conjunction with other measures conducive of the best interests of my country, I have done so—and from a high sense of duty I owed to my country, and my God—not for self aggrandisement, nor the emoluments of office. In 1848 the Whig party of the nation ignored its former declared principles upon the question of slavery, and nominated a man in unison with slave power. Its action caused the Free Soil party to come into existence. It had its mission—and in due time accomplished its work. From it the Republican party emanated, and was recruited by the liberty loving voters of all parties; and appeared upon the political arena in 1856 as a factor for the above parties. It became apparent to the slave power that the slumbering spirit of freedom was aroused. and by compromise and otherwise it sought to allay its onward march. In 1860 the Republican party entered the political field in all earnestness. It nominated its ticket, and adopted its platform in this city of Chicago, and went forth to conquest. In my native State (Mass.) the spirit of 1776 had been revived long ere this. The people of the State pooled their political strength as to the encroachment of the slave power, and in 1852 sent that champion of religious and political liberty to the United States Senate—Charles Sumner, a man who sacrificed his life and strength to the cause so near and dear to his heart, the *people's rights*. Your humble servant believes he aided in Sumner's election. The town had not sent a representative in eight years. A coalition of Free Soilers with the liberal Democrats elected a member of the Legislature by one majority. I brought to the polls the last voter that voted the successful ticket, and at a Sumner supper, given at Holliston after the election, State Senator Wilson, afterward U. S. Senator, and later Vice-President of the United States, said: "To Lucian Prince belongs the credit of electing your member of the House, and his vote, after a hundred and fifty-one ballots, elected Charles Sumner." Thirty-eight years later I look back to the event as the proudest political act of my life.

In 1856 the Republican party was organized in Worcester, Mass., where I then resided, and it was at that meeting that I renounced the Democratic party, and gave the following as my reasons for so doing: President Pierce, in his inaugural address, said: "No act of mine shall reopen the agitation of the question of slavery." We soon found him running neck and neck with squatter sovereign Douglas, seeing who could cringe the lowest to the slave power. I said in the above named meeting that

Pierce had forfeited all right to the confidence of the people, and for one I repudiated him and his party—and to this day I have had no occasion to regret it. I have been an active participant in all that conduced to the good of the government my fore-fathers came to this country in 1631 to help establish in Massachusetts.

By a vote of the Tippecanoe Club of this city I was requested to write and present my own biography. I have ever felt proud of the part my ancestors took to establish religious and civil liberty in the early days of this republic. The name of Prince is coeval with the settlement of Boston. 1631 Rev. Job Prince, a blind Episcopal minister, settled in Boston. On the voter's list has appeared the name of Prince to this day. Many of them have filled important civil and political offices. On my mother's side, the Gore's came to Roxbury (now Boston highlands) in 1637. The name can be found among its voters from that day to this. Gov. Gore was a man of wealth, and spent most of his life within the political arena of his State—at one time acted as U. S. Senator. My great-grandfather emigrated from Roxbury to Dudley in 1729, and the name of Gore was upon the voter's list of that town for one hundred and forty years.

In the meeting of the Tippecanoe Club heretofore alluded to, I spoke of the part I took in the erection of a monument to the memory of Col. Bigelow, of Worcester, Mass., of the Continental line, in 1860. It was erected by his grandson, Chief Justice Bigelow, of Boston, on the Central Park of Worcester. This man Bigelow left Worcester on the 19th day of April, 1776, as Captain of the Minute Men, who had organized to go upon the first signal informing them that the war had commenced. It was upon this ever memorable 19th day of April that the war messenger from Boston came into town on a white horse, at break-neck speed, shouting at the top of his voice: "*To arms! to arms! the war has commenced! Minute Men turn out!*" It was understood by these Minute Men what was to be the signal. When the messenger made his announcement the old South bell was to be rang vigorously. There were to be three signal guns fired also. At the dedication of this monument it was the wish of the entire

community that the scenes of April 19th, 1776, could be re-en-
acted. Preparations were made to do so. The city government
entered into the arrangements heartily. They caused Main street
(over which this war messenger rode) to be cleared of all carriages for a mile, so the man who rode the horse could do so
with safety while announcing his message. Your humble servant
acted as that messenger. The city dailies, in giving an account
of the same, said: "The stentorian voice of Mr. Prince, who acted
as the war messenger, could be heard for a long distance. It
was truly a thrilling scene—one long to be remembered." I
should have said ere this, that those Minute Men left the old
South Church in one hour and forty minutes after the news was
communicated to them — after the Rev. Mr. McCarty united
with them in prayer. They started upon the double-quick for
the first mile out of the forty-five to Boston—so says the historian, the Hon. George Bancroft, a native of Worcester.

I desire to allude to the part I took on the 19th of April, 1861.
A notice came to the Worcester Light Infantry, from Gov. Andrews, to appear on Boston common at twelve o'clock, noon, next
day, armed and equipped as the law directs, to join the Massachusetts Sixth, which would leave the State for Washington, D.
C., as soon as may be. This Worcester company left their
armory at ten o'clock A. M., under escort of the citizens of Worcester, to the Boston depot, by order of Maj. Lamb. The right
of the line was accorded to your humble servant. I early sought
to become a volunteer to help to put down the rebellion—and
was rejected, as I had but two whole fingers on my right hand. I
expressed my indignation, and said: "You will be glad to get
three-fingered fellows before this rebellion is squelched." I acted
upon important committees to encourage enlistments during the
war. The Massachusetts Twenty-First, Twenty-Fifth, Thirty-
Sixth, and Fifty-Fourth Regiments left the Agricultural Grounds
of Worcester for the war. I resided in the hall upon the grounds.
As these regiments left the grounds I announced to them that I
should keep open house during the war, and any soldier would
be welcomed, day or night, to my hospitalities, and many were
the times I arose and welcomed these defenders of my country

as they were homeward bound, by reason of wounds or furlough. My whole soul was aroused at the audacity of the leaders of the rebellion, and its among the pleasant events of my life that I did all I could, directly and indirectly, to enforce the laws of the land—embodied as they were in the platform of the Republican party, as laid down in this city of Chicago upon the nomination of our lamented President Abraham Lincoln in 1860. The closing scenes of 1888, I rendered by voice and vote all the power I was in possession of to oust the Democratic president and seat in his place our worthy president, who, I hope, will guard well the government which has overcome, for the second time, the slave power—who never dared to have free suffrage extended to the entire citizens of this republic. Long may he live—much of good may he do—and when the scenes of earth shall recede from his view, may he go on to the grand home celestial.

> " To a land of deathless beauty,
> Where no shadows dim the view;
> Where are many shining mansions,
> Waiting for the kind and true."

Is the prayer of his friend and well-wisher, and that of the nation; governed, as I hope it will ever be, by the principles of the Republican party as now understood, henceforth, now and forever, and forevermore.

ALONZO RAWSON

Was born in Richmond, Chesire county, New Hampshire, February 28th, 1809. His father, Jonathan, Rawson, was a merchant in that town for more than thirty years, and was elected to represent the town in the legislature of New Hampshire for a number of terms, besides holding many other offices of trust in the town. Alonzo came west to Cincinnati, Ohio, in 1829, where he resided for about three years, and from that place went to Louisville, Ky., where he was in business as a merchant for nearly thirty years, and while in business there served one term as president of the Board of Trade, and as a director of one of the leading banks for nearly ten years. He removed to New York City in 1863, and

was engaged in business there for about three years, and from
that city came to Chicago, where he has since resided. He voted
for Gen. W. H. Harrison in 1840, and has always since he became
a voter been an unwavering Whig and Republican. During the
Rebellion he was an outspoken Union man. Edward Rawson, a
native of England, and first secretary of the Colony of Massachusetts Bay, was the progenitor of his family, and as far as can
be ascertained, of all bearing the name of Rawson in the United
States, with two exceptions.

ALANSON REED.

I was born in Warren, Worcester county, Mass., November
14th, 1814, my father being a farmer of New England's rugged
hills. At the age of sixteen I was a mechanic in the piano factories of Boston, and in 1840 was appointed one of the vigilante
committee for Ward 10. After hearing our Daniel Webster and
and Henry Clay speak of the principles of the Whig party, I
worked with a vim to help elect Gen. Wm. Henry Harrison in
1840. My heart and vote went together into the ballot-box.
Success crowned our efforts. In 1842 I moved to Ohio, and settled in Columbus, the capitol city. In 1859 removed to St. Louis,
Mo., and in 1861, owing to the civil war, again removed to Chicago, which since that time has been my home. My last presidential vote I gave for Gen. Benjamin Harrison, and again
success was with our party. Were I to live seventy-four years
more I would vote on that line.

HENRY A. REW

Was born on April 9th, 1813, in Bloomfield, Ontario county, New
York; lived in Rochester, N. Y., until 1842, when he came to Illinois. He was an "Old Line Whig," and voted for William
Henry Harrison in 1840, and for every Whig candidate for the
presidency until the formation of the Republican party, and has
voted for every nominee of that party until, and including November, 1888, when Benjamin Harrison was the man of his
choice.

A. SPENCER REYNOLDS

Was born in Greenfield, Saratoga county, New York, June 21st, 1819. He lived in that county until August, 1838, removing to Jackson, Michigan, where he resided until 1842. He voted for William Henry Harrison in 1840 at Jackson; in June, 1842, he returned to Ballston Spa, Saratoga county, New York, and engaged in the mercantile business. He remained there until 1846, when he moved to Oswego, Kendall county, Ill., and from thence to Chicago, in 1855, where he has resided ever since, voting in 1888 for the grandson of " Old Tippecanoe."

WILLIAM RIPLEY.

The father of the writer was born in Connecticut, May 27th, 1782; married Susan Bingham, daughter of John Bingham, at Lisbon, Conn., March 31st, 1805. He moved to Ellsworth, Ohio, in the spring of 1806 (requiring seven weeks to perform the journey, as at that day there were no public conveyances). They suffered many privations and hardships for several years, as they were among the early pioneers in Trumble county, where they settled—being annoyed more or less by Indians—who still remained in that portion of the State.

I was the sixth of seven children, born July 9th, 1818. My father was a farmer by occupation. At the age of twelve I engaged as a clerk in a country store, which position I occupied until I myself embarked in the mercantile business at Berlin Centre, Ellsworth and Poland, covering a period of sixteen years. In the year 1854 I moved to Madison, Wisconsin, and at once engaged in the lumber business, having for a partner Mr. Wm. A. Mears. After a residence of eleven years at Madison, following various pursuits, I moved to Chicago, May 1st, 1865, (the day our lamented Lincoln lay in state in the court house) and have since then been directly and indirectly engaged in the lumber business.

July 18, 1839, at Ellsworth, Ohio, I married Ann Eliza Fitch— daughter of Richard Fitch; one of the children by this marriage, Orianna, born October 2, 1844, married Hampton B. Smith, and is now living at La Crosse, Wis. August 7, 1848, at Ellsworth, Ohio, I married my second wife, B. Eliza Allen, daughter of Asa W. Allen—two of the children by this marriage, Gordon and Bradford W., are associated with me in the lumber business at 238 So. Water Street, Chicago.

Politically, I voted the first time, in the fall of 1840 for Gen. William Henry Harrison for president of the United States, and the last time for the grandson, Gen. Benjamin Harrison in the fall of 1888. By this record, I think I am entitled to the honor of being, by lineage, a consistent Republican. I could not, and would not know how to be a Democrat.

THOMAS H. ROGERS

Was born in the State of Vermont, town of Cavendish, county of Windsor, on the 10th day of October, 1809. In 1840 he voted for General William Henry Harrison, for president, in Wampsville, town of Lenox, Madison county, New York. In 1862 he enlisted in the service of the United States army, and at the battle of Perryville, Ky., was captured a prisoner.

THOMAS ROBERTSON

Was born in Argyle, Washington county, on the 27th of August, 1811, of Scotch-Irish parentage, and lived with his father—working on the farm—until his fifteenth year. He then went to Cambridge, and served a regular apprenticeship at the tanning and currying business with his uncle, John Robertson. He remained in Cambridge until the spring of 1838, when he went to Troy, N. Y., and formed a partnership with his brother, in mercantile business. There he married Mary Shaw, of Greenwich, N. Y., on the 14th day of May, 1840; remained there until the fall of 1848, when he removed to Lakeville, Washington county, N. Y., and went back into his old business of tannery and currying, and grist milling. Here he remained for thirty years, and in the fall of 1871 he sold all of his property—having lost his wife and half of his family within about two years—and started for the far West,

WM. RIPLEY.

changing about from place to place, until finally he came to Chicago, in the year 1881, where he has remained ever since. He is now making his home with his son, A. S. Robertson and his family. He was a Whig of the old school; voted for Henry Clay for president in 1832, and William Henry Harrison in 1836 and 1840. He became a member of the Associate Church in early life, and has endeavored to maintain a con.:stent Christian character.

SENECA ALONZO SANFORD

Was born in Shoram, Vermont, June 9, 1816.   Came to Defiance, Ohio, in 1836, where, in the year of 1840, he voted for William Henry Harrison, of which he is very proud, and in 1888 for Benjamin Harrison.   He is the proud posessor of a clarinet—one hundred and twenty-five years old—which was used in the campaign of 1840, and was on exhibition in the club room of the Old Tippecanoe Club.

HENRY SAYRS

Son of Josiah and Sarah Van Kleeck Sayrs, was born in Po'keepsie, New York, July 1st, 1819.   Received his education at the Dutchess Academy, from whence, in 1836, he went to the City of New York, and engaged as clerk in a wholesale grocery house. On September 17, 1839, he married Miss Sarah C. Lockwood, of Newburgh on the Hudson, who, as time rolled on, became widely and favorably known for her philanthropical work.   Her biography, to 1869, is contained in the history of "The Loyal People of the Northwest."   She died on the 21st of April, 1888.

In 1840, Mr. Sayrs entered the wholesale grocery business in his own name in the City of New York—soon thereafter taking a partner, when the firm became Sayrs & Storm, and remained in said business until 1845, when, with his family, he moved to Milwaukee, Wis., where he was engaged in mercantile business, operating considerably in real estate.   He was a member of the common council in 1847-'48—its presiding officer and acting mayor—and was a delegate to the Harbor and River Convention held in Chicago in 1848.   Before the convention that nominated

HENRY SAYRS.

him for the legislature of Wisconsin in that year, he distinctly affirmed, that if elected, he would vote for no candidate for U. S. senator (two senators were to be chosen) who did not first assure him, over his signature, that if elected, he would introduce and advocate in the senate of the United States, an act to abolish slavery in the District of Columbia.

In consequence of their continual ill health, Mr. Sayrs moved with his family to Johnstown, Wis., in 1849, where he engaged in general trade, and was postmaster under President Taylor. He came to Chicago in 1853, and entered commercial business; was burned out at 54 and 56 Michigan Avenue in the general conflagration of 1871, immediately after which calamity he commenced importing and wholesaling teas, which business he continued until 1884, when, after forty-four years service on his own account, he retired from active pursuits.

Beside other positions of honor and trust, he was president of the Chicago Wholesale Grocers' Exchange, and the first president of the Merchants' Exchange; president of the Third Ward Republican Club in the Hayes and Wheeler campaign, uniforming, at his own expense, a company of one hundred wide-awakes, and presenting them with a large and elegant flag, behind which they marched to victory, under the name of Sayrs' Guards. Mr. Sayrs was an ardent Whig until the party north merged into the Republican; since then he has been an unswerving, uncompromising Republican. His first vote was cast for "Old Tippecanoe"— General William Henry Harrison—thereafter he voted for Henry Clay, Taylor, Scott, Fremont, Lincoln twice, Grant twice, Hayes, Garfield, Blaine and General Benjamin Harrison, grandson and inheritor of the principles of "Old Tippecanoe."

CHICAGO, MAY 15, 1889.

In connection with the foregoing biographical notice, I ask the privilege of recording here my admiration of the character of Mrs. Henry Sayrs. My long acquaintance with whom, in her efficient service rendered to me during my presidency of the Soldiers' Home, through and after the war, convinced me that she was the very embodiment of active, practical and judicious charity.

THOMAS B. BRYAN.

Extract from the History of "The Loyal People of the North-West."—1869.

" Among the first ranks of ' new women ' raised up to us by the late civil war, stands prominent the name of Mrs. Henry Sayrs. Her fine presence and able address might have won distinction as a lecturer; her diversified talents would have been legions of strength in any department of these thrilling times— but *works*, not *words*, told the story of her life. Her deeds of kindness are written in grateful joy upon the inmost heart of the soldier and his family. She has drawn tribute-tears from hardened hearts, and blessings from dying lips; she has brought hope to the hopeless, strength to the weak, and light to the obscure abode of the desolate widow and orphan; she has, in the fullest sense, ' fed the hungry, clothed the naked, taken in the stranger, visited the sick and in prison,' and toiled night and day for years to build comfortable homes for the ' war-scarred heroes,' daily pouring into them. Clara Barton worked on the field, Mrs. Sarah C. Sayrs *worked at home*. Elizabeth Cady Stanton thrilled thousands from the public forum, but the subject of our sketch thrilled thousands who received the kind benefaction from her hand, and moved to great patriotic deeds scores of Chicago capitalists, and her name was among the leaders of every patriotic enterprise."

In the same history, 1869, Rev. Robert L. Collier paid the following tribute: " Mrs. Sayrs is pre-eminently a woman of moral force. Remarkable for dexterity, she seldom waits for the slow dictates of reason when the keen sensibilities of her heart are touched. The history of her services for the poor and suffering armies, which only the good angels have witnessed, will, in eternity, and do, in her own conscience, outweigh in worth all public accomplishments. I doubt if any one person did more for the war than she did. She has a true Christian spirit, is a broad, liberal minded woman, and her church is one of the homes of her heart. She is ever on the alert to relieve the wretched and raise the fallen. No beggar is ever turned unsatis fied from her door, and no more hospitable mansion does Chicago afford than the one over which she presides with such grace and enthusiasm. She gave freely to the cause of her toils, her heart and her means. She is a true wife and mother—a steadfast friend, and lives in the esteem of all who can appreciate real womanly worth."

To Mrs. Henry Sayrs.

FROM THE INTER-OCEAN. BY EMMA E. MERRICK.

From out my heart these words I send
　To thee—a birth-day greeting;
With sincere pleasure of a friend
　As on these years are fleeting.

Thy three-score years—already past—
　Are faught with honest labor,
In memory will forever last
　To family, friend and neighbor.

God gave your heart an impulse strong,
　And hand that's ever ready,
With principle to right the wrong
　And help the poor and needy.

You've been a true and loving wife,
　A blessed, faithful mother;
No greater good can come of life
　For this world or the other.

You've filled a mission broad and gr;
　Wherever your work was needed;
Have helped the soldiers of our land,
　The orphans' cry you have heeded.

And when at last your work all done,
　Amid the blest you're sleeping,
A "crown of glory," justly won,
　Waits in your Master's keeping.

Feb. 29, 1888.

IN MEMORIAM.

*Recited by Rev. Jenkin Lloyd at the funeral of Mrs. Sarah C. Sayrs,
wife of Henry Sayrs, April 24, 1888.*

Fold reverently the weary hands
　That toiled so long and well;
And, while your tears of sorrow fall,
　Let sweet thanksgiving swell.

That life-work, stretching o'er long years,
　A varied web has been;
With silver threads by sorrow wrought,
　And sunny gleams between.

These silver hairs stole slowly on,
　Like flakes of falling snow
That wrap the green earth lovingly
　When autumn breezes blow.

Each silver hair, each wrinkle there,
　Records some good deed done;
Some flower she cast along the way,
　Some spark from love's bright sun.

O, gently fold the weary hands
　That toiled so long and well;
The spirit rose to angel bands
　When off earth's mantle fell.

She's safe within her father's house,
　Where many mansions be;
Oh, pray that thus such rest may come
　Dear heart to thee and me.

JOHN SCHMIDT

Was born March 5th, 1826; a native of the village of Horath, in the Rhinish Province, Prussia; arrived in New York on the 15th of July, 1840, after a stormy passage of fifty-three days. On the day subsequent to their arrival Mr. Schmidt's father, and a dozen of his companions, declared their intentions of becoming citizens of their adopted country, subsequently making their declarations good by taking out their naturalization papers and giving us five boys citizenship rights. About a month after the party removed to Cleveland, Ohio, where Mr. Schmidt had his first experience in a presidential campaign, which, by reason of his age, consisted in " swelling the line, hurrahing, and drinking good hard cider to the health and prosperity of Tippecanoe and Tyler, too." In 1846 he removed to Chicago, and has resided here ever since. He cast his first vote in 1847, experiencing considerable difficulty in so doing, as he was a Republican, and in those days Republicans in the Seventh Ward found it hard work to reach the ballot-box. He voted for Gen. Benj. Harrison in 1888, and all the Republican candidates in the interim.

WINCHESTER D. SCOTT.

I was born in Washington county, Ohio, February 14th, 1819, on a farm, on the Muskingum river, one mile below where the town of Beverley now stands. Lived there until I was thirteen, then moved with my people to Etna, in Licking county, Ohio, on the line of the National Turnpike, which was then building. Was taken into my brother's store and remained two years; went to Columbus, Ohio, to learn the drug business; remained about one year; after that went to school and sold goods in Etna and Columbus until 1839, when I went into a store at Tiffin, Ohio; remained in Tiffin selling goods fifteen years on my own account and five years as a clerk, until 1859, when I moved with my family to the town of Rulo, in Richardson county, Nebraska, and engaged in farming and stock-raising. Removed to Chicago in 1880 and established a patent medicine business. While at Tiffin I was selected as a delegate to the State Convention at Columbus,

Ohio, February 22, 1840, that recommended Gen. William Henry Harrison for president. Was an active Whig thereafter, being made chairman of the Chippewa Club, and on various committees in the campaigns of Generals Scott, Taylor and Fremont. While in Nebraska was a delegate to the first State Convention at Platsmouth, which authorized the people to vote for or against coming in as a State—also to nominate Republican candidates for State officers. Was then made chairman of the State Executive Committee for Richardson county, and canvassed it, which gave two hundred and fifty majority for State.

In 1872 was elected a State Senator from the First District, and in 1873 was elected a Regent of the State University of Nebraska. During my twenty years residence there I was in some minor public capacity nearly the whole time, such as member of School Board, Mayor of Rulo, Grand or Traverse Juryman in the Federal and State Courts. Was made State agent and superintendeo the building of the first ten miles of the Burlington & Southern Railroad (now the Atchison & Nebraska), of which organization I was a charter member. During the war we saw rough times, there being no sure mode of egress or ingress, and no markets for the first three years, and the country was overrun by bands of thieves. We organized a Union party for mutual protection, and for political purposes, which we maintained during the war.

At the close of the war a great change came. Our river was opened to traffic, we came in as a State, and the railroad commenced to build, emigrants came flocking in and locating, changing the scene from one of destitution, doubt and uncertainty to one of the greatest prosperity.

WILLIAM SKINNER

Was born June 9, 1805, in Franklin county, Penn.; was raised on a farm, and in 1818 went to learn the tanners trade, and in 1823 bought the tan yard and stock there. In 1831 started a general store in Holidaysburg, Pa.; in 1834 went west, dealing in land and cattle; in 1862 moved from Lake county, Ind., to Chicago,

WM. SKINNER.

where he has been engaged in grocery—general commission—business, until burnt out in the big fire, October 9, 1871.   In 1875 moved to Wisconsin, to oversee his grist mill for four years, sold out, and returned to Chicago in 1880, where he has lived most of the time since then, and is still hale and hearty at the age of eighty-four.   Has four sons and a daughter living.

WILLIAM D. SEARLES.

I was born in Fairfield county, Ohio, December 8, 1808; learned the tinner's trade in Lancaster; married and located in Tiffin, Ohio, in 1831; went into business then, and remained until 1865, when I moved to Rulo, Richardson county, Nebraska, where I engaged in the house-furnishing business.   I was appointed postmaster of Rulo, the same year, and held it until 1874, when I resigned, and moved to the City of Buffalo, State of New York, since which time I have not been engaged in business, living part of the time in Buffalo and part of the time in Chicago. While at Tiffin, I supported the Whig and Republican parties. Voted for William Henry Harrison, for president, in 1840, and have taken part at the various Whig and Republican campaigns since that time, my last vote being for Benjamin Harrison.

JAMES SHOURDS

Is of English ancestry, his father having been born in 1762, but soon removed to America, where, in 1807, on January 22, at Little Egg Harbor, New York, the subject of this sketch was born. Later the family removed to Cayuga county, and Mr. Shourds remained there until he reached his majority, when he started out to "shift for himself," living at various places in Ohio and New York, and 1840 found him a resident of Rochester, N. Y., where he voted for Gen. William H. Harrison.   After twenty-five years' residence in Rochester he located in Chicago, where he still resides, hale and hearty, at the age of eighty-two, and where he, in common with one son and other family connections, voted straight for Harrison and Morton "too."

D. E. STEDMAN.

DANIEL BAXTER STEDMAN

Is a descendant of Isaac Stedman, who came to America in his ship "Elizabeth," arriving in the year 1635, first settling at Scituate, Massachusetts, removing in 1650 to Muddy River (now Brookline), Mass., where he did business as a merchant. D. B. Stedman, son of Josiah Stedman, was born in Boston, Mass., on the 18th day of April, 1817. Commenced business in 1837 as importer of china and earthenware, under the firm of Atkins & Stedman, afterward D. B. Stedman & Co., which business he was in until the disastrous fire in Boston in 1872.

He voted in Boston in the year 1840 for Gen. William Henry Harrison for president, and at Chicago, in 1888, for Gen. Benjamin Harrison, and has always—without an exception—been an ardent supporter of the Whig and Republican parties. He was elected Representative to the Massachusetts Legislature for the session of 1866 and 1867.

DAVID SHEPPARD SMITH, M. D.,

Was born in Camden, New Jersey, on the 28th of April, 1816. His father, Isaac Smith, was a native of Salem county, in that State. His mother's family name was Wheaton, of Welch descent. His parents were noted for marked decision of character. The son inherited a robust constitution and received excellent youthful training, and feels especially indebted to the influence of his mother for his moral and intellectual inclinations. He very early conceived and strove for a high order of mental culture, and evinced an ardent desire to study the healing art, and at the age of seventeen years entered as a student of medicine in the office of Dr. Isaac S. Mulford. He attended three full terms of lectures at the Jefferson Medical College, in Philadelphia, and graduated from that institution in 1836. That college was then, as it is now, one of the foremost medical schools in the country, and its diploma could only be earned by genuine merit. Armed with this diploma and a determination to succeed, the young physician came West, and settled for practice in the then small town of Chicago. In 1837 he married Miss Rebecca

D. S. SMITH, President.

Ann Dennis, formerly of Fredonia, N. Y. The marriage has been blessed with four children, two of whom survive, the eldest Mrs. Whitehead—widow of the late Major F. F. Whitehead; the other—Caroline—the wife of J. L. Ely, of the city of New York.

During a visit in Camden, Dr. Smith became deeply interested in investigating the then novel doctrines of Hahnemann on homœopathy, and procured all the works he could gather on that subject. These books he studied assiduously. In 1842 he returned to Chicago, imbued with full confidence, from what he had learned by practical experience and observation, in the doctrines of Hahnemann, and the following year he fully adopted that system in his practice, and was the *first* physician to introduce it west of the lakes. It grew rapidly in public favor, and Dr. Smith had more calls for his professional services than he could respond to. Other practitioners were attracted to his side, and soon the advocates of the new school of medicine formed a medical body whose power has kept pace with other great factors in the production of wonderful Chicago. Homœopathy, no longer an experiment, has indeed taken deep hold on the convictions of the loftiest intellectual powers and the noblest personal worth, and now challenges the considerate judgment of the civilized world. Dr. D. S. Smith has justly won for himself the appellation of the " Father of Homeopathy " in the West. The ranking physician of both the schools of practice in Chicago, he procured from the Illinois Legislature of 1854–5, the charter of the Hahnemann Medical College in Chicago, and wrote the original draft of this charter in the law office of Abraham Lincoln. He held the position of President of the Board of Trustees of said college from its commencement until 1871, and after the death of Dr. Small, his successor, he was again elected to the presidency. In recognition of his eminent services, an honorary degree was conferred on him in 1856 by the Homeopathic Medical College of Cleveland, Ohio. In 1857 he was elected secretary of the American Institute of Homeopathy; in 1858 he was chosen president, and in 1865 treasurer of this national association. In 1866 he visited Europe, and while there studied the hospitals and colleges

with keen observation and profit, receiving the friendliest attentions and marks of distinguished consideration from men of
learning and eminence. In 1867 he returned to Chicago with
invigorated health, and renewed his extensive practice of his
profession.

He has witnessed the growth of Chicago from the time it was
a mere hamlet until it has become one of the largest and most
important cities in the Union, and his influence and varied public
benefactions are indelibly stamped upon its history. He is a
man of religious convictions, and a respected member in the
worship of the Methodist Episcopal Church—a man of unquestioned integrity, simple in his habits, dignified, urbane, generous
and hospitable, an attentive listener, a ready debater, a strict
disciplinarian, was president of the Second Ward Republican
Club in its palmiest days, and is now the honored and popular
president of the Old Tippecanoe Club of Chicago.

ENOS SLOSSON.

The existence of the Old Tippecanoe Club of Chicago is due
to this old patriot, who, so soon as General Benjamin Harrison
had been placed in nomination for president by the Republican
National Convention of 1888, set to work with enthusiasm to organize an Old Tippecanoe Club, going about it in a business way,
and with a measure of success beyond his anticipations. How
well he did let this completed volume tell.

Born February 16th, 1817, at Berkshire, Tioga county, New
York, from the best of thorough American lineage, his whole life
has been more or less identified with the good of our common
country, and his best efforts have been directed toward the success of the Whig and its legitimate successor—the Republican
party.

The grandfather of Mr. Slosson, who was also Enos Slosson,
emigrated from England in the stirring times which preceeded
the outbreak of the Revolutionary War, settling at Lenox, Massachusetts. Events at Lexington and Bunker Hill aroused the
patriotism of the country, Slosson shouldered his old flint-lock,

and for God and his country fought manfully and well; was promoted in the army to the Captaincy for meritorious conduct, till
at Yorktown the crushing defeat and surrender of Cornwallis
opened the gates of peace and American independence.   Mr.
Slosson also shared the honor to be under direct command of
Gen. Washington, and of sharing in the privations of Valley
Forge. After the war he settled in Berkshire, a valley in the
State of New York, where the subject of this sketch was born in
1817.

Enos Slosson, the father of the present Enos Slosson, was
born in Massachusetts in 1782, and although he died at the age
of thirty-eight, had attained prominence as a soldier, holding a
Colonel's commission in the War of 1812, signed by Daniel D.
Tompkins, the famous War Governor of New York. He was
also elected to Congress, but died before taking his seat. The
grandfather of Enos Slosson the third, on his mother's side, came
also from Old England to Connecticut, where he, too, joined the
Revolutionary army, being in many battles promoted to the Captaincy; sharing also in the privations of the memorable winter at
Valley Forge with Washington, and participated in the surrender of Cornwallis at Yorktown.

Enos Slosson, the third of the same name, engaged in commercial pursuits when but fourteen years of age, and has ever
been a commercial man, being successful in business.   For
eighteen years he was of and with the firm of Parkhurst &
Slosson; and at its dissolution engaged in the lumber trade, and
on the Stock Board at Harrisburg, Pa.   He voted for Gen. William Henry Harrison at Elkland, Tioga county, Penn., in 1840.
He soon after was appointed postmaster by Gen. Taylor, then
president, at Osceola, Tioga county, Penn.--now a good sized
town—with whose interests he was greatly identified in building
up, and giving it the name of Osceola.

At this time in the Twelfth Pennsylvania Congressional District he performed another very great deed for future generations—leading along down the many ages, resulting in none
other than generous and humane by the nation, by bringing forward the Hon. Galusia A. Grow as the successor of the distin-

ENOS SLOSSON, FIRST VICE-PRESIDENT.

guished author of the great anti-slavery proviso for Texas—
(Hon. David Wilmot) for a seat in Congress, the motion coming up before the convention, of which Enos Slosson was president in the Twelfth District. The ballots were many without a
majority. At last the unanimous voice of the convention called
for a descision of the Chair. The chairman gave the casting
vote for Hon. Galusia A. Grow, being equivalent to an election,
as was proven soon after. Upon the assemblage of Congress
Grow was elected Speaker. When the committee reported the
bill in the House, he left the Chair and made a vigorous speech
thereon. The bill passed; went to the Senate; it was approved,
lingered but a short time there; was sent to the executive—the
great Abraham Lincoln, President of the United States. He
only required a single glance, and seizing his pen wrote the word
"Approved," with Abraham Lincoln thereunder, after once
being vetoed by James Buchanan. It was a law of the nation
that one hundred and sixty acres of the national domain was al-
lotted to each landless man and woman, and up to this date a
law of the nation—thanks to its early friends.

A great and spontaneous demonstration was successfully inaugurated at Osceola, Pa., in the campaign of the Free Soil
party, composed of Democrats and Whigs, in southern New
York and northern Pennsylvania. It was a gathering at once the
largest, the best, the most opportune, and the first held by the
Free Soil party in the republic –culminating in the establishment
of the great Republican party. Its importance was widely recognized and acknowledged by the press, conspicuously the New
York *Tribune*, the great leading Republican journal of the world at
that time. Think what has been the destiny of our country, influenced a thousand times to greatness by the Republican party,
which sprung from the small, impulsive Osceola move, seconded
by David Wilmot, and eulogized by Horace Greeley, with the
mighty and immense following of them both. Think of the
masterly achievements of this host of freedom; the manumitting
of three millions of slaves and the conquering of eighteen millions of enemies; the reinstatement of a united government of
forty-two millions (now sixty millions) of people, and the inaug-

uration of the best system of finance the world ever witnessed, the propagation of a free school idea, popularizing our form of government, and enhancing the wide-spread prosperity of the nation. It was greatly through his solicitations that Gov. Alexander Ramsey, the first Territorial Governor of Minnesota, accepted the appointment from Taylor; and he was also deeply engaged in engineering Minnesota into the Union.

Mr. Slosson was admitted to the bar of the Supreme Court of Minnesota, to which State he removed some time previous. Upon the breaking out of the Rebellion he removed to Chicago, where he was also admitted to the bar, and has ever since resided, always with the Republican party on every question, and subscribing largely to the first government 7-30 bonds—the money going to the army boys at the front—an honest man, a good citizen, well-to-do financially, and surrounded by hundreds of devoted friends. His last days will assuredly be peaceful ones as a valued citizen of Chicago.

ALBERT SOPER

Was born the 9th of January, 1812, at Rome, Oneida county, N. Y. He secured a good common school education, under instruction of Mr. Oliver D. Grosvenor, then in charge of the principal academy. Among the schoolmates of that day and class are found the names of Judge Anson S. Miller, now of California, the late Norman B. Judd, of Chicago, Thomas Wright, of Rome, and Henry R. Hart, of Utica. He began business in early life as a contractor and builder, and soon afterwards established the first lumber and planing mill business, in which he continued, at Rome, N. Y., until 1866, when he came to Chicago and organized the lumber business with which he is still connected. He is president of the Soper Lumber Co., of Chicago, besides being interested in the Menominee Bay Shore Lumber Co., of Menominee, Mich., and the Michigan Shingle Co., of Muskegon, Mich. He has also been for several years one of the directors of the Hide & Leather National Bank, of Chicago. In the spring of 1837, being in impaired health, and having a desire to see something of the then great West, he accepted an invitation from his former instructor, Mr. Grosvenor, to accompany him on a trip thereto. So, taking a packet boat on the Erie Canal, that being the only rapid transit available at that day, and passing through Syracuse, Lyons, Palmyra, Rochester, Lockport, and other thriving villages, they in due time arrived at Buffalo, from whence they took steamer for the Upper Lakes, stopping at all places, receiving and discharging passengers and freight between Buffalo and Macinac; thence to Green Bay, Sheboygan, Milwaukee, Racine, Southport (now Kenosha), Little Fort (now Waukegan), being detained at each of these places—*deliberately*, discharging cargo—finally arriving at the pier at Chicago. No busses or cabs—passengers were compelled to grab their carpet-bags, and wade a long distance through slush and mud before reaching terra-firma, and then, to reach the Lake House, on Rush Street, near the river, had to walk a single plank. The Lake House was just being completed as the best hotel in the place, and the " North Side " was the favorite. Having stopped over a few days, our travelers were not favorably impressed with the situation. Streets were not graded, and, at sections, some of the most important of them were impassable for teams, and boards were stuck up in their midst inscribed: " No Bottom Here!" The town was a swamp, intermingled with sloughs, bull-frogs, malaria, and— some adventurers—an uninteresting, uninviting place—its denizens looked disappointed, tired, woe-begone, as though they had got to the end of their purse, or did not know where else to go; and those of them who owned anything wanted to sell out. Except via. lake it was a difficult place to get away from, of which fact Mr. Soper and friend had ample evidence, for, wishing to view some of the adjacent farming country, they started in a lumber wagon and soon after crossing a bridge at Lake Street came to thick, muddy water, through which, from one to two feet in depth, they were compelled to travel most of the way to Widow Berry's Point, now the beautiful suburb, Riverside. From there they went on through mud until they arrived at Joliet, where they were agreeably surprised to find so promising and eligibly located a town, surrounded by fertile lands.

ALBERT SOPER, Treasurer.

Democracy ruled in Chicago, in Illinois, and in the nation, and the full force of Jackson's unfortunate administration was being felt the bubble had burst, and as speculation in real estate had thus far been the specific *industry* of Chicago, the laborers in that vineyard were now out of employment, and no danger of strikes apprehended.   However, as whisky cost only ten cents per gallon, the numerous saloons run a lively competition for Michigan " Wild Cat " money, that constituting most of the circulating medium of the northwest.   Van Buren was President, representing a party opposed to internal improvement among the States, and as there was no money in the National Treasury, he ordered the sale, by auction, of the dredging machines, and all other machinery that had been purchased and used for, and was still needed to dredge the harbor and river of Chicago, and they were sold at a great sacrifice.   The town, the State, and the nation were alike bankrupt, and consequently without credit.   The bonds of the State were almost valueless.   The general outlook was discouraging, and the wildest imagination could never have dreamed that the mire called Chicago, from which the tourists departed on their return home in 1837, would, by any freak of circumstances, become fifty-two years thereafter (having meantime in one year, viz.: in 1871, been nearly destroyed by fire at a loss of $200,000,000 of property) the second city in population, magnificence and business in the United States.

In 1837 Mr. Soper was married to Esther Farquharson, of Rome, N. Y.   They recently celebrated their golden wedding, which was attended by their children, grandchildren and many friends.   Seven children have been born to them, of whom five are still living—Arthur W. Soper, of New York City; Mrs. Geo. Merrill, of Eau Claire, Wis.; Alex. C., and James P. Soper, of Chicago, and Mrs. Wm. Penn Smith, of Eureka, Cal.

In politics Mr. Albert Soper was an unswerving Whig until the formation of the Republican party, since which time he has been loyal and devoted to its principles.   He voted for William Henry Harrison in 1836 and 1840.   Was one of a large delegation who went from Rome, via. the Erie Canal, to Syracuse, N. Y., to attend the grand State rally of the Harrisonians at that place.

Such an enthusiastic assemblage had never been known in the
State. With log-cabins, flags, banners, and numerous bands of
music, the delegations moved up the hill to hear Hon. W. H.
Seward, Gen. Baker, of New Hampshire, and others, who, with
their arguments and eloquence, contributed to bring us a great
victory. He voted for Henry Clay in 1844, and for every Whig
or Republican candidate for President of the United States since,
and November 6th, 1888, for Benjamin Harrison for the same
high office. Mr. Soper is the treasurer of the Chicago Tippecanoe Club.

CALVIN SHAW

Was born in Plymouth county, Mass., on the —— day of - —— -
——————, and moved to Ohio in the year 1839. His first vote
was cast at Chillicothe, Ohio, in 1840, for Gen. William Henry
Harrison, and attended a very large convention that was addressed by General William Henry Harrison, during that campaign, and was one of a company of young men who acted as an
escort. Mr. Shaw voted for every Whig up to the birth of the
Republican party, and has since then voted for the candidates of
the latter, including Gen. Harrison in 1888. He lived in Ohio
until 1887, when he moved to Chicago, and has resided here ever
since.

BENJAMIN SMITH

Was born in Ridgefield, Fairfield county, Conn., January 12, 1815.
His parents, Amos and Sarah (Keeler) Smith, were known far
and near throughout the country as one of the oldest hotel-
keepers in the State, on the site that his father, John, before him,
kept until the close of his life. His grandfather, Ebenezer, was
one of the original thirty settlers of the town, receiving this with
a tract of land as his portion of the township, purchased from the
survivors in September, 1708. The company selected a ridge of
land in the central portion, some eight hundred feet above Long
Island Sound, fifteen miles distant, which it overlooked. This

property never left the Smith family, being yet occupied by the younger brother, Samuel, and sister, Emma, who married George Smith.

Benjamin remained home —working on the farm—till seventeen years old, when he left to learn the tailor's trade, which he finished in the city of New Haven. In the fall of 1837 he came to Chicago, and with J. W. Hooker, engaged in the grocery trade, on Lake street. In August, 1838, he was married to Rachael Van Nortwick, the daughter of William Van Nortwick, in Batavia, Kane county, Ill. The result of this union has been four daughters— the eldest, Sarah I. Clarim, the wife of Doctor Edgar D. Swain; the second—Martha Marie—is the wife of Daniel B. Andrews; the others died young.

While with Mr. Hooker, he traded for a lot, fifty by eighty feet, on north-west corner of Dearborn and Washington streets, and built a comfortable home on it, but after residing a few years on it, lost it by engaging in business with Joseph Johnston. In 1846, purchasing a patent reaping machine, commenced the manufacture of the same, and after a trial it was found worthless, but by making changes and improvements, succeeded in making a successful reaping machine. In 1846, he made the first successful crooked sycle, cutting it himself after having it forged out of steel and iron. In the fall of 1847, he removed to Batavia, Kane county, built a shop, and continued to manufacture till 1857 successfully with all the reaping machines that came into use. Returning to Chicago soon after, built a home on Peoria street, between Lake and Randolph streets, where he resided until 1870, when, disposing of that home, removed to 63 Aberdeen street, corner of Aberdecen, where he still resides, practically retired from business.

W. G. SMITH

Was born in New Haven, Rutland county, September 6th, 1816, and resided in Sudbury, Vt., in 1836, where he took an active part in the unsuccessful canvass of Gen. Harrison; and in 1840 worked and voted for the successful election of that gentleman. In 1888

Mr. Smith resided at Wheaton, Ill., and worked and voted for Benjamin Harrison, and was inexpressibly pleased at the result.

ICHABOD STODDARD

Was born April 14th, 1808, in the county of Leeds, Province of Ontario, Canada. In 1837 he removed to Illinois, later residing in Porter county, Indiana, where, in 1840, he cast his first vote as an American citizen for Gen. William Henry Harrison, and again forty-eight years thereafter—cast another ballot for the grandson—Gen. Benjamin Harrison—this time in Illinois. Is enthusiastic over the Tippecanoe Club.

GEN. ALEX. MILLER STOUT

Was born January 8, 1820, near Shelbyville, Shelby county, Ky. His father was a soldier of the War of 1812, and three of his family were officers in the Revolutionary army. His early life was spent on the farm. Was educated in Bardstown, Ky., finishing his course in 1840. Worked hard for Gen. W. H. Harrison's election, and attended his inauguration. He completed his study of law at Cambridge University, and was city attorney at Louisville. From 1857 to 1861, on the breaking out of the war, he volunteered his services, and with the rank of Colonel engaged in the recruiting service, going to the front shortly after as Colonel of the 17th Kentucky Infantry. He was at Donaldson, Shiloh, Chicamauga, Atlanta, siege of Nashville, Franklin, and elsewhere, coming out of service with a commission as Brevet-Brigadier-General of Volunteers. Had his horse shot under him at Donaldson. His son was killed at Shiloh, and he himself was severely wounded in the same fight. Subsequently he was elected Representative in the Legislature of Kentucky, and nominated by a Republican caucus as Speaker of the House. He was also, from 1866 to 1868 acting Commissioner in charge of the Patent Office, subsequently resigning that position to practice "patent law." He moved to Chicago in 1879, and like all the rest of the "Tippecanoes," voted for Gen. Benj. Harrison in 1888.

JOHN HENRY TAYLOR

Was born near Little Beaver Falls, Columbia county, State of Ohio, February 26, 1818. He received his education at Rutledge, and commenced his business career at fourteen years of age as bookkeeper in a paper mill. In 1843, the family moved to Steubenville, Ohio, where his father and himself were employed in the paper mills at that point, the heads of which institution were all ardent for protection of American industry, and supporters of Henry Clay in his American system. Mr. Taylor through these associations inherited the political opinions as proclaimed by the Whig and Republican parties. He embarked in business on his own account in 1836, but after the panic of 1837 he became pedagogue, subsequently acting superintendant of the Steubenville, Ohio, public schools. He attended a large mass meeting of the Whigs of southeast Ohio and northwest Virginia, held at Steubenville, in the summer of 1840. This meeting was addressed by W. H. Harrison, Tom Corwin and other eminent speakers. Harrison's speech was a scathing rebuke of Jackson and Van Buren reigns. It is needless to say that Mr. Taylor cast his first vote, in 1840, for Gen. Harrison. He moved to Illinois in 1855, where he held various positions of trust, until 1866, when he returned to New York. He has resided in Chicago since 1879, and in 1888, while favoring the nomination of Blaine as first choice, he received the nomination of General Benjamin Harrison with delight, and his election with equal pleasure.

JOHN B. TAYLOR

Was born in the county of Kilkenney, Ireland, March, 1813. He moved to the United States, and settled in Kentucky in 1831, and in 1832 came to Illinois, where he voted for William Henry Harrison in 1836 and '40, at Springfield. He came to Chicago in 1858, and has voted for every one of the "Old Line" Whigs and Republicans, save when he voted for James Buchanan, for which Mr. Taylor says—in parenthesis—"God forgive me." His family of seven, are all staunch Republicans, and in all probability never have occasion to repeat their parental ancestor's prayer of "God forgive me."

E. P. TEALE

Was born in the village of Whitehall, State of New York, in 1808. His residence in 1832 was in Waterford, N. Y., where he voted for W. H. Harrison in 1836. In 1840 he resided in Ypsilanti, Mich., where he again voted for W. H. Harrison. Mr. Teale is now a resident of Chicago, and voted for Gen. Ben. Harrison in 1888, and adds, as do the majority of the Club members, "I am proud of my political record."

T. TEN EYCK.

Born in New Jersey, August 5, 1819; came west with his father, Gen. James Ten Eyck, in 1835, settling in Michigan. In 1840 he became a voter, and voted and worked enthusiastically for the election of General Harrison. Was a member of a band, and was present at nearly all the large meetings held in Michigan during that eventful campaign; moved to Wisconsin in 1846; lived at Green Bay, Wis., when the Rebellion commenced. He enlisted in the Twelfth Wisconsin Volunteers in August, 1861, as a private, and served with his company until February, 1862, when he was commissioned a captain in the regular army, by President Lincoln, being assigned to Eigthteenth United States Infantry served about ten years in above mentioned grade— and was honorably discharged in January, 1871, having been brevetted major for faithful service during the war.

He has voted for every Whig and Republican presidential candidate since 1840 to, and including, our present Harrison, except Abraham Lincoln; could not vote for him in '60—being then in Colorado Territory—and in '64, was paying a compulsory visit to our southern brethern in South Carolina.

WILLIAM THOMAS.

In 1840 he resided in Detroit, Michigan, and although too young to cast his vote at the election, worked hard through the entire campaign, attending log cabin meetings in Detroit, Cleveland, Canadaigin, and other places, taking more interest actively

JOHN HENRY TAYLOR.

than in any other campaign since. In 1844 he voted for Henry
Clay, later for Martin Van Buren, Fremont, and since then for all
the candidates of the Republican party. Mr. Thomas, in closing
his biographical sketch, adds: "In looking back over the thirteen presidental elections, I feel that I have made no political
mistake—none that I would change—and I only wish that I may
have the opportunity to cast one more vote for Benjamin Harrison, or the nominee of the Grand Old Party.

M. M. THOMPSON

Was born on the —— day of ————————, and removed to the
West August 28th, 1834, being one of the first to organize the
Bureau Committee in this State. He voted for Tippecanoe in
1836 and in 1840, and cast his vote for Gen. Benj. Harrison on
Nov. 6th, at Wyanette, Ill., which he believes to be his last vote,
but let us hope otherwise. Proud of the Tippecanoe Club badge.

A. G. THROOP

Was born July 22d, 1811, in Deruyter, Madison county, N. Y.
Was in Clyde, St. Clair county, Mich., in the year 1840, and cast
his first vote for Wm. Henry Harrison at that place. Later on
Mr. Throop located in Chicago, where he held positions of trust
and political preferments. He is at present a resident of Pasadena, Cal., where he voted for Gen. Benj. Harrison. He is now
serving the citizens of Pasadena as a member of the council.

EDWARD TIFFANY, M. D.,

Was born in Rochester, New York, May 11th, 1817. His early
life was uneventful, and in 1839 he commenced the study of medicine at Alden, Erie county, N. Y., afterwards attending Harvard
University and the lectures in the Massachusetts General Hospi-
tal. In 1844 he moved to Meigs county, Ohio, where he practiced medicine for thirty-six years, with the exception of some

EDWARD TIFFANY.

months when he attended lectures on his chosen vocation at various standard colleges Was married July 8, 1847, in Alden, N. Y., to Miss Martha A. Kellogg. During the four years of the war he represented his county in the Lower House of the Ohio Legislature, and was appointed by Gov. David Todd a member of the county military committee for the same period. Politically, the Doctor has always been a strong adherent of the good Republican party, voting for W. H. Harrison in 1840, and for Gen. Benj. Harrison in Chicago, 1888.

CALVIN TOWNSEND

Was born in Dixfield, Maine, April, 1819. His political preferences have always been with the Whigs and Republicans. His first vote was cast for General William Henry Harrison in Welton, Maine, in 1840, and his last vote, in Chicago, for Harrison the second.

DANIEL TRUE,

Born February 10, 1813; in the town of Goshen, Cheshire county, New Hampshire. Moved to New York in 1823. Enlisted in the army in 1831; served five years during the Black Hawk and Seminole wars. Voted for General William Henry Harrison in 1836 and 1840 at Albany, New York, and for every Whig and Republican nominated for the presidency, from 1836 to 1888 inclusive.

A. S. VAIL.

My father and mother moved from Dawley, Vermont, to a town in Canada, by the name of Dunham Lane; left there during the war of 1812, and moved to Dawley, Vermont, where I lived most of the time until I came to Illinois, where I have lived nearly fifty-three years. I came to Iroquois county in 1836, took part in election of William Henry Harrison but could not vote, as I had not been here as long as the law required; voted for him in 1840 and for Benjamin Harrison in 1888, and if his record is good and I should live, will vote for him in 1892 if he is nominated. I like the Old Tippecanoe Club of Chicago.

C. R. VAN DERCOOK,

Son of Michael S. Van Dercook, was born in Pittstown, Rensalaer county, New York, on the 20th day of May, 1819. His grandfather was a commissioned officer in the Revolutionary war. The family are legal heirs of the famous Anke Jantz, whose estate, many years in litigation, embraces, as alleged, the Trinity Church property of New York—worth many millions of dollars. The subject of this sketch came to Chicago in 1838; his occupation being that of a clerk. His first vote was cast for William Henry Harrison, for president, in 1840. Believing the Whig party to represent the best interests of the country, especially on the tariff question, he consistently acted with that party until it was absorbed by the Republican party, since then he has been actively identified with the latter—casting his last presidential vote for General Benjamin Harrison. In 1841-'42 he was one, of nineteen, who organized and built Trinity Episcopal Church. Sad to relate, all of his compeers in that transaction, excepting Wm. W. Bracket, have gone to that bourne from whence no traveller returns. Since the early days of Chicago, Mr. Van Dercook has been prominent in very many of its social and charitable societies. In 1846 he became identified with the masonic bodies, and through his individual effort, the debts of the Apollo Commandery were paid and its charter saved—this is said to now be the largest commandery in the world. In 1843 he was elected, and served as treasurer of the Young Men's Library Association. In 1846-7 Van Dercook & Co., cast and built the first stove manufactured in Chicago, employing about two hundred men, and turning out fifty stoves daily. For more than twenty years Mr. Van Dercook was employed in the city water department. In 1880-'82 he organized the company which constructed and operated, with good success, a dummy railroad from Fortieth street, Chicago, to Harlem. With a record of unremitting business

activity Mr. Van Dercook's present physical and mental condition pays eloquent tribute to his mode of living, and gives
cheering promise of many more years of usefulness among his
fellow citizens.

B. VAN VELZER

Was born August 12, 1818, at Syracuse, New York, and removed
to Chicago in 1836. Was engaged on the canal in Ohio in 1840,
and cast his vote for Gen. William Henry Harrison in a small
town near Akron. Afterward he returned to Chicago, engaging
in the hotel business, and made his permanent home here. Has
always been a consistent Republican, and took special pains to
vote for Benjamin Harrison.

ARCHER R. VANHOUTTEN

Was born on the 5th of October, 1812, in Tarrytown, New York,
and when fifteen years of age was bound out- as was the custom
in those days— to a cabinet maker, and has followed that trade
and other branches thereof, during the greater portion of his life.
He voted for Gen. William Henry Harrison in 1836 and 1840, and
Benjamin Harrison in 1888.

As a carpenter he was called upon to build the arches on
Broadway, Pearl and other New York streets for the Whig processions of 1836 and 1840, and also a large log cabin exhibited at
the same time.

JAMES A. WAKEFIELD

Was born in Cherryfield, Maine, April 30th, 1819. Received his
education in common schools and the Academy of Cherryfield.
His business in Maine prior to leaving for the Western States,
was chiefly lumber and mercantile business, often superintending
lumber operations and the erection of mills. In 1861 and 1862
was one of the " select men" of Cherryfield, and in 1861 was ordered by Adjt -General of Maine to enroll the " militia," and
during the war recruited many men for the service. In 1866 left

Maine for Minneapolis, Minn., where he resided eight years. In 1874 came to Chicago, Ill., where he has since resided. In 1884 he cast his vote for James G. Blaine for president—his decided preference. The first vote he ever cast was for William Henry Harrison in 1840 for president, and in 1888 he voted for the "grandson."

A. G. WARNER

Was born in Le Roy, Genesee county, N. Y., February 22d, 1817. His father, Thomas Warner, died at Ypsilanti, Mich., in 1828, where he had gone to prepare a home for his family, consisting of his wife and seven children, whom he left in Le Roy awaiting his return, when the news of his death, instead of his presence, was received. The bereaved, but courageous mother, was left in poverty to rear and care for the seven children, of whom A. G. was the third in age.

In 1835 he left the widowed mother's home in Le Roy to enter a business life at Rush, Monroe county, N. Y., where he cast his first presidential vote for William Henry Harrison in 1840. He was a staunch Henry Clay Whig—was one of one hundred selected by the Whigs of Monroe county to attend the convention at Baltimore in 1844 to influence the nomination of their party idol -Henry Clay—and was one of twenty-five selected from the hundred to proceed to Washington the next day to greet the illustrious nominee and ratify his nomination. In 1853 he came to Chicago to reside, and entered the " Eagle Works " manufacturing establishment of P. W. Gates & Co., as book-keeper, his older brother, E. S. Warner, being a member of the firm. In 1856 he was admitted a member of the firm, under the name of Gates, Warner, Chalmers & Fraser, taking charge of the office work during the existence of the co-partnership.

In 1867 he removed to Englewood, Cook county, Ill., where he now resides, and cast his last presidential vote for Benjamin Harrison. Although a pronounced anti-slavery and temperance man and worker, he has always voted with the Whig and Republican parties from 1838 to 1888 inclusive, always deprecating national third party movements, fully believing that slavery could never be abolished until the true party of reform, the grand old Whig party, should identify its power in the movement, which it did do in 'adopting a new name—the Republican party; and as with slavery, so it will be, in his estimation, with the liquor traffic. Prohibition, he thinks, cannot be accomplished by the third party movement. Political Prohibitionists must return to the real party of reform and progress - the glorious and reliable Republican party—and whether under that name, or a new name that may be chosen hereafter, prohibition, he thinks, will, in the near future, be the watchword of the party of reform, and in the natural course of events be victorious.

ABIAL H. WILLIAMS

Was born in the town of Lyman, State of Maine, October 13, 1818. Cast his first presidential vote for Gen. Wm. Henry Harrison, at Atkinson, in said State, in 1840, and voted the Whig and Republican tickets down to and including the election of Benjamin Harrison to the presidency of the United States. Mr. Williams is yet quite vigorous, and has enlivened the meetings of the Club by singing with great effect some of the old-time campaign songs, notably the one entitled " The Sword of Bunker Hill."

M. D. WILLIAMS

Was born in Saratoga, New York, July 15. 1816. His political career has been that of a private citizen, consecutively and persistently for the success of the Whig and Republican parties. Voted for General William Henry Harrison in Fulton county, New York, in 1840, and for the younger Harrison in 1888.

WILLIAM R. WILSON

Was born at Ashland, Ky., August 9, 1817. His father was a Whig, living in the same town with Henry Clay, for whose political opinions he had the highest regard, and was a warm, personal and political friend up to the time of his death, in 1837.

Mr. Wilson followed in the political footsteps of his father, and lays claim to being a Whig from 'way back. In 1836, lacking just two years a legal voter, he was unable to vote, but in 1840 cast his first vote for " Tip and Ti," at Greensborough, Ind., and from that time to 1852 he voted for the Whig nominees. In 1864 he voted for Abraham Lincoln, and ever after he gave his support to the Republican party. Mr. Wilson closes his short biographical sketch of himself by saying " My only political regret is, that I did not have the courage of my convictions to vote for Abraham Lincoln in 1860."

ALBERT WINGATE

Was born at Hallowell, Kennebec county, Maine, June 15, 1817; removed to Penobscot county in 1839. September 6, 1842 started by team for the far West as Illinois was then called— reaching the Ten Mile House, now Auburn, kept by John Smith and Merrill Kile, October 17, and on October 26 commenced housekeeping in a log cabin in the present town of Worth, Cook county, Illinois, and has lived in the same school district ever since. Mr. Wingate has always been a farmer, and comes of a long line of distinguished ancestors. John Wingate was a planter at Hilton's Head, now Dover, New Hampshire; served in King Phillip's War in 1658, and died Dec. 9th, 1687. Joshua Wingate held the rank of Colonel in the army that captured Louisburg, in 1745, and died February 9th, 1769, aged ninety years. Rev. Paine Wingate was pastor of the Second Congregational Church in Amesbury, Mass., for sixty years, and died February 19th, 1786, aged eighty-three years. Joseph Wingate, popularly known as " Farmer Wingate," died in Hallowell, Maine, September 18th, 1826, aged seventy-five. Paine Wingate, Albert's father, died at Hallowell, Maine., January 12th, 1849, on a farm which he had cleared of the dense forest that covered it in 1806, when he first got it. All of his ancestors owned and lived during a portion of their lives on a farm.

Joseph Wingate was a Federalist, Paine Wingate a Federalist and Whig, and Albert Wingate cast his first vote for president for Wm. Henry Harrison, at Orono, Penobscot county, Me.; voted for Clay in '44; missed '48; voted for Scott in '52, Fremont in '56, and all the Republican candidates since that date, including Benjamin Harrison in 1888. Mr. Wingate has never used glasses, and his sight is good today.

EMORY B. WOLCOTT

Was born on the 19th of September, 1806, at Trenton, Oneida county, New York. In politics, Mr. Wolcott has never been other than Whig and Republican. He voted for Gen. William Henry Harrison in 1836 and 1840 at Rome, New York, and was one of a large party who, in 1840, went from Rome to Utica in wagons, making a portion of a three-mile procession in celebration of Gen. Harrison's election, which was followed by a ball in the evening. Mr. Wolcott voted in 1888 at Fernwood, Ill. It is entirely unnecessary to say for whom that vote was cast.

A. J. WRIGHT.

Born August 6th, 1817, at Dunstable, county of Middlesex, Massachusetts. His father was a Clay Whig, and voted for Wm. Henry Harrison in 1836 and '40. His grandfather served in the Revolutionary War. Mr. Wright took an active part in the campaign of 1836, but by reason of his age did not vote; but did vote for William Henry Harrison, in Nashua, New Hampshire, in 1840, and has voted the straight Republican ticket ever since. Mr. Wright has been in business in Chicago since the year 1854, being quite well known to our citizens in general.

JOSHUA PALMER YOUNG,

Dealer in real estate, was born at Brockport, N. Y., March 18, 1818. He voted for Gen. W. H. Harrison, at Brockport, in 1840.

He came to Chicago in 1848, and built the first house on the West Side south of Polk street. He early became interested in city and suburban property, managing many important transactions. In 1856 he purchased and platted eighty acres of land on which most of the village of Blue Island is located, where he has since resided, and where he voted for Benjamin Harrison in 1888. Mr. Young was a man of great business sagacity, and all his dealings were characterized by uniform integrity. His business life was paralleled by his devout Christian character and his sincere religious life. He founded the Congregational Church at Blue Island, and was its main pillar till his death, May 26th, 1889.

N. STARR CARRINGTON

Was born at Middleton, Conn., Dec. 12, 1816; came to Chicago October 1, 1836; settled on a farm in Lyons, Cook county, Ill.; the same year; married Miss Flora Butler, of Norfolk, Conn., Aug. 16, 1841; voted for Wm. Henry Harrison in 1840—always Whig and Republican.

Letter of Benjamin Harrison, the Signer.

Benjamin Harrison, the signer of the Declaration of Independence, received an appointment under General Wayne, and
intended accompanying him on the expedition against the northwestern Indians, but was unable to do so in consequence " of
having three of his ribs broken near the backbone, also loosened
from his breast, and one broke near the middle." Under these
circumstances he determined to send his son, Wm. Henry, even
in the humble capacity of private soldier, as will be seen by the
following extract of a letter written to Maj.-Gen. Charles Scott,
afterward Governor of Kentucky:

OCTOBER 10, 1792.

And now, before I take my leave, permit me to tell you, my son, a youth
of nineteen years of age, I have sent forward in the character of a private soldier, under Captain Rollins. His youth and inexperience, I make no doubt,
will stand in need of your friendship; therefore, I pray you, teach him the
duties of his station, and if any accident should happen him, pay some attention to him. Your obedient and humble servant.   BENJAMIN HARRISON.

From a Popular Campaign Song of 1840.

Oh, what has caused the great commotion, motion, motion?
Our country through?
It is the ball that's rolling on
For Tippecanoe and Tyler, too!

Tippecanoe's Triumphal March to Washington.

Tuesday, January 26, 1841, crowds of the citizens of Cincinnati congregated in front of the Henrie House, to see for the last time previous to his entering upon the important duties of office of President-elect, Gen. Wm. Henry Harrison.

The day was cloudy and the streets were muddy. A carriage had been provided, but the General preferred walking, and was escorted by several military companies, and a large number of citizens, to the river, where lay the steamboat "Ben Franklin," waiting for the distinguished passenger. The crowd upon the wharf was immense for those days, and was estimated at twelve thousand. Gen. Harrison was most deeply affected when, from the deck of his little steamboat, he briefly addressed his friends and neighbors. He spoke of the difference in his feelings at that time from those experienced when he first landed at the spot an humble ensign in the army of his country; and contrasted the present scene with that of his arrival, when only an occasional log cabin could be discovered, and all around was a dense, dark wood, the silence of which was unbroken, save by the scream of the panther and fierce yell of the savage. He spoke of the part he had borne in all these changing years, and of his love for the great West. He said he fully realized the vast responsibilities of the duties he was about to enter upon, and that the nation's weal would be his compass and polar star. When he was found deviating from the high road of genuine Democracy he felt that he would merit their condemnation and rebuke. He closed his remarks with words of farewell, and amid the cheers of the multitude, the martial music, and the cannon's boom from either shore, the little boat steamed away upon its journey, and, as it sadly proved, General Harrison left his beloved West forever.

THE JOURNEY.

He was accompanied by half a dozen intimate friends, and several grandsons, whom he was taking East to college. The boat was crowded with eminent citizens of Indiana, Kentucky and Ohio, and a Company of Military, who escorted him as far as Pittsburg. Thursday, at one o'clock, a signal gun, to which the cannons in the city of Wheeling responded, announced the expected arrival of " Ben Franklin," with the President-elect on board. Flags were unfurled, bells rung, and shouts and cheers from the thousands gathered at the wharf welcomed his coming. He was escorted from the boat to the hotel by the reception committee in an open carriage, followed by bands, military and citizens, and also a reception committee and military company from Pittsburg. On his arrival at the hotel he was formally received by a prominent citizen, and made a short and happy speech in reply, after which he was taken by the hand by thousands of the citizens of Wheeling and the surrounding country. From the hotel he was escorted to the house of an old friend, where great preparations had been made for his reception, and during the evening many of Virginia's fair daughters called and paid their respects. At ten o'clock the party resumed their journey. About three o'clock Friday afternoon the boat reached Pittsburg, where another gratifying reception was accorded the General. From a member of the company on board it was ascertained that there were at least twenty-five thousand people on the shore when the " Ben Franklin " approached.

On the edge of the bank several military companies were stationed to keep back the crowd and open a passage way for the carriages sent down for the presidential party. The " Ben Franklin " landed at the foot of Wood Street, and when General Harrison mounted the hurricane deck a deafening shout arose. He soon went on shore, and escorted by the committee and military that met him at Wheeling, made the circuit of the city in an open barouche. He stopped at the Pittsburg Hotel, and through that evening and the following morning he received the congratulations of the citizens. At eleven o'clock Saturday he addressed an immense audience in front of the hotel, and it is said that for squares in all directions there was a dense mass of human beings eager to get a glimpse of the coming chief magistrate.

An escort of Pennsylvanians then took charge of Gen. Harrison, and in a vehicle provided for the occasion, the presidential party proceeded to Brownsville, where they took passage in a stage-coach for Baltimore. At every point at which he stopped, if only for an hour, he met with demonstrations of the most flattering kind, and finally arrived in Washington on his sixty-eighth birthday—the 9th day of February—and fourteen days after he had embarked at Cincinnati.

AT THE CAPITOL.

He was warmly greeted upon his arrival at the depot by a large concourse of people, and was briefly welcomed by the Mayor. The reception committee and Tippecanoe Clubs escorted him to the City Hall, where the Mayor made an address of welcome, and Gen. Harrison responded in a short speech. He left Washington February 11, for Richmond, Va., for the purpose of placing in school the grandsons who accompanied him.

The celebration of Washington's birthday was observed with great eclat in Richmond, and on that occasion Gen. Harrison and Gov. Tyler met for the first time in public life. In the morning the Governor of Virginia, in behalf of the State, presented elegant swords to nine officers of the army and navy—who were natives of Virginia, and distinguished themselves in the then late war—in the presence of the distinguished guests, and the members of the legislature, and others. After the ceremonies of the presentation were over, the whole body were escorted to a large hall over the market-place, where they were tendered a banquet, and where Gen. Harrison entertained them with a speech, followed by Tyler, and other persons of prominence.

During the visit of the General to Richmond, he amused himself by visiting the scenes of his boyhood, and, notwithstanding the fatigue of entertaining, which he continually underwent, he was up by day-break, walking about the city, looking in at the markets, pricing grain and other products, asking questions, and hunting up the old places he knew so well. He searched out the building where he was a student of medicine, and, although he found in the old, tumble-down house a grog-shop, he entered it and explained to his companions, much to the surprise of the keeper: " Here, fifty years ago, I worked the pestle and mortar in compounding medicines."

Gen. Harrison went from Richmond to Petersburg, by invitation, and thence to Berkley, on the James River, and by way of Annapolis he reached Washington Monday, March 1. For the three days previous to his inauguration he was the guest of the Mayor of the city, where he received, at all hours of the day, the visits of his many friends and admirers. For days and weeks the city had been gradually filling with strangers, who traveled in various ways. They came by land and water, in wagons, carriages, and on foot.

At eight o'clock the morning of March 4, the military companies, Tippecanoe Clubs, and delegations began to form, and at ten o'clock the procession moved from the head of Four-and-a-half Street, when a salute of three guns announced their march toward the quarters of the president-elect.

THE CEREMONIES.

At this point Gen. Harrison, who, it is said, was mounted on a magnificent white charger, and accompanied by his suite of personal friends, took his place in the procession immediately after the officers and soldiers who fought under him. On his right were seven citizen Marshals, and on his left the Marshals of the District of Columbia and four aids.

The enthusiasm was intense along the line of march among both participants and lookers-on, and when at the last the President-elect stepped forth upon the platform, prepared over the portico of the east front of the Capitol, he was received with tumultuous and long applause. When the uproar had subsided he proceeded to read his address in a clear and distinct tone, the commanding voice never flagging until he had finished. After the oath of office had been administered, the deafening shouts were renewed and prolonged, and a pealing cannon announced that the country had a new chief magistrate. The procession again formed and proceeded along Pennsylvania Avenue to the presidential mansion, cheered by the crowds that lined the Avenue and filled the doors and windows along the route.

Extract From President Wm. Henry Harrison's Inaugural Address, March 4th, 1841.

I deem the present occasion sufficiently important and solemn to justify me in expressing to my fellow citizens a profound reverence for the Christian religion, and a thorough conviction that sound morals, religious liberty, and a just sense of religious responsibility, are essentially connected with all true and lasting happiness; and to that good Being who has blessed us by the gifts of civil and religious freedom, who watched over and prospered the labors of our fathers, and has hitherto preserved to us institutions far exceeding in excellence those of any other people, let us unite in fervently commending every interest of our beloved country in all future time.

Harrison's Family Tree.

BY MR. BLACKFORD.

Master John Harrison—first Governor of Virginia—1623.
Benjamin Harrison, of Surrey—born 1645.
His son, Benjamin Harrison, of Berkley—died April, 1710.
His son, Benjamin Harrison—killed by lightning.
His son, Benjamin Harrison, great-grandfather of the President.
His son, Wm. Henry Harrison, President of the United States.
His son, John Scott Harrison, father of the President.

W. DEWEY

ICHABOD STODDARD,

L. W. PARKE

A. H. MORRISON

L. V. BADGER.

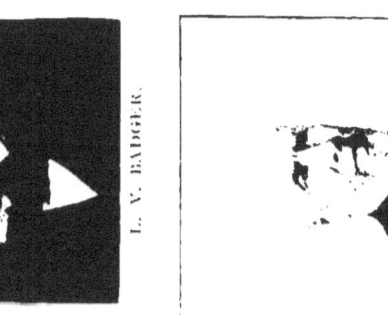

J. M. PERRY.

J. C. KILGORE.

S. WEBSTER-M.

NATHAN DYE.

Report of George S. Knapp.

Having represented the Old Tippecanoe Club, of Chicago, in Washington, at the inauguration of Gen. Benjamin Harrison as President of the United States, on the 4th of March, 1889, I beg leave to report that as such representative I was everywhere received with demonstrations of respect, and treated with the highest consideration. Dressed in plain black, wearing the badge of the Club upon my breast, and bearing aloft the time-honored flag which floated in the breeze in the presidential campaigns of Grant, Garfield, Blaine and Harrison, and which saluted General Grant on his return from his trip around the world—myself always the ensign—that flag which represents the principles of civil and religious liberty, for which my grandfather, Captain Simeon Crandall, struggled on Bunker Hill, and throughout the war of the Revolution. I was assigned a place in the line of march directly in rear of the regiment of veterans who served under General Harrison in the war of the Rebellion. Arriving at the capitol, I had an excellent opportunity to hear the President deliver his able and patriotic address to the people of the United States. I was then an invited guest to the reviewing stand of the President. The sight from this position is never to be forgotten by those who were so fortunate as to witness it—was so sublime as to baffle description.

At the inaugural ball—a dense forest of people, all nations represented, moved, unostentatiously and serene the cynosure of all eyes, the chosen ruler of sixty millions of freemen.

"On with the dance, let joy be unconfined!"

'Tis morning! Now, as the king of day salutes the summit of Washington's Monument with a kiss, a welcome summons greets the ear: "The President will, this A. M., receive all Clubs from outside the city." Thereupon, your obedient servant, accoutered as on the previous day, passed through the door of the White House, and halting in the presence of the chief magistrate, said:

Mr. President:—Representing on this occasion the Old Tippecanoe Club, of Chicago, comprising some five hundred veterans,

G. S. KNAPP.

I congratulate you, and I am authorized to pledge the Club to the support of your administration with the same zeal and devotion that it manifested in your election. In accordance with my promise, I now and here, in the White House, in the name and in the honor of the Old Tippecanoe Club of Chicago, take pleasure in waving this flag of our Union before you.

Whereupon the President replied substantially as follows:

Mr. Knapp:—I thank the Old Tippecanoe Club of Chicago for its active and efficient service in the recent campaign, especially for the uniform kindness shown me. My home is open to all the Old Tippecanoes, and I should be pleased to have them call on me when here.

Levi P. Morton, Vice-President of the United States,

Was born at Shoreham, Vermont, May 16, 1824. His father was the Rev. Daniel P. Morton, a Congregational minister of small means, and a lineal descendant of George Morton, who came to this country from England in 1623. Levi received a common school education, was a clerk in Concord, N. H. In 1850 he became one of the firm of Beebee, Morgan & Co., merchants in Boston; in 1863 he founded the banking house of Morton, Bliss & Co., in New York, and Morton, Rose & Co., in London, England. The two companies assisted largely in funding the debt of the United States, enabling the government to save several millions of dollars. The Wall Street firm has since that time been one of the most conspicuous in America. Mr. Morton entered political life in 1876. In 1878 he was elected to Congress from New York by a majority exceeding the entire vote of his opponent, and at once took a commanding position on finance. As Minister to France he was extremely agreeable and prominent at the French capitol, and his house became singularly popular. With the coming into power of the Cleveland administration, Mr. Morton, of course, returned home. In January, 1885, his name was before the Republican caucus in Albany for nomination for United States Senator, when Mr. Evarts was chosen and elected. Mr. Morton uses his vast wealth so that his name has become synonymous with benevolence. A notable instance was his fitting out, in 1880, the ship "Constitution" with provisions for the starving people in Ireland. His contribution to this worthy object amounted to a small fortune. He enjoys the full confidence of the party which elected him to his high office, and the whole people feel assured that in any emergency the country could safely be entrusted to his care.

Facts About Presidents.

The table below gives at a glance the political history of the Presidents. The letter " o " signifies that the President whose name is opposite filled the specified offices before he was called to guide the ship of State:

Names.	Born.	Mility Rank.	Legislature.	Congress.	Governor.	U. S. Senate.	Cabinet.	Vice-Pres. Minister.	Minor Offices.
Washington	1732	Com.	o	o					
Adams	1735		o	o	.	.		o	o
Jefferson	1743		o	o	o	.	State.	o	
Madison	1751		o	o	.	.	State.	.	.
Monroe	1758	Capt.	o	o	.	o	State.	o	.
J. Q. Adams	1767		o	o	.	o	State.	o	.
Jackson	1767	Mj. G.	.	o	o	o		.	Judge.
Van Buren	1782		o	.	o	o	State.	.	o
Harrison	1773	Mj. G.	o	o	o	o		o	Tr. Sec.
Tyler	1790		o	o	o	o		o	
Polk	1795		o	o	o	.			
Taylor	1784	Gen.	.	.	.	.		.	
Fillmore	1800		o	o	.	.		o	Com.
Pierce	1804	Bg. G.	o	o	.	o		.	D. Atty.
Buchanan	1791		o	o	.	o	State.	o	.
Lincoln	1809	Capt.	o	o	.	.		.	Post M.
Johnson	1808		o	o	o	o		o	Ald.
Grant	1822	Com.	.	.	.	.	War.		
Hayes	1822	Bg. G.	.	o	o			.	City Sol.
Garfield	1831	Mj. G.	o	o	o			.	
Arthur	1830	Gen.	.	.	.			o	Col. Pt.
*Cleveland	1837		.	o	.			.	Mayor.
Harrison	1833	Bg. G.	.	.	o			.	Ct. Rep.

* Cleveland was Sheriff and Assistant District Attorney.

History does not bear out the general belief that a seat in the Cabinet or a position at a foreign court ends a man's Presidential ambition, for Jefferson, Madison, Monroe, Quincy Adams, Van Buren and Buchanan each served as Secretary of State. All of them except Madison and Van Buren represented the nation abroad as Ministers. Gen. Grant was Secretary of War. Seven Vice-Presidents reached the higher office. They were John Adams, Jefferson and Van Buren, who were elected to it; and Tyler, Fillmore Johnson and Arthur, who succeeded the four Presidents who died in office, viz: Gen. Harrison, Gen. Taylor, Lincoln and Gen. Garfield.

Only three Presidents occupied office after vacating the Presidential chair—Quincy Adams, who afterwards spent seventeen years in Congress; Monroe, who became a Justice of the Peace; and Johnson, who was elected United States Senator in 1875.

The Speakership of Congress has not proved conducive to the Presidency. Only one man who presided over the House has reached the Chief Magistracy, and that was James K. Polk. Two of America's most brilliant sons—Henry Clay and James G. Blaine—are cases in point. Both were sent to the Legislature when young, and they became the Speakers of their respective Houses. They were elevated to Congress and each became Speaker of the House. Both served in the Senate and in the Cabinet as Secretary of State. They were also unsuccessful candidates for President. Each was defeated by a comparatively unknown man—Clay by Polk, and Blaine by Cleveland.

Virginia has furnished no less than seven Presidents—Washington, Jefferson, Madison, Monroe, "Old Tippecanoe" Harrison, Zachary Taylor and John Tyler. Harrison was a resident of Ohio and Taylor of Louisiana when elected.   ·

The two Adamses, John Adams and John Quincy Adams, were both natives of Massachusetts. Franklin Pierce was born in New Hampshire, and Gen. Arthur was a native of Vermont. Thus New England has had four representatives in the White House.

Five of the men elevated to the office were either natives or residents of Ohio, and soldiers—viz: "Old Tippecanoe" Harrison,

Gens. Grant, Hayes and Garfield, and Gen. Benjamin Harrison. All but Gen. W. H. Harrison (a Virginian by birth) were born in Ohio. Grant became a resident of Illinois and Benjamin Harrison is an adopted son of Indiana. Hayes had a singular experience in his political career. He was elected Governor of Ohio three times, defeating each time a Democrat of national reputation—Allen G. Thurman, George H. Pendleton, and "Old Bill" Allen. The first two named were unsuccessful candidates for Vice-President. It was Thurman who admitted Hayes to the bar.

New York has furnished four Presidents—Van Buren, Fillmore, Arthur and Cleveland. The first two were natives of the State, Arthur was a Vermonter, and Cleveland a native of New Jersey. It is an odd coincidence that Fillmore and Cleveland were residents of Buffalo.

Illinois never sent a native of the State to the White House, but two of the most illustrious Presidents—Lincoln, the emancipator, and Gen. Grant—were citizens of the State when they were raised to the Chief Magistracy.

It is a singular fact that the three citizens of Tennessee who occupied the White House—Jackson, Polk and Johnson—were natives of North Carolina. The first two named lived in or near Nashville.

As to education: Washington, Jackson, Van Buren, Taylor, Fillmore, Lincoln, Johnson and Cleveland were not college men. Except Van Buren and Cleveland, who were educated in small academies, the others received only the commonest kind of an education. Johnson could neither read nor write until his wife taught him those accomplishments.

Both the Adamses, father and son, were Harvard College graduates. John Quincy Adams was a professor at Harvard.

Madison graduated from Princeton College, and Jefferson, Monroe and Tyler received their sheepskins at William and Mary College, Virginia.

Old Gen. Harrison graduated from the Hampden-Sidney College, Polk from the North Carolina University, Pierce from Bowdoin College, Buchanan at Dickinson College, and Grant at West Point. Williams College was Garfield's alma mater, Hayes was trained at Kenyon College, Arthur at Union College, and Harrison at Miami University.

No less than eleven Presidents had military titles won on the battlefield. Washington and Grant were commanding Generals; Jackson, William H. Harrison, Taylor and Garfield, Major-Generals; Pierce, Hayes, and Benjamin Harrison, Brigadier-Generals. Monroe was a Major and Lincoln a Captain. Washington, Monroe and Jackson took part in the Revolution; Jackson, Harrison, and Taylor in the War of 1812; Taylor, Pierce and Grant went through the Mexican war; Lincoln fought in the Black Hawk war, and Grant, Hayes, Garfield, and Benjamin Harrison in the war of the Rebellion.

All the Presidents except Jackson, Taylor, Grant, Arthur, Cleveland, and Benjamin Harrison served in their State Legislatures. All of them except Taylor, Grant, Arthur, Cleveland, and the new President were Congressmen.

Jefferson, Jackson, Van Buren, Harrison, Tyler, Polk, Johnson, Hayes, and Cleveland were Governors of their respective States for one or more terms. Both Harrisons, the younger Adams, Monroe, Jackson, Van Buren, Tyler, Pierce, Buchanan, Johnson, and Garfield were United States Senators. Garfield was elected, but he never served, having been elected President shortly afterward. Jackson never spoke in the Senate.

Seven of them were Cabinet officials. Jefferson, Madison, Monroe, John Quincy Adams, Van Buren, and Buchanan served as Secretaries of State, and Gen. Grant as Secretary of War for five months. Both the Adamses, Jefferson, Monroe, Tippecanoe Harrison, and Buchanan were Ministers to foreign countries.

Only one President was a Sheriff; that was Cleveland. Only one an Alderman—Johnson. Both Johnson and Cleveland were Mayors. Gen. Grant was the youngest President, 47, and "Old Tippecanoe" the oldest, 68. Monroe, Grant, and Arthur were residents of New York City when they died.

In business life Washington was a surveyor; Jackson worked in a harness shop, sold cotton and mules; Taylor, a farmer; Fillmore, a clothmaker's apprentice; Lincoln, a boatman and woodchopper; Johnson, a tailor; Grant, a tanner; Garfield, a canaler;

John Adams, Arthur and Cleveland, teachers.

Several Presidents had nicknames, Jackson was "Old Hickory"; W. H. Harrison, "Old Tippecanoe"; Taylor, "Rough and Ready"; Buchanan was called "Old Buck"; Lincoln, "Old Abe," and Gen. Benjamin Harrison, "Little Ben."

Tippecanoe Entertainment. Held April 4, 1889.

When the Old Tippecanoe Club announced a musical and literary entertainment, to be given under their auspices, everybody knew it would be a good one, because the old Tippecanoe veterans have done well everything they have tried since the old days of '40, when they helped elect "Tippecanoe and Tyler, too." Last night they deserted the Wigwam for Central Music Hall, where they assembled in large numbers, with many of their friends, to listen to a most attractive program of musical and literary selections. The stage was effectively draped with American flags in profusion, and at the right was the portrait of William Henry Harrison, the unveiling of which was the second number on the program. Mr. Harrison Wild played on the organ with his customary success an opening number, which ushered upon the stage the members of the club to the number of about one hundred. It was an imposing and affecting sight to see the array of aged, who have been active and enthusiastic in political affairs for over forty years. Here and there a dark head was seen, but a large majority were white, and there were a good many canes, which came in excellent play for applause later in the evening. After the unveiling of the portrait Hon. Thomas B. Bryan delivered an address, substantially a follows:

FELLOW CITIZENS:

In this venerable presence it seems to me that silence would best become a stripling of only three score years.

Despite, however, my protest, several hundred of these sprightly octogenarians have summoned me to this platform.

As the elections are over, and the discussion of politics would not accord with the proprieties of this occasion, my compliance with the request for an introductory address shall be limited to a few words, uttered in deference to age. In passing, however, and speaking generally, it may not be amiss to declare that no danger so threatens the permanence of our Republican institutions as do the hot-beds of corruption in the politics and administration of cities. In this respect a somewhat extended comparison has forced upon me the painful conviction that our American cities present a mortifying contrast to those of Europe. It behooves our legislators and patriotic citizens to devise some plan of municipal government that will divorce, as far as possible, party politics from the control of our city administrations, so that oft-recurring municipal elections may not tempt excited and eager partisans to vie with each other in courting the support of the worst elements of society. The best men of both the political parties that battle for city prizes, acknowledge the evil, and in expressions that may be condensed in some such epigram as this:

> Twixt the Iroquois and the Tippecanoes
> In our city elections there's little to choose;
> For with either's defeat (horse, foot and dragoons)
> There yet flourish alike the dens and saloons.

As banks and great commercial houses are confided to men of business capacity, without regard to their political antecedents and connections, why should not the more complex affairs of great cities be entrusted, without regard to politics, to those possessed of the requisite business qualifications? But a truce to this grave topic!

Could the years of these fathers, now occupying this stage, be regarded as not contemporaneous, but be extended to the past in a continuous chain, with links of three score years and ten or more, it is startling to think that it would reach to a remote age of hundreds of centuries ago. Such a reflection upon the present pervading atmosphere of antiquity about this platform recalls my impressions when first pacing the streets of Pompei, and fancying them peopled as of old.

And this is a club! A club not of commercial men; not of dancers; not of scientists; not of "them literary fellers;" but, apart from its political affiliations, a club of silver beards and glistening heads.

Some may call it hobby-riding. But shall the riding of hobbies be confined to the young? Why should old men voluntarily shelve themselves? Death of the mind is worse than total death, which it often precipitates. With man's faculties disuse is decay. The genial prince of anglers occupied his ninetieth year with successful authorship. In our own day two continents listen with eager interest to every utterance of Bismark and of Gladstone. Just homage to age is intensified when the old evince intelligent interest in current affairs.

Not a few are the compensations of age. Among the chief of these is the feasting of memory. Youth rarely occupies itself with thoughts of age, but

THOS. B. BRYAN.

age continually reverts to youth. Rarely indeed do we hear—once only have I ever heard—an old man quote:

> "O Memory! Thou lingering murmur
> Within joy's broken shell,
> Why have I not, in losing all I loved,
> Lost thee as well?"

These gentlemen delight to recall the earlier presidents, and especially the elder Harrison, for whom, as for his illustrious grandson, they worked and voted —with an interval of nearly half a century between the two. Some have described with accuracy to me the personal appearance of the first, for as Geo. Elliott says: "Old men's eyes are like old men's memories; they are strongest for things a long ways off."

Then, too, this club, like that of the "Old Settlers," is a club of peculiar experience. A third or a half a century in Chicago is equal to a whole age of Methuselah in some sleepy hollow. What marvels of growth since we waded through the muddy village, with its varying grades, necessitating climbing and descending steps from block to block, familiarizing one with the ups and downs of life! Now behold a mighty metropolis boldly aspiring to commercial supremacy among the cities of the earth! Was there ever before so great an alembic, in which, with like rapidity, old customs and conservative sluggishness, were dissolved, and results of genuine and startling progress attained? Not among these aged eye-witnesses of that progress can be found one man to question the mighty destiny of Chicago. Such a doubter could only find comfort in Pascal's consoling observation, that "Man is necessarily so much of a fool that it would be a species of folly not to be a fool." Then, too, these old men, unlike some of the opposite sex, whose age some growler declares to be the only secret they keep inviolably, rather plume themselves upon their years. And well they may—for experience such as theirs is apt to purify the mind, and strengthen the judgment. They ought, as a body, to exercise a salutary influence over us all, especially at times of election when man's morality is rather a loose-fitting garment. Look at these men, and say if their honest faces do not answer effectively the ill-natured comment of that scoffer at mankind, Heine, when speaking of La Fayette as the only honest man, and that "at his death the situation was vacant."

Whatever may be their infirmities of body, however heavy and labored the step of some, they seem at least light-hearted. And so men should be; realizing that if man is the only animal that knows he must die, he is also the only animal that knows how to laugh. Extremely rare are those whose life lease is ninety-nine years, and none with a clause of renewal in this—what the Book of Ecclesiastes might call—grasshopper country. But, though, as with most scarce things, the fewer the days left us, the more precious they should be, I have no patience with the man who makes of himself a sand-glass, constantly brooding over the descending sand, instead of being a sun-dial ever brightly reflecting the goodness and mercy of God.

The glowing remark of one of this club, a day or two since, and of one, too, who was in active business when I was still in the cradle, that he loves now, more than ever, both his country and the women who glorify it, amused and gratified me not a little. The love of country takes deep root in congenial soil, grows with one's growth, and endures to the end. That the heart which has pulsated for over eighty years with the love of woman, should by that time fully appreciate so good a thing, is not unnatural, nor should such a flame in a good old heart occasion any more surprise than that green wood kindles less quickly than that which is old and thoroughly dry.

I well remember seeing Grant, Sheridan and Sherman together in a social company in Washington, the last the liveliest of the illustrious trio. He amused himself, and everybody else, by his frolicsome snatching of kisses from young women, whose ringing laugh attested their willing tribute to his age and distinction. If all his enemies had but one neck Nero would have severed it at one stroke. If all the fair of our land had but one pair of lips, and our greatest surviving General were anywhere in reach, terrific would be the concussion.

Two things are entitled, as a rule, to especial respect, long lives and short speeches. My aged friends having insisted upon my being their mouth-piece, I greet you warmly, brothers, in their behalf. And the cordial greeting extends to you also, my fair auditors, who can best enlighten me on all the duties of a mouth-piece. One thing, however, is certain, the lip-salutation of these veteran worshippers of women could not, even were they willing, be warmly and effectively tendered by proxy.

Then Rev. Dr. Withrow recited in the spirit of its author—Oliver Wendell Holmes—the humerous poem, entitled "The Boys."

After a march on the organ by Mr. Wild, the Imperial Quartette sang in its usual successful manner, and later in the evening again, both times responding to well-merited encores. A recitation, Susan Coolidge's "Ginevra," by Miss Hattie Fleming, was one of the most pleasing things heard in many a day in Chicago. Miss Fleming has not appeared in public before, but by her charming grace and finished reading of the poem she captivated her audience. She was followed by Miss Mary Shelton Woodhead, who sang in highland costume, "A Hundred Pipers." Miss Woodhead is always well received, and last night added laurels to her reputation. Later in the program she sang "Annie Laurie," and as an encore "The Land o' the Leal," which always captures an audience when she sings it. The dancing of Miss Cora Spicer, a little girl, was very good, and gave general plea-

sure. The old song, "The Sword of Bunker Hill," was sung by Mr.
A. H. Williams, an aged member of the club. He carried an old
sabre which saw service at Bunker Hill in the hands of Captain
Simeon Crandall, from whom it had descended to his great-grand-
son, Mr. G. S. Knapp. After this song, Mrs. Josephine Turck-
Baker recited two selections from "Josiah Allen's Wife," giving
much satisfaction to the highly pleased audience. Two recitations by Mr. Eugene Hall were well received. Mr. Fenton B.
Turck gave some excellent impersonations, "doing" Professor
Swing and Dr. Lorimer, to the unmistakable delight of the audience. The program concluded with a most pleasing series of
characteristic pieces played by Mr. Paul Olah's Hungarian
Orchestra from the Eden Musee.

The Sword of Bunker Hill.

AS SUNG BY MR. A. H. WILLIAMS.

He lay upon his dying bed,
    His eye was growing dim,
When with a feeble voice he called
    His weeping son to him.
"Weep not, my boy," the veteran said,
    "I bow to Heaven's high will,
But quickly from yon antler bring
    The Sword of Bunker Hill."

*   *   *   *   *   *   *

Now sixty millions bless the sire,
    And Sword of Bunker Hill.

A. H. WILLIAMS.

A Notable Gathering.

People who happened to be on State, between Washington and Randolph streets, Thursday evening, a little before eight o'clock, heard the shrill tone of a fife and the sharp rat-a-tat of a tenor drum. Then there passed through the dim light of the gas-lamps a procession, headed by two American flags and a banner, in which marched men two by two, going toward the north.

The voicings of the fife were a trifle querulous, as if the wind of the player were scant, and the tones of the drum were somewhat quavering and uncertain, as if the hands that held the sticks were a little weak and shaky. There was a peculiar accompaniment to the hesitating utterences of the instruments—that of the tapping of metal on the stone of the sidewalk. It was the impact of canes carried by the members of the procession, each of which struck the pavement as if it were impelled by a heavy weight.

One could not see the faces of the individuals of the procession, in the obscurity; but one could see that many of them stooped as they walked, as if there were a powerful attraction pulling them toward the earth. Some of their legs were stiffened so that movement was an awkward sort of hop-and-skip; some of the heads were dropped well forward so that the chins almost touched the breasts. All the way the canes played a conspicuous staccato accompaniment to the march.

A little later the audience in Central Music Hall saw on the stage a dense mass of black which was covered with fleecy white as from a covering of virgin snow. Under the strong glare of the footlights the individuality of the procession from the street became distinct. It was the Old Tippecanoe Club, men who had voted for the original log-cabin candidate, and who, on the anniversary of his death, had gathered to do honor to his memory. It may be that the assembling on the 4th of April was not intentional; if not, the coincidence was a curious one.

It was something to inspire reverence, almost awe, the spectacle of this snow-thatched aggregation. There was much that was pathetic in their attitudes as they patiently stood, with bowed figures and leaning heavily on their canes, during the long preliminary performances. Their rheumatic legs must have hurt them, and their poor old backs ached, as for almost a full hour they were forced to stand without opportunity for a change of position.

It is a half century since the youngest among them was old enough to vote for "Tippecanoe and Tyler, too." Some of them voted eight years before the advent of Harrison, which would place them now in the eighties. Some of them are as old as the century.

It was a curious speculation on the part of some of the audience as to what these old men were thinking of as they stood thus in a solid mass. Did the contact, the numbers, strengthen them and make them reflect, each one thinking: "I am not the only one who is aged, white-haired and failing. All these men are the same as I, and I will not have to cross the river alone." Did the fact that there were so many of them afford a species of grim consolation?

That they thought of the past cannot be doubted. Their memories took them back to 1840, when hard cider was a party beverage and a rallying cry; when the country blazed with bonfires; when log cabins ranked higher than palaces, and the nation was crazed with an enthusiasm which has not since been rivaled. And possibly, too, they thought of their victory, the interposition of cruel death, and that in the re-election of the grandson of their venerated chief there was something in the nature of a compensation.

One could not avoid thinking as he gazed on the gray, stoop-shouldered men, leaning heavily on their sticks, of the contrast between them and their former selves. Then these men, with the wan faces and shriveled forms, were rose-cheeked, full as to chest and muscle, with hair brown, raven and dense, and with voices, not as now, thin, weak and tremulous, but stentorian as they shook the ground with their mighty huzzas.—*Herald.*

NOTE.—The above mentioned "coincidence" was undesigned, and the "banner" referred to was displayed in the convention which nominated Gen. William Henry Harrison for President in 1840.

Members of the Old Tippecanoe Club.

Abbott, S. G.
Abernethy, J. W.
Ackerman, James
Ackley, Benj.
Adams, James
Aiken, Daniel
Ames, Cheney
Ashbury, Capt. H.
Askin, Robert Y.
Atkins, Henry M.
Averill, A. J.
Avery, W. B.
Ayers, E.
Ayers, W. B.
Babcock, John N.
Backer, Fred
Badger, Leonidas
Baker, John P.
Baldwin, Henry
Baldwin, Wm. G.
Ballard, O. W.
Barbour, L.
Barber, Lillibridge
Barnard, R. H.
Barnes, A. H.
Barnett, Alexander
Bartlett, Joseph P.
Bartlett, E. L.
Bassett, Jared
Bates, A. T.
Battershaw, M.
Beecher, Jerome
Beecher, Wm. Henry
Beefield, William
Bennett, R. J.
Beckwith, C. H.
Becker, J. W.
Beidler, J.
Beidler, Henry
Benton, R. O.
Biglow, L. H.
Bishop, G. O.

Billings, A. M.
Billings, Henry L.
Booth, Judge
Bone, J. C.
Bonham, G. W.
Bosworth, A.
Bosttetter, J.
Boyden, Jas. W.
Boyington, Wm. W.
Brace, Wm.
Brackett, Joseph W.
Bradley, Wm. Henry
Bradley, D.
Bradley, Frances
Brayton, J. W.
Brayton, E. F.
Brooks, J. W.
Brown, Charles E.
Bristol, George S.
Blackall, A. H.
Blair, M. R.
Blair, William
Blakesley, Levi
Blakestee, L.
Blodgett, Phineus M.
Buel, James W.
Burroughs, Phillip
Burley, Arther H.
Burley, Arther G.
Burns, A. H.
Burns, Patrick
Burbank, T. W.
Burt, A. S.
Butlers, M. R.
Carr, Dr. Watson
Carrington, N. S.
Cary, John M.
Carter, Thos. B.
Carpenter, Geo. W.
Castle, Col. E. H.
Case, S. S.
Campbell, B. H.

Cannon, M. S.
Chadwick, James N.
Chadwick, Wm. B.
Chessmann, N.
Chalmers, Thos.
Chapin, L. R.
Chapin, Henry L.
Chase, J. R.
Churchill, Stillman
Clark, J. H.
Clark, Dr. W. E.
Cleaver, Chas.
Clement, J. C.
Clement, Stephen H.
Coale, Isaac
Cobb, S. B.
Cobb, Lucius I.
Cobb, G. W.
Cool, Benj.
Coon, P. H.
Coffin, Fred W.
Coffin, R.
Cogswell, F.
Colby, E.
Colbson, J. H.
Cole, Israel
Colton, C. W.
Conkey, W. H.
Converse, Henry
Connally, A. P.
Coultright, J.
Crana, D. E.
Craig, C. W.
Crawford, John
Crawford, H. P.
Cross, Asahel T.
Crittonton, E. O.
Crim, Dr. M.
Crure, Dr. M.
Currey, James
Dame, Capt. John
Davis, F. M.

Corey, F. E.
Danly, G. L.
Davis, J. R.
Davidson, W.
Dean, D. H.
Dewey, Washington
Dewey, Solomon P.
De Wolf, W. F.
Doddridge, J. G.
Dodge, George,
Downs, M. D.
Douglas, Frank
Dickey, J. P.
Dickinson, W. P.
Duffield, C.
Dunning, C. A.
Dunham, John H.
Durant, J. T.
Durley, Madison
Dye, Nathan
Eddy, Ira B.
Edwards, S. W.
Elliott, Wm. Sidney
Emory, Franklin
Eschen, J. T.
Farnsworth, L. L.
Ferguson, D. C.
Ferguson, J. C.
Fisk, D. B.
Finnelly, Benj.
Follett, J. D.
Foster, Charles G.
Follett, M. P.
Forbes, S. D.
Frailey, W. P.
Frank, H.
Freer, L. C. P.
Frisbie, M. L.
Frost, S. D.
Fulton, L. H.
Fuller, Andrew
Fry, John E.
Gage, John
Gage, H.
Garlick, Leman W.

Garnett, Wm.
Garner, G. P.
Gates, P. W.
Gale, Stephen F.
George, L. F.
Gerden, B. W.
Gibbs, Aaron Dr.
Gibbs, O. F.
Gidron, Capt. G. W.
Gill, J. H.
Gifford, Calvin
Goodman, Thos.
Goodrich, Grant
Goney, S.
Gookins, F. Y.
Grath, P. M.
Gray, F. D.
Gregory, J. H
Griggs, F. C.
Griffing, W. A.
Grunnip, L.
Hair, Uriah
Haggard, Samuel B.
Haggard, J. V.
Haight, F. T.
Hall, T. W.
Harris, Geo. P.
Harrison, W. H.
Harmon, Joseph W.
Hardy, Dexter
Hammond, M. W.
Hammond, Rev.H.L.
Hatch, J. C.
Hawley, C. M.
Hayden, Amos
Hewitt, Wm. P.
Higgins, Judge V. H.
Higginson, Geo. M.
Hillard, L. P.
Hinckley, Watson S.
Holden, R.
Hoine, D. H.
Holt, George
Holmes, Rev. D. G.
Hoffin, Samuel

Hough, D. L.
Hough, R. M.
Houston, A. Van
Howe, John D.
Howland, Isaac
Hoyt, A. L.
Hubbard, Thomas
Hubbard, W. R.
Hull, J. B.
Huntley, Silas
Huntington, John
Hurd, Thomas
Husted, H. H.
Huston, Brice Viers
Hutchinson, J. D
Hyde, William
Hyde, J. T.
Ingraham, Wm. W.
Ingersoll, Frederick
Jack, Mathew W.
Jackson, Chas. P.
James, John
Jenks, Chancellor
Jenks, M. W.
Jessel, E. H.
Jones, Cyrus
Jones W.
Johnson, John
Kealy, E. P.
Keeling, William
Kennedy, John M.
Kerr, J. M.
Kent, B. A.
Kilgore, Isaac C.
Kile, John
Kinne, Isaac D.
King, John, Jr.
King, T. B.
Kingsley, W. S.
Kirby, James
Knapp, G. S.
Kinnly, J.
Kunbark, M. N.
Kyle, O. G.
Lane, John

Lane, E. S.
Laning, Capt. James
Langhurst, Wm.
Law, J.
Lawrence, M. A.
Lawrence, W. H.
Leake, Jas. B.
Loomis, James W.
Loomis, J. M.
Lovejoy, M.
Lovejoy, F. C.
Lord, J. F.
Little, D.
Lyman, N. R.
Macauley, M.
Magee, W.
Magee James K.
Mann, O. L.
Marsh, Isaac
Marshall, James A.
Mason, Carlisle
Mason, J. E.
Mason, Nelson
Mathews, P. P.
Matthews, G. L.
McCulloch, C. G.
McCulloch, L. G.
McDaniels, A.
McHenry, Capt. H.
McKindley, James
McLean, John
McMaster, B. D.
Mears, J. C.
Mears, Nathan
Mears, C.
Merrill, J. B.
Merrill, Nathan F.
Merrill, Benj.
Merriam, Jas. L. ·
Mendsen, William
Meyers, Henry
Mills, Luther Laflin
Miller, John
Mills, Wm. Bruce
Miller, T. L.

Miller, Dr. A.
Miner, G.
Mitchell, F. M.
Mitchell, Thos. F.
Moore, A. J.
Moore, Warren
Moore, Geo. S.
Moore, Thos. C.
Morrison, Col. A. H.
Morrison, E.
Morrison, C. E.
Morrison, L.
Morton, Chas. H.
Munger, C. W.
Murray, E. D.
Myrick, W. F.
Newell, J. W.
Nichols, Chas. H.
Nickerson, W. H.
Norton, E. H.
Northway, E. H.
Nourse, Francis
Nourse, John
Nowlin, Lewis
Officer, A.
Olcott, Orville
Osborn, W. A.
Osborn, Judge A. L.
Osborn, Henry
Osborn, S. S.
Osgood, Isaac
Packard, J. A.
Paplin, N. S.
Parks, L. W.
Parker, Thos
Parsons, A.
Pattle, Moses L.
Patterson, Wm.
Patterson, W. H.
Pease, W. H.
Peck, C. E.
Peck, C. M.
Peck, J. C.
Perry, James M.
Perkins, W. S.

Phillips, M.
Plummer, B.
Pomeroy, G. W.
Pope, Geo. G.
Pote, Robert
Potter, John O.
Powers, Levi
Powers, Amos H.
Platt, Maj. O. H.
Preble, J. G.
Pridmore, W. H.
Prince, Lucian
Pringle, Thos.
Pringle, Thos. J.
Pritman, V. C.
Pullman, A. B.
Pullman, G. M.
Pulisfer, Samuel
Ramsey, O. D.
Ranny, A. D.
Rawson, Alonzo
Raymond, A. N.
Reed, Alanson
Reed, H. B.
Reiter, W.
Rew, Henry A.
Reynolds, A. S.
Richards, Rawson
Richmond, H. M.
Rin, D. A.
Ripley, Wm.
Ripley, Geo. C.
Risbig, Levi
Robertson, Thomas
Robinson, J. N.
Rodgers, W. B.
Rogers, Thos. H.
Rogers, Thomas
Ross, R. C.
Roundy, D. C.
Sanford, S. A.
Sayrs, Henry
Searles, Wm. D.
Sedgwick, Dr. S. P.
Severence, J. F.

Sawyer, D. B.
Sayers, R. F.
Scammon, J. Y.
Schaffer, J.
Schmidt, J.
Scott, Gen. Horace
Scott, Geo. W.
Scott, W. D.
Scribner, Wiley S.
Shaw, Calvin
Shepard, W. W.
Sherwood, P.
Shipman, Geo. E.
Shourds, Benj.
Shourds, James
Sieber, Josiah
Sinclair, Jayson
Skinner, Wm.
Slater, F. A., M. D.
Sloauneb, A. D.
Sleeper, J. A.
Slocum, E. F.
Slosson, Enos
Smith, Benj.
Smith, Benj. E.
Smith, Dr. D. S.
Smith, H. R.
Smith, O. A.
Smith, W. G.
Soper, Albert
Spear, S. L.
Spry, John
Staples, R. B.
Start, John

Steel, E. P.
Stedman, D. B.
Stevens, Isaac
Stevens, James P.
Stitt, John
Stoddard, Ichabod
Stone, W. B.
Storey, Geo. H.
Stout, Gen. A. M.
Stovle, C. U.
Tait, John
Tanner, Henry
Taplin, M. S.
Taylor, J. B.
Taylor, J. H.
Teale, E. P.
Ten Eyck, T.
Thomas, B. W.
Thomas, T. D.
Thomas, Wm.
Thompson, Jared
Thompson, M. M.
Throop, Amos G.
Tiffany, Dr. E.
Toms, Collins S.
Townsend, C.
True, Daniel
Turner, John
Turner, J. V.
Turnor, J. A.
Tuttle, Fred
Vail, A. S.
Van Dercook, C. R.
Van Houtten, A. R.

Van Velzer, B.
Viberts, John
Wakefield, James A.
Walrath, H. M.
Warner, A. G.
Washington Geo.
Watkins, Elias J.
Watson, B. A.
Watts, Robert
Weigslebaum, B.
Wells, M. A.
Wheeler Hiram
Whitbeck, H.
White, C. B.
Whitney, E. H.
Willard, A. J.
Williams, Asa
Williams, A. H.
Williams, M. D.
Williams, Chas.
Wilson, Washington
Wilson, W. R.
Wingate, Albert
Winslow, J. H.
Winston, N.
Wolcott, E. B.
Worster, Asa
Worthington, D.
Wright, A. J.
Wright, E. L.
Wright, J. G.
Wright, S. F.
Yates, H. H.
Young, J. P.

HONORARY MEMBERS.

Blaine, Hon. James G.
   Sec. of State of U. S.
Drake, John B.
Douglas, Stephen A.
Fifer, Hon. Joseph W.
   His Excellency
Harrison, Benjamin,
   President of the U. S.
Mercer, Rev. L. P.

Roach, Hon. John A.
   Mayor of Chicago
Withrow, Rev. Dr. J. L.
Bosworth, Mrs. Albert
Burroughs, Miss K.
Collins, Mrs. Thomas
Cooke, Mrs. A. Augusta
Dewey, Mrs. Mary

Elliot, Mrs. Minerva K.
Garlick, Mrs. Annah S.
Hall, Mrs. S. C.
Harrison, Mrs. A. I.
Hopkins, Mrs. Mary M.
Knapp, Mrs. G. S.
Remington, Mrs. Belle
Ten Eyck, Mrs. Thos.

The Old Guard.

— —

The Old Tippecanoe Guard will not be the least among the attractions at the forthcoming centennial celebration. It is exceedingly graceful, as well as appropriate, that these veteran voters should be given an honored place at an assembly convened to observe the anniversary of the inauguration of the first President of the republic. Some still survive who participated in, or witnessed the semi-centennial which was commemorated the year before Old Tippecanoe led the log-cabin, coon, cider, and song campaign that retired forever " Little Van " to private life, and wrought so potentially upon the Whig conscience of nearly fifty years ago.

The political canvasses of 1840 and 1888—of Old Tippecanoe and Young Tippecanoe—were both peculiarly picturesque. An effort was made to transform the bandanna into the semblance of a sentiment, but campaign exposure and evasion early took shape and form out of it and left only a shapeless, colorless shred, no more like what it started out to be than a rag compared to the stars and stripes. But the attractions of the simple, sincere canvass of log-cabin days never failed to awaken patriotic impulses, to quicken the public life into high resolve, to animate the people, and at the same time to expel the gall of bitterness from a campaign that became famous in song and story. The strong Americanism of the campaign of 1840 was healthful to the nation, just as that decided bias was last year which Young Tippecanoe gave to his party and the people in all his public utterances. There had been much in politics that was too practical or too professional. The change from this side of selfishness and place-seeking to the other of patriotic endeavor, of generous service for the industrial classes, of simple worth against sham and shoddy, that was brought about by both Tippecanoes was refreshing and hopeful for the republic. So unusual was it that the people felt its picturesqueness and cherished the change. A new literature was introduced. New music came. The song-writers of the war for the Union had for the most part passed

away, and this fresh field was peculiarly grateful. These inno-
vations introduced amenities into the campaign such as had not
appeared for a generation in political history. And the nation
continues to enjoy proofs of health and hope from that experience.

The influence of the Old Tippecanoe Guard is not confined to
last autumn's election. It will be felt for many quadrennials to
come, just as the campaign of 1840 is even now more than a mere
cold historical fact. The white-haired men who voted for General Harrison in 1840, and again for General Harrison in 1888, are
comparatively few and feeble, and by another presidential election many will be laid away to rest. Their influence will continue, however, and the men of Whig convictions in 1840, and of
Republican belief in 1888, will have sons and grand-sons that may
be expected to lead the van in every great public improvement
and good work. The history these Old Tippecanoe Guardsmen
leave is already luminous with their labors for the liberty of
every race, color and condition. They and their sons will be
found at the front in every forward movement. And while the
veterans remain let them be given the largest consideration, and
more especially in the centennial of the nation whose history
they are so large a part of, and to whose highest welfare they
have contributed so much.— *Inter Ocean.*

Death of Wm. H. Harrison

PUBLISHED IN APRIL, 1841.

The western firmament is spread
With festoons of a mighty woe ;
Upon each Alleghany's head,
Each forest and each vale below,
And o'er each rolling inland sea,
Is heard a nation's wail for thee,
Thou, ruler of a day.
Hear ! Chanted by the breezes wild,
The requiem of freedom's child,
Where, circling the northern pole,
The hurricanes of winter roll,
Cold's revelry and sway.
Hear ! Wafted on the prairie's breath,

The tidings of the patriot's death,
A dirge, by nature sung ;
But echoing still the anthem high,
That burst the freedom, when the cry
Of Independence rung.
For when that Heaven born spirit gave
Her charter from the ocean wave,
Of Atalanta's throne,
And bade America awake,
(In accents that made empires quake,)
And armed a Washington,
The very triumph that she gave
Roll'd o'er the ashes of the brave,
And saddn'd victory's swell,
And though no mighty battle's breath
Burst around thy bed of death
And bore afar thy knell.
Thou, honored brother of the free,
A nations tears are shed for thee.
Ye potentates of Europe, you
Of old hereditary sway,
Who battle holiest truth-- if new,
And not the faith of grandsires—say,
If all the pageants that have shown
The picture of an empty throne ;
Or all the hired peals that ring
Around the coffin of a king ;
Or all the mercenary gloom
Of mourners at a despot's tomb,
Can equal that spontaneous tear
Wept over a worth to freedom dear.
As sunlight to the gem,
A worth that shed a holier glow
Around the patriot hero's brow
Than empires diadem.
No ! Though the millions weeping, bend
O'er St. Helena's empty tomb
And monarchy dead, a glory lend
To Russia's frozen womb.
Though sepulchres embannered vie
With columns trophied to the sky,
And pyramids of marble dare
To shoot beyond the tides of air,
To heaven's empyreal blue,
Though proudest ministers o'er your
     shrines,
Are decked from farthest India's mines
In fettered gold for you.
For him a nobler trophy springs
Than decks a dateless line of kings,
Which time can never dim,
Till skies wrapt up in doom shall be,
Deep in the hearts of millions free.
Behold the shrine of HIM !

President Harrison's Tribute to the Tippecanoes.

WASHINGTON, D. C., May 9. The Association of Veterans of 1840, composed of members of the Tippecanoe Club, who assisted in the election of President William Henry Harrison, called at the White House today in a body, for the purpose of paying their respects to the President.

There were about seventy veterans in all, including ex-Minister Schenck, ex-Senator Pomeroy and ex-Public Printer Clapp. The latter acted as chairman of the delegation, and made an address. The president responded as follows:

Mr. Chairman and Gentlemen: -I beg to assure you that I appreciate very highly this evidence of your respect and confidence. If I were to set before me an ambition which would insure the success of my administration, it would be that I might continue to hold fast the respect and confidence of *such men as yourselves*, matured of mind and unbiased in judgment. I thank you for coming, and for your kindly words.

www.ingramcontent.com/pod-product-compliance
Lightning Source LLC
Chambersburg PA
CBHW031428020726
47499CB00005B/1636